The Only Best Place

The Only Best Place

Carolyne Aarsen

NEW YORK BOSTON NASHVILLE

Scripture taken from the HOLY BIBLE:
NEW INTERNATIONAL VERSION®. Copyright © 1973, 1978, 1984
by International Bible Society. Used by permission of
Zondervan Publishing House. All rights reserved.

Warner Faith

Hachette Book Group USA
1271 Avenue of the Americas, New York, NY 10020
Visit our Web site at www.HachetteBookGroupUSA.com.

Warner Faith® and the "W" logo are trademarks of Time Warner Inc. or an affiliated company. Used under license by Hachette Book Group, which is not affiliated with Time Warner Inc.

Printed in the United States of America

First Edition: September 2006
10 9 8 7 6 5 4 3 2 1

Library of Congress Cataloging-in-Publication Data
Aarsen, Carolyne.
      The only best place / Carolyne Aarsen.— 1st ed.
          p. cm.
      ISBN-13: 978-0-446-69681-4
      ISBN-10: 0-446-69681-1
      1. Farmers' spouses—Fiction.   I. Title.
      PR9199.3.A14055 2006
      813'.6—dc22   2006006559

For my beloved family;
Richard, Jesse, Cheyanne, Fern, and Amiel.
You are the best part of home.

Acknowledgments

hough the front cover lists only one name, the reality is that this book was not written alone.

First off, I owe a huge thanks to Karen Solem, who believed in this book and found its home. You are a super agent, Karen.

Then, thanks to Anne Goldsmith, who helped me shape this book and find its focus. I appreciate your patience and humor and ideas.

A heartfelt thank-you goes to Corinne Aarsen, my dear sister-in-law, and Diane Wierenga, my dear friend, and Michelle Klosterman for all their help with E.R. nursing information. Any mistakes that other nurses may find in this story can be blamed on me, not them.

Also, thank you to Rev. Jack Huttinga for his help in researching the beautiful area in which the book took place.

Finally, Linda Ford, what would I do without you to run ideas past and struggle with story ideas? Thank you, thank you.

The Only Best Place

Chapter One

mile. Think happy thoughts. Take a deep breath and . . .

"Hello. I'm Leslie VandeKeere, and I'm a farmer's wife."

No. No. All wrong. That sounds like I'm addressing a self-help group for stressed-out urban dwellers.

I angled the rearview mirror to do a sincerity check on my expression and pulled a face at my reflection. Brown eyes. Brown hair. Both the polar opposite of the VandeKeere signature blonde hair and blue eyes repeated throughout the Dutch-based community of Harland.

I cleared my throat and tried again. "This will be interesting."

Worse yet. Most women could break that code faster than you could say "fifteen percent off." *Interesting* was a twilight word that veered toward either the good or the dark side.

Right now my delivery was pure Darth Vader. A quiet and subdued Darth Vader.

I had to keep my voice down so I wouldn't wake my two

kids. After four *Veggie Tales* and a couple of off-key renditions of "The Itsy Bitsy Spider," they had finally drifted off to sleep and I didn't want to risk waking them. The trip through two states and one time zone had been hard on us. They needed the rest. *I* needed the rest, but I had to drive.

I stretched out hands stiff from clutching the steering wheel of my trusty, rusty Honda, the caboose in our little convoy. My husband, Dan, headed the procession, pulling the stock trailer holding stage one of our earthly goods. Next came his brother-in-law Gerrit, pulling his own stock trailer loaded with our earthly goods, stage two.

I had each bar, each bolt, each spot of rust on Gerrit's trailer indelibly imprinted on my brain. Counting the bolt heads distracted me from the dread that clawed at me whenever I saw the empty road stretching endlessly ahead of me.

A road that wound crazily through pine-covered mountains and wide-open, almost barren, plains. Now, on the last leg of our journey, we were plunging into a large, wide basin flowing toward rugged blue mountains. The fields were broken only by arrow-straight fence lines and meandering cottonwoods. Tender green leaves misted the bare branches of the poplars edging the road, creating a promise of spring, which I hadn't counted on spending here.

I hadn't gone silently down this road. I had balked, kicked, and pleaded. I had even dared to pray that a God I didn't talk to often would intervene.

Of course, I was bucking some pretty powerful intercessors. I'm sure the entire VandeKeere family was united in their prayers for their beloved brother, son, cousin, nephew, and grandchild to be enfolded once again in the bosom of the family and the farm where they thought he belonged. So it was a safe bet my flimsy request lay buried in the avalanche of petitions flowing from Harland.

The one person I had on my side was my sister, Terra. But she talked to God only when she'd had too much to drink. Of course, in that state, she chatted up anyone who would listen.

The friends I left behind in Seattle were sympathetic, but they all thought this trip would be an adventure. An *interesting* adventure, my friend Josie had said when I told her.

I glanced in the rearview mirror at my sleeping children. Nicholas shifted in his car seat, his sticky hands clutching a soggy Popsicle stick. The Popsicle had been a blatant bribe, and the oblong purple stain running over his coat from chin to belly would probably not wash out. A constant reminder of my "giving in."

Since Missoula, I'd been tweaking my introduction, and now that we had turned off the interstate, the miles ate up what time I had left. I had only ten minutes to convince myself that I'd sooner be heading toward the intersection of "no" and "where" otherwise known as Harland, Montana, than back in Seattle.

We would still be there if it weren't for Lonnie Dansworth—snake, scumbag, and crooked building contractor. The $90,000 worth of unpaid bills he left in the "Vande-Keere Motors" inbox tipped Dan's fledgling mechanic business from barely getting by to going under. The Dansworth debacle, in turn, wiped out the finely drawn pictures I'd created in my head of the dream life and home

Dan and I had been saving for. The home that represented stability for a marriage that had wobbled on shaky ground the past year.

The second push to Harland came when Dan's stepfather, Keith Cook, booked a midlife crisis that resulted in him doing a boot-scootin' boogie out of hearth, home, Harland, and the family farm, leaving a vacuum in the VandeKeere family's life that Dan decided we would temporarily fill.

Temporary had been a recurring refrain in our life so far. The first two years of our marriage Dan had worked for a small garage in Minneapolis while I worked in the ER at Abbot Northwestern Hospital. When a large company in Dallas needed a maintenance mechanic, we went south to a land of heat and long vowels. Two years later an opportunity to be his own boss came up in Seattle. When we packed up and moved, Dan promised me this was our final destination. Until now.

"It's only a year," Dan assured me when he laid off the employees, pulled out of the lease on the shop, and filed away the blueprints we had been drawing up for our dream home. We could have lived off my salary while Dan got his feet under him—worked on our relationship away from the outside influences of a mother Dan still called twice a week. But Dan's restless heart wasn't in it. Being a mechanic had never been his dream. Though I'd heard plenty of negative stories about his stepfather, Keith, a wistful yearning for the farm of his youth wove through his complaints. We were torn just like the adage said: "Men mourn for what they lost, women for what they haven't got."

The final push came when a seemingly insignificant matter caught my attention. The garage's bilingual secretary. She could talk "mechanic" and "Dan" and seemed far too interested in the state of our marriage. Her name showed up too often on our call display when I worked evenings. I confronted Dan. He admitted he'd been spending time with her, but was adamant they had never been physically intimate. Though the relationship had been over for a few months, she still worked at the garage.

I was angry, Dan was chastened, and her name never came up again. But her shadowy presence reminded me of how fragile a relationship can be.

Now, with each stop that brought us closer to the farm and Harland, I'd seen Dan's smile grow deeper, softer. The lines edging his mouth smoothed away, the nervous tic in the corner of one eye disappeared.

Mine grew worse.

A soft sigh pulled my eyes toward the backseat. Anneke still lay slack jawed, her blanket curled around her fist. Nicholas stirred again, a deep V digging into his brow, his bottom lip pushed out in a glistening pout. Nicholas was a pretty child, but his transition from sleep to waking was an ugly battle he fought with intense tenacity.

I had only minutes before the troops were fully engaged.

My previous reluctance to arrive at the farm now morphed into desperation for survival. I stomped on the gas pedal, swung around the two horse trailers, and bulleted down the hill into the valley toward my home for the next year.

My cell phone trilled. I grabbed it off the dashboard, glancing sidelong at Nicholas as I did.

"What's up?" Dan's tinny voice demanded. "What's your rush?"

"The boy is waking up," I whispered, gauging how long I had before his angry wails filled the car.

"Just let him cry."

I didn't mean to sigh. Truly I didn't. But it zipped past my pressed-together lips. In that too-deep-for-words escape of my breath, Dan heard an entire conversation.

"Honestly, Leslie, you've got to learn to ignore——"

Dear Lord, forgive me. I hung up. And then I turned my phone off.

I hadn't perfected Dan's art of selective hearing. He could let Nicholas cry while he calmly read the paper. The phone would ring and he wouldn't even look up.

Ignoring the phone was a genetic impossibility for me. Call display only increased my curiosity. Why had Josie phoned me at nine o'clock at night? What did the hospital want from me on my day off?

As for ignoring Nicholas? Not even an option. My little tyrant pushed and demanded until I paid attention, and then, when he got it, exacted more. Ignoring Nicholas was as easy as ignoring the guilt that had been my constant companion ever since I found out I was expecting an unexpected second child.

My master plan included one child, Anneke, followed by a maternity leave wherein I suitably bonded with my daughter, then enrollment in a day-care center chosen for its forward-looking program and trained caretakers. After Anneke's arrival, I returned to work as an emergency room nurse, doing a job I loved while saving up money needed for the large down payment on the dream home Dan and I had been planning since our wedding day.

God, it seemed, had a sense of humor. Twenty months after I ushered Anneke into the world, I found out I was pregnant again.

I didn't put on maternity clothes until the very last button refused to go into its buttonhole on my largest pair of surgical scrubs. I worked until the head nurse pried my fingers off the vital-signs monitor and pushed me out the door. When Nicholas fought through twenty hours of excruciating labor, I knew it was this child's way of getting back at me. I wondered if I could truly love this child the same way I loved Anneke.

However, as soon as the nurse brought that tight little bundle of flannelette that was my son—cap of dark hair, his unfocused eyes slightly crossed—a drowning wave of love and guilt washed over me.

How could I not have wanted this beautiful child? How could I have resented this innocent being? This perfect little person with fingernails like fragile shells, eyelashes that were a mere whisper across delicate eyelids. As I touched him, felt his realness nestling in my arms, I prayed for forgiveness to a God I had acknowledged only briefly before.

But Nicholas wasn't as forgiving and quickly started making me pay for my sins. All the kisses and cuddles snatched between housework and night shifts couldn't eradicate the debt he thought I owed. Nicholas was a tiny, unrelenting loan shark and guilt, his nasty skip tracer. No matter how hard I worked, how often I played with him, sang to him, told him I loved him, the interest on the loan kept accruing.

Nicholas now jerked awake, his head twisting to one side, his hands thrust out in front of him as if denying his entrance into wakefulness. He arched his back and launched directly into a full-fledged wail, his hands grabbing at the restraint holding him in.

"Honey, it's okay," I said ineffectually, hoping my soothing voice and nonsense words would calm him down.

Silly Mommy. Declaring things to be "okay" just inspired him to prove otherwise. In a nanosecond his cries filled all available sound space in the car, pushing away every fragment of peace and quiet.

I careened down the gravel road, driving too fast and not even caring. By the time I pulled into the yard, Nicholas's cries pounded against my tired head. I jumped out of the car and closed the door on my sobbing offspring. Nicholas on the verge of a pediatric coronary and Anneke sobbing her poor little heart out and I, Lord forgive me, stepping away from the car.

I craved a few moments of silence. Of separating myself from the tentacles of motherhood and wifehood tugging me in unwelcome directions.

The old two-story farmhouse, our home for the next year, stood solidly anchored to the ground, its foundations softened by shrubs and plants, and sheltered by a thick windbreak of planted trees.

The few times Dan and I had visited, I thought the house quaint. Now it simply looked old and tired and abandoned.

I drew in a long breath, then another, but I couldn't push away the muffled cries of my children. Forcing myself out of my selfish spat, I turned back to the car. Mommy once again.

The door of the house slapped shut, echoing sharply in the silence and as my mother-in-law stepped out of the house, inevitability laid a chilly hand on my shoulder.

"You're finally here," Wilma called out, waving to me from the back door.

Note to self: Ignore the "finally." She's had a hard time. Do not—repeat, do not—look for hidden agendas.

I had to give her credit, though, I thought as I checked out her khaki Capris and pale pink shirt. She certainly didn't look like she had been recently jilted by her husband.

And my goodness—makeup and earrings?

I tried not to glance down at my own stained T-shirt and wrinkled sweat pants. I had aimed for ease of movement and comfort for our trip out here, not knowing when I would have to leap a car seat in a single bound.

Wilma strode down the cracked and slanted sidewalk, looking past me. Her usual modus operandi. "Where's Dan?"

"He should be coming soon," I said, pushing down a pinch of hurt at her quick dismissal of my presence. "I got a little ahead of him and Gerrit. Nicholas was crying, so I wanted to get here before he burst a blood vessel. . . ." *And stop right now before she thinks you're a complete idiot instead of the incomplete version you're already projecting.* I opened the back door of the car, releasing the blast of my children's sorrow and pain into the great wide world.

Wilma's eyes snapped from the driveway behind me to my offspring. "Oh, you poor children," Wilma cooed in sympathy as she opened the door beside Nicholas. She pulled my tightly wound son out of his car seat, his back arching in anger. She held him close, stroked his damp hair away from his face, then glanced down at his coat. "Oh, my goodness. You're all sticky." She flashed me a quick patronizing smile, hitting the guilt bull's-eye in one shot.

"I'll take him," I murmured, holding out my hands for my son. "He probably won't settle for you."

Mothers should never, ever, utter such provocative statements. Especially around a child as contrary as Nicholas.

He gave out one more long wail, but I could hear his heart wasn't in it. Then he hiccupped a couple of times and wilted against his grandmother, making me look like some loser who would have known more about her child had she spent quality time with him instead of working evening shifts so she could keep him clothed in Baby Gap and Please Mum outfits.

Little traitor.

"Poor baby," Wilma clucked, stroking Nicholas's pale hair, a shade lighter than her own blonde hair, away from his flushed and damp face. "You've had a bad trip, haven't you?"

I did, too, I felt like saying, but, of course, mothers aren't supposed to want sympathy. I tried a smile on her, but Nicholas held her fussy attention so I bent over and pulled out a still-sniffling Anneke.

"Hey, pumpkin. That was hard to listen to Nicholas cry, wasn't it?" I said, lifting her into my arms.

She nodded, sniffed again, and peeked shyly over my shoulder at Wilma.

"Hello, Anneke," Wilma said quietly.

Anneke ducked her head down and clung to me. Okay, I confess I'm not above a little maternal smugness. Anneke's clinging warmed my heart and negated Nicholas's easy defection and Wilma's casual brush-off.

"Say hi to Grandma," I urged Anneke, ready to share her now. But Anneke only burrowed deeper into the neckline of my worn T-shirt.

"Oma," Wilma corrected as her prim smile glanced off me, then warmed as she stroked Anneke's hair. Anneke flinched and grunted her displeasure. Wilma's smile shifted into a disapproving frown.

Okay. Things were slithering right along. I needed points. Fast.

"I'm really thankful you and Judy were able to help us move," I said, injecting a hale and hearty note into my voice.

Wilma shifted Nicholas in her arms, her brisk nod accepting my little peace offering. "We were finishing up in the kitchen," Wilma said over her shoulder as she walked toward the porch door. "I thought that would be your first priority."

Wilma gave me more credit than I deserved. Right now my first priority was a selfishly long hot bath and a good book while Dan entertained the children. Such a dreamer I am.

As we stepped onto the empty, echoing porch with its gleaming floor, I wondered if I should take my shoes off upon entering the hallowed ground of the VandeKeere home place.

I glanced around, feeling the weight of history and responsibility slowly settle on my uneasy shoulders. Dan's father had grown up in this home with his siblings, and he and his wife, Wilma, had raised their children here.

Once Dan and I moved in, we would temporarily hold the keys of the kingdom.

I heard footsteps coming down the stairs above the porch, followed by the sound of humming. In spite of the weariness fuzzing my mind and dragging at my limbs, I smiled.

Where Dan's older sister Gloria was forceful and uptight, Judy was easygoing and friendly. Not hard to decipher which of the sisters I felt closest to.

Judy looked up as we came into the kitchen. The same wispy blonde hair that tufted Nicholas's head these days drifted out of the elastic holding the rest of her hair away from her face. Her sloppy, faded shirt and sweats couldn't camouflage her generous size—the polar opposite of her slim and put-together mother and sister. And when she smiled, I thought for the first time since we packed up the vehicles, *I can do this.*

Judy grabbed me in a quick hug and cupped my face in her hands. "Hey, Leslie. Don't you look adorable? I like the sassy haircut."

"Just got it done before we came." I threw out the comment as if the new me was something I had planned. Not done in a fit of anger when I discovered the loss of Dan's business. The sudden splurge was supposed to make me feel lighter, cheer me up. In the end it gave me one more bill to add to the "pay it or skip it" file.

"Suits you," Judy said, lowering her hands and resting them on my shoulder as her expression grew serious. "I'm so glad you and Dan and the kids are here. I know you're going to miss Seattle and your job and all, but you can make a home here, too." Judy's voice rose in a hopeful question. She touched Anneke's cheek, then slipped her arms around my shoulders again, encompassing both of us. She held on for that one extra split second, turning her hug from a polite gesture into a warm, welcoming greeting.

When she pulled away, Anneke stared up at her, soft hazel eyes still puffy from crying. "Who are you?" Anneke asked, sniffing.

Whoops. This she was supposed to know.

"Oh, c'mon, Anneke," Wilma chided. "That's your Auntie Judy."

"Do you remember me now?" Judy tilted her face to one side to catch Anneke's eyes.

Anneke shook her head.

"We have a picture of Auntie Judy and Uncle Dayton on our bulletin board. By the phone, remember?" In light of Anneke's momentary lapse, I needed them to know I hadn't neglected the legacy that was the VandeKeeres'. I took seriously the responsibility of the family pictures entrusted to me each year in Christmas cards and letters.

Judy winked at me, a small gesture that connected and forgave. "You'll remember us all soon enough, Anneke. But for now, we sure know who you are. Do you want to go upstairs and look at the rooms? Maybe if your mommy lets you, you can pick which one you want to sleep in."

Another solemn nod and then, to my surprise, she wiggled out of my arms to the floor and took Judy's proffered hand.

I looked around the large empty kitchen. The avocado green flooring I'd seen in pictures of Dan as an eager toddler did what it was bought to do. Last. The bright yellow painted cupboards almost hurt my eyes. I knew Wilma had painted the cupboards and chosen the flooring, and I felt her eyes watching me as I inspected my new kitchen. To insult her handiwork was to insult her.

Though Wilma was always unfailingly polite, I knew she didn't care for me. In her eyes, I had committed a number of cardinal sins of omission and commission. Where Dan and I had met headed the list of offenses. When Dan first introduced me to the family, he told the story of our meeting in the bar and laughed. Wilma gave me a glacial smile and never really warmed up to me after that. Though she never overtly referred to it, the subtext of her comments was that I had been the brazen hussy whose siren song lured Dan away from church and turned him into a lush. From that auspicious beginning, things went decidedly downhill. I was the daughter of an absent single mother, which had made the wording of our wedding invitations an awkward situation I got to hear about until Dan and I said "I do." In Wilma's mind, to not have a father was a misfortune, but to misplace both parents was irresponsible.

In addition to the lack of parents, I had a sister who smoked too much and laughed too loud when she drank too much. Which she did. At our wedding.

I was the home wrecker who kept her beloved Dan in Minneapolis, then dragged him to Dallas and finally Seattle—all places too far away for casual visits. Easier to blame me than acknowledge that Dan's restless spirit had us packing up and heading out every two years. Wilma even cast me as the impediment to Dan's return to the farm, when that sinister role obviously belonged to Dan's stepfather.

To add to the growing list, I had put her dear grandchildren in day care while I sauntered off to make bags of money saving up for an extravagant home that Dan would have to work all hours to keep up and furnish.

But my worst offense was superseding her as the number-one woman in Dan's life. The battle for supremacy had been declared when she insisted on a church wedding and when she demanded an expensive supper followed by a reception large enough to invite even the most removed of Dan's relatives. I smiled, nodded, then told her we couldn't afford all of that. She pushed; I held firm. End result? One afternoon wedding held outside to avoid the hypocrisy of a church wedding, followed by a stand-up reception that Terra almost ruined with her crazy in-your-face behavior.

The push and pull continued the first year of our marriage as I slowly weaned Dan off calling her every night to report on our life. I encouraged him to quit asking her for advice he never took.

Our combined debt load made it difficult to travel back to Harland for Christmas, so we decided to celebrate in our apartment in Minneapolis rather than at the family farm as she insisted we do.

Over time, our relationship became a one-way trip from bad to worse as Dan slowly became more my husband and less Wilma's son.

Now we were back in the sheltering, smothering bosom of the family. Though I knew I would have to make a solid stand, I also realized I needed to be sensitive to Wilma's current emotional state.

I glanced at Wilma, trying to catch some hint of the humiliation and sorrow I was sure she felt at the moment. It had been only a few months since Keith left. Wilma had been crushed in a public way and now stood in the house where she'd enjoyed much happier memories. I tried to imagine how difficult it must be for her.

"So, how have you been doing?" I asked, lowering my voice in an attempt to sound sympathetic, warm, and friendly.

Wilma gave me a puzzled frown. "I'm fine. Had a bit of a cold the other day, but otherwise, I'm fine."

And the sharing moment collapsed like a cheap tent in a light breeze.

Okay. On to chirpy and mundane.

"I see you left the electric stove behind."

"The last renters didn't have any appliances." Wilma glanced down at Nicholas. "I'll go clean him up."

As she swept out of the kitchen, I sucked in a big breath. Suddenly I had room to breathe and allow myself a little bit of pity. Compromise had brought me here and, as with so many compromises, it resulted in two unhappy people.

I glanced around trying to see positives. I had more space in this kitchen than in our two-bedroom condo . . . and more cupboards. I swept the room with a glance. My gaze snagged on the large, fly-specked window facing south. Through it I saw the unfamiliar expanse of fields, fences, and hills rising to the mountains.

Open, empty spaces.

If my life were a movie, this would be the moment when the soundtrack would get all quiet, intimate, and trembly and the focus would go soft. I would gracefully drift to the floor, holding my head in my hands and curling into the fetal position to chew on the cuffs of my sweater and mutter incoherently.

Okay, so it wouldn't be an Oscar-winning moment, but the way I felt, it had the elements of pathos, if not elegance. All the way here I had tried to be positive and upbeat, putting on my smiley face whenever Dan asked me how I was doing. But right now, faced with the reality of where we would be living for the next year and with whom, I felt a jolt of panic, if not Oscar-worthy emotion.

Upstairs, I heard Anneke bopping along behind Judy. Downstairs, water ran in the bathroom off the kitchen as Wilma repaired the damage done to Nicholas's jacket. Then, above that, the rattly growl of a diesel engine.

The truck pulling the trailer lumbered into the yard and drew up behind my little car. Dan had arrived with the remainders of our other life. Time for smiley face number three.

After a moment Dan stepped out and stretched, twisting his upper body the way he always did when he wound down after a stressful day. His dark blonde hair looked as if he had run his fingers through it in five different directions. But as he walked away from the truck stretching out his arms above his head, I could see that the smile creasing his face was one of a man arriving at the promised land.

"Dan's here!" Judy called out from upstairs. Her feet beat out a joyous tattoo down the stairs, Anneke close behind her.

"My boy is home." Wilma's soft exclamation from the hallway laid further claim on him. Still holding Nicholas, she strode out of the house down the walk, waving her free arm. Calling out his name.

Dan turned and ran toward his mother, like a soldier returning from battle. He caught her in his arms, Nicholas and all, pulling them toward him in a hug that shouldn't have made me jealous.

From: tfroese@hotmail.com
To: lesismore@montana.net

I can't believe U took three hundred and sixty-five Lindor chocolates along to Harland. U really are serious about this countdown thing, aren't U? How are U going to keep track if U suddenly have a snack attack, or Dan finds them? BTW— love the new e-mail name. How's life in La-la-land? Has Wilma told U she loves U yet? :) Will be a full-time job keeping her claws out of handsome hubby. I still can't get over how she ignored me at UR wedding, though I did my best to let her know I was there. Ha. Ha. Put a crust around that soft heart of URs. Don't let her get to U. Thankfully U got me giving pithy advice. Pithy I don't live closer. :) Keep UR house money in term deposit, else U will have nothin' when U head back to Seattle. I think UR crazy not to work. U'll find a job like that (me snapping finger) and U can use the money. I'm off to San Francisco next week. Try to find a job there. Kiss the kids. I'll send pics when I have some. Heard anything from Mom? Me neither. Sigh.

Terrific Terra Testing the Tides

P.S. Did U ever hear more about that chick Dan worked with, the one U said could speak two languages? Forgot her name.

From: lesismore@montana.net
To: tfroese@hotmail.com

I forget her name too. Not. I figured I would let sleeping dogs lie, if you get my drift. Near as I know she moved back home to Canada. And the three hundred and sixty-two chocolates are in a box under the bed. Oh. Goody. It's almost 6:00. Supper time and time for another chocolate. Must snack.

Lonely Leslie

From: lesismore@montana.net
To: josiepussycat@yahoo.com

Hey, Josie. I'm here. And, well, I'm here. And, like you said, things are interesting. Please keep me posted on what's been happening at the hospital so I'm not so out of it when I come back.

Les

Chapter Two

irst thing tomorrow we should empty the rest of the boxes," Dan whispered as he slipped into bed late Friday night. We had been here three nights already, and I was still in the throes of moving-denial, which meant that not all our stuff had been unpacked yet.

"I won't need the stuff out of them," I whispered back. I had been all for leaving them back in mini-storage in Seattle, creating an anchor that would eventually draw us back there. "Half those CDs qualify as antiques and the other half as poor taste and most of the books are covered in three inches of dust, one from each state we've lived in."

"You might want to read them," he said. "You might even have time to start a hobby."

"Right, Dan. Hobbies and me are nodding acquaintances— I read about them in the obituaries of older women." I stifled the jitters bubbling in my chest at the thought of being home day after day, trying to fill my time with knitting and tatting, baking—things I knew nothing about. For a moment I regretted my decision to stay home and nurture my relationships with kith and kin instead of going to work.

When I was younger, my sister, Terra, and I had made a list of must-haves for what we considered a normal life. Husband, kids (in that order), all safely ensconced in a new house in the suburbs of a suitably sophisticated city. My job and Dan's business had been ways to achieve these must-haves. For now I could put a check mark beside two of my goals.

The house would have to wait.

"I think the roof leaks," I said, counting the water spots on the ceiling of the upstairs bedroom.

"I don't understand why we couldn't take the downstairs room." Dan yanked on the blankets and shifted around, making his usual nest.

"There is no way I'm sleeping in the same room you were conceived in."

"Over-sharing, Leslie," he groaned.

"Besides, I want to be close to the kids," I whispered. "They're not used to this house yet." Nor was I. It smelled wrong and made me feel disoriented. The last time we'd been here, Dan and I had slept in the spare room, Anneke and Nicholas in this room. Though our furniture graced most of the house now, this still seemed like Wilma's domain.

Dan cuddled closer, a contented sigh drifting over his face. And why shouldn't he be feeling all jovial? Things were tipping heavily in his favor. We were in his old house, in his old yard. His territory.

"Gloria phoned last night," Dan said, pulling me close.

"She thought maybe we could have a family dinner here sometime. Maybe after church."

Family? Dinner? All those VandeKeeres in this house? Wilma and Gloria walking through the house doing minute inspections of my kitchen and bathroom, critiquing my furniture and towels and snooping through my medicine chest?

"That sounds like a good idea, but really, Dan, I'm still an apprentice in this whole family-supper course." And if it was after church, the implication would be that we should attend the service. Though this subtle morphing of my husband to his pre-Seattle days wasn't a shocker, it created a low-level fear that we were making incremental shifts away from our goal.

"Leslie, you're a great cook." He lifted himself up on his elbow, and in the half light of the bedroom, his eyes shone down on me.

"If it's tacos or barbecued steak you want, hey, I'm your girl. But Sunday dinner? I've never met a turkey that I didn't dry out. I hate cooking ham, and I don't know how to make my own croutons." I pulled out a list of excuses, determined not to get railroaded again by his crooked smile and soft voice. In the months before we moved here, I hadn't seen much affection from Dan but now, it was as if back in his home place, he was slowly reverting to the man I had fallen in love with. Loving, attentive, and caring. Though the shadow of Miss Bilingual still hung like a silent specter over our marriage, she was slowly getting eased away by the obligations and expectations I was sure Dan felt from his family.

"Leslie," Dan said, going down softly on the *ie* part of my name. I hate that light intonation even when I know it's coming. It signals his intention to be long-suffering and patient with the woman he promised to stay faithful to until death do us part, but Oh, Lord, it shouldn't have to be this hard. "It doesn't have to be Sunday dinner. We can buy pizza and ice cream and have them over during the week. We haven't gotten together in this house since Mom and Keith moved out."

"I don't know what kind of pizza they like."

"It would be fun to have a dinner here, in the old house. For Mom's sake."

The burden of moving into the flagship of the Vande-Keere line dropped like a yoke on my shoulders. This house had been built by Dan's grandfather, replacing the older house now overgrown with willows and poplars, which replaced the small dugout that Great-grandfather Willem VandeKeere had moved his young bride into when they first came to Harland from Holland.

This yard was a veritable museum of VandeKeere history, and I had taken reluctant possession of one piece of it. And if Dan's sisters wanted to have a family supper, it was a sure bet that in the long run I was helpless to stop the plans. But for now, the home was mine and the control was mine.

"Let me think about it, okay?" I said, reverting to Ambiguous Wife as I turned to him, trying to re-create the faint moment of warmth he had kindled in me.

"Sure. Whatever." Dan flopped onto his back, replying with What's-So-Hard-about-This Husband.

I deflected my automatic sigh. No need to fan the flames with that outpouring of breath.

"Oh, by the way, Mom's coming over tomorrow," Dan said.

"Does Wilma think we need more help?" I had used my limited powers of persuasion to convince her to stay home today. I couldn't maintain a loving façade and deal with another litany of "suggestions" on how to arrange the kitchen or veiled criticisms about the number of appliances I owned. So what's wrong with having a crepe maker *and* a waffle iron? "Isn't she tired from helping out all day yesterday?"

"She said she'd like it if you'd call her Mom." Dan's comment was delivered in quiet, reasonable tones.

Not happening, though. I already had a mom. Not the best mom, but she was *my* mom.

"She wants to talk about our finances," Dan said, dropping that bomb as casually as I would a dirty diaper. "To give us some advice."

I pressed my hand to my thumping heart, trying to keep it in my chest. *Swallow,* I commanded myself. *Breathe . . . and relax. Again. Good girl. Now you can talk. Use short words and . . . smile . . . and you're on.*

"That's okay, Dan. I'm sure we don't need her help."

"She doesn't mind."

Obviously the smile had worked too well. I needed to lay down hard and firm boundaries. With each dish I put away and each item of clothing I hung up I felt tiny threads anchoring me to this unfamiliar place that was Dan's home and territory. "We've managed for years without her help, I'm sure we'll be fine now." Nice firm delivery, strong intonation. Much better.

"But the farm belongs to her."

"I don't see the connection."

"She'll be writing the checks."

Don't panic. Do not panic.

"Mom's real good with money. She can help us out. Said she had a budget drawn up for us."

"I don't think . . . We never really . . . Budget?" I couldn't grab the right words from the hundreds that swirled around my head. "I thought you would be doing the finances."

He looked up at the ceiling, avoiding me. "Mom asked if you would mind if she kept doing it. I said sure. It will make things easier for us, and it gives her something to do."

Dread spiraled in my stomach and made a home. Wilma. In charge of the farm finances. Our finances. It didn't take a gourmet cook to know this was a recipe for disaster. "But how is she going to figure out . . ." I faltered, still trying to absorb this latest information. "Why didn't you ask me—"

Dan feathered a quick kiss over my forehead. "You had enough to do getting the house set up. I didn't want to bother you."

"If we're going to be talking finances, are you going to tell her about the assessment?"

When Dan and I talked about giving a year of our time to help out his mother, we decided it would be in our best interests to have an assessment done of the farm. We assumed once we left, the farm would be sold. I knew Dan. Every place we'd lived in, he'd fixed up. Every place we lived, his work hadn't been recognized. This time I wanted to make sure that Dan was paid for any improvements he did.

"It seems a bit soon for that," Dan hedged.

I was about to encourage him to do it anyway, when I

heard Nicholas let out a loud wail. Kiddy timing. I could have let him cry but inherent guilt won over the current crisis. Our boy needed me so seldom, I didn't want to miss any chance to connect.

"Let him cry," Dan grumbled.

"He's in a strange bed in a strange place . . ." *Like me,* I thought, glancing around the room that still had Judy's posters on the wall. "I'll be right back." We weren't done with Wilma and the budget thing yet.

But as I walked down the hall, Nicholas's already loud cries grew in intensity, and by the time I got to his door, his screams filled the room and he thrashed about, kicking his feet, his adorable face squinched so tight that his eyes disappeared.

This is going to take a while. I lifted Nicholas, a stiff and unyielding bundle of terry cloth, out of his crib, his screams piercing my ears.

Anneke appeared in the doorway as I tried to rock Nicholas out of his snit. She sidled up to me, sniffing. "I'm scared!" she called out above Nicholas's cries.

And I knew that by the time I got back to the bedroom, Dan would be snoring.

The farm has to support two families now." Wilma folded her hands over the checkbook as if defending it from my grasping clutch. Her gaze flicked from me to Dan and back again. The significance of the equal triangle we formed around our circular kitchen table wasn't lost on me. Dan sat equidistant from me and his mother—torn between two women again. I almost felt sorry for him. Emphasis on *almost.* "We will have to watch every penny," Wilma continued.

Considering that Wilma already had that department well in hand, I didn't think the pennies needed my eagle eye on them, as well. I glanced at Dan, sitting across from me at the kitchen table, wondering what he thought of the check that lay on the table in front of him.

Dan had been up before me this morning so before I could tell him I didn't want his mother coming over, she was striding up the sidewalk, farm books in hand and a take-no-prisoners look in her eye.

"We won't have lots of expenses." Dan stroked his chin with one hand as he picked up the check with the other. "If the farm pays for fuel for the truck, power, and upkeep on the house, we won't need to use this for more than our personal stuff." He smiled up at me. I felt heartened by the glimpse of disappointment I caught in his eyes.

"Of course, if things go well this year, I'm sure I'll be able to give you extra money." Wilma smiled as if she had just granted us stock options in a blue-chip company. "Though I think the amount you are getting is a fair bit."

A fair bit? If she knew how much I could make in a week, she would choke on her decaf.

"Now if you will look at this budget, you'll see that it won't be hard to live on what you are getting." She handed me a paper. Call me stubborn, but I didn't spare it so much as a glance. Dan, however, dutifully picked it up and looked it over, nodding his approval.

"I did put in an entry for contributions to the church . . ."

Wilma let her sentence drift off, her eyes on her son. "That is, if you will be coming to church. Of course, there's no obligation . . ."

Of course, there *was*. While her words were meant to let us off the hook, the raised eyebrows and the tilt of her head caught Dan neatly in a snare of expectations.

"It would be wonderful if you could come."

"Of course we will," Dan said, sitting back, setting the paper down. I caught the question in his eyes as he looked at me and I subtly shook my head.

"I wouldn't be comfortable," I said. "I'm not familiar with church."

"C'mon, Leslie. You've gone at Christmas and Easter." Dan's awkward laugh made me nervous. "And you, your mother, and sister used to go when you could get . . ."

"That's enough, Dan," I said sharply, cutting off his sentence.

Wilma's eyes darted from Dan to me and then back again, as if hoping she could weasel out what I had stopped. Not a chance.

"Well, I hope you will reconsider coming to church." Wilma continued, as always brisk and efficient. "And look over that budget and tell me what you think."

I already knew what I thought of it. Not much. But she was the payer and we were the payees. Powerless and puny.

"There's one more thing. I would really like to have the family together to talk about the farm. We are in a bit of a cash crunch . . ." She paused and I immediately thought of Keith, but she rallied and forged ahead. "So if Gerrit and Dayton could offer us some advice, that would be helpful."

"That's a good idea," Dan said.

"Your Grandma VandeKeere has been asking after you and the kids," Wilma said to Dan. "Once seeding is done you should go."

"I haven't seen her since Christmas. How is she doing?"

Wilma leaned a bit closer, as she brought him up to speed on the care and maintenance of the family tree.

I picked up my coffee mug and washed it out as their conversation covered all the twists and turns of names and connections I doubted I would ever master. I didn't feel left out. Not a bit.

How was I going to make it for another eleven months, two weeks, and five chocolates?

Wilma finished her coffee, wound down the conversation, then went to the living room to see Anneke and Nicholas.

"Sorry about that church comment, Leslie," Dan said as he set the coffee cups beside the sink. He touched me on the side of my neck, then pulled me close in a hug. I really needed the hug and turned gratefully to him, letting his strong arms hold me close. "I shouldn't have . . ."

"It's okay," I muttered against his shirt. I didn't want to talk about my past; I had my husband, I had my children. And, oh yes, I had a budget. But we would get through that as well.

I leaned back, holding his face between my hands. I let my eyes linger over his blue eyes, his long nose that veered ever so slightly left, his high cheekbones all framed by hair that needed to be cut.

"Hey, you," Dan whispered, brushing a strand of hair out of my eyes.

"Hey back." I smiled at him. He was here, with me. He was smiling at me. He was lowering his head.

"I'm going now," Wilma called out. I jumped.

He wasn't going to kiss me.

"Thanks for coming, Mom." Dan let go of me. Then gave Wilma my kiss.

"Bye, Leslie," she said, tossing me a quick wave. "Dan, I was wondering if you could have a look at my car. There's a funny knocking sound in the engine."

As they walked out the door, Wilma took him by the arm and pressed her head against his shoulder. Dan bent closer and gave her a hug. They talked a moment as Wilma brushed her fingers over his cheeks.

I really wanted to give her the benefit of the doubt. I really wanted to be a good person and feel sorry for her. But as I watched her clinging to Dan, I felt that although Miss Bilingual had been left behind she had been replaced by another, more powerful combatant for my husband's heart.

From: tfroese@lakeshore.com

To: lesismore@montana.net

So Dan is making noises about going to church? So not fair. Tho I figured that would happen once he got back to mommy. She's got a hold of him U gotta watch. And the whole finances and Wilma thing? Lee-lee, be afraid. Be very afraid. I don't think this woman has met a dollar she couldn't put in a bank account. Speaking of, mine should be out of the red soon. Got a job. Not great, but we can't all be brilliant nurses. And hey, I think I have a right to push U back to work. After all, I had a part in UR edjumacation, sugar plum. If anyone can prove the Froeses can be productive members of society U are the one. Two kids, one husband that UR still married to. :) Give my darling nephew and niece a hug kiss from their

Adventurous Aunt, Alive and Adorable

From: lesismore@montana.net
To: tfroese@hotmail.com

The noises about church have become actions. He went this morning and took Anneke with him. I just remind myself to grow accustomed to this phase—once we're back in Seattle we get normal back.

Laconic Leslie

From: lesismore@montana.net
To: josiepussycat@yahoo.com

Hey, Josie. You alive? Write to me. Talk to me. Buy a coffee at Starbucks for me.

Les

Chapter Three

hat are you doing?" Dan bent over my shoulder, the scent of hay and warm masculinity teasing my nose. It was a kinder, gentler smell than the gag-me-in-the-throat odor of oil and gasoline fumes that usually swirled around him after a day of mechanic work.

Farm chores had turned Dan into a kinder, gentler man. Seattle Dan would never have had time for lingering in the kitchen, watching me work. Then again Seattle Leslie would not have been frowning over the arrangement of cookies on a plate for company.

"I'm trying to make these cookies look tastier than they are," I said.

"I don't know why you bothered." Dan slipped his arms around my waist. "My mother and sisters said they'd bring dessert."

"Well, I felt duty bound to provide my own temptation." I sighed as I moved away from him. Much as I wanted to, I didn't have time to nuzzle. I had domestic duties to perform and an obligation to bring the family shrine up to Vande-Keere specs. Nuzzling was on the B list.

When Dan had come home from church on Sunday, it was to inform me that his mother, Gloria, Gerrit, and their kids were coming over on Tuesday to help with the cows. This was said with an expectant look that I could translate only as, "Could they stay for supper?" In a moment of insanity I caved in to familial pressure. Then, as if to make my breakdown complete, I invited Judy and her family to join us for pizza afterward, as well. This necessitated making a quick run to the grocery store in Harland to buy said pizza and, of course, cookies that I didn't have to bake myself.

Wilma had made her bi-daily visit yesterday with her take-no-prisoners attitude . . . and a pile of cookbooks. She had helpfully folded over the pages that held Dan's favorite recipes. It wasn't like I didn't have cookbooks of my own. It was just that I read recipes the way I read science fiction—with skepticism and disbelief that people could even think this stuff up. I put the books in an obscure corner of a cupboard and closed the door of self-preservation on them. I may not be in charge of the farm checkbook, but I was in charge of this home and this home *bought* cookies.

"C'mon, be a sport." Dan rubbed his nose along my neck. "We haven't done this for ages."

In Seattle, I worked night shifts so Anneke and Nicholas would spend minimal time in day care. When Dan's business declined, he started working extra hours in a futile attempt to save it. That gave us time for nothing more than an occasional heart scrawled on a Post-it note slapped on the fridge. Hardly enough to keep the fires of passion burning brightly.

Now it seemed he had time. I could hardly complain about his desire to indulge in some marriage maintenance.

So I closed my eyes, concentrated on Dan, and allowed myself a quiet moment of leaning, concentrating on the welcome warmth of his shoulder, the rough hairs on the back of his hands layered under mine. I had always loved Dan's hands. The first time he kissed me, his fingers played over my face as if reading my features by Braille.

"Do you think you'll have enough temptation for later?" Dan growled, his voice heavy with innuendo.

And now I was thinking about "her" again, juxtaposed against images of a female praying mantis who ate her males after they mated.

The forgetting would come, I assured myself as Dan's arms held me close. A time would come when I wouldn't imagine her in Dan's arms. When I wouldn't wonder if that faraway look in his eyes was about her.

"What do you mean, later?" I asked hoping the right amount of flirtation slipped into my voice, reassured that he still found me attractive.

"For the meeting. After supper."

"Oh." My heart downshifted with a mixture of relief and disappointment. He meant cookies.

"I talked to Gloria and she agreed that we should get together like Mom suggested to bring me up to speed."

Meanwhile I was trying to switch lanes, switch gears, get in sync with the direction of my husband's thoughts. "Good idea." I pressed my lips together to stop a surprising tremor. I still loved him. It was his feelings for me I was unsure of. Meanwhile, we had practical issues at stake, and I knew he wasn't ready or able to face down his family en masse. The burden of our future lay on my size-eight shoulders. Lovely.

"Are you going to talk about doing the assessment, then?" I asked.

Not the best thing to say given his mood, but someone had to look to the future—away from this place.

"We agreed to make sure the year we are here is recognized. At least a little bit." Wilma's visit last week had made this a priority.

Dan sighed and pulled away, and the brief moment of marital togetherness twisted toward the usual Business of Being Married. "I don't think tonight is a good time. We've got other important things to discuss with the rest of the family."

"The longer we wait, the longer your family is going to think we're staying." Dan's stern expression made me feel like a negotiator in a hostile takeover. I wanted to be on the same page as Dan, but the hard stuff was important, too. We had to be practical. Take care of our little family. "Once the year is over, we're moving back. It's not fair to raise your family's expectations and then dash them."

We had gone over it all before we came here. Talked about it endlessly while we checked out all our options. He couldn't switch allegiances on me now.

His resigned sigh told me that he was shifting back to my side. "Okay. I'll try to work it into the conversation tonight."

The hard block of tension that had lodged in my chest

dissolved. I gave him a look that hopefully transmitted love, but to cover all the bases, I added a cookie to the gesture.

"Thanks," he muttered, then leaned back against the counter as he ate, cupping one hand under the other to catch the crumbs. "I remember eating cookies straight out of the oven in this kitchen," he said with a smile.

It was a throwaway memory, but saying it in this kitchen where thousands of homemade cookies had been baked added a bit of a sting. "Good thing you didn't marry me for my baking skills," I said with a quick smile to show him I was okay with the memory, on the surface at least.

"I married you for other reasons." Dan leaned over and kissed me again. Though his declaration was imprecise, his kiss was a good kiss and as I looked into his eyes I thought, *I love this man.* A warmth I hadn't felt in a while curled around my heart and I reached over to touch his cheek.

The screen door slapped open, and Anneke burst into the house. "Mommy, Mommy, I found a worm!" She held it up, a long pink string that bunched and pulled and made my stomach curl.

Okay. Calm voice. Soothing voice. Don't make her drop it. "Honey, Mommy doesn't like worms in her kitchen." Surely it was too cold for worms. Where had it come from?

Anneke held it up in front of her face, inspecting it further. Then, with a light shrug, she turned and ran directly into her little brother, who had followed her in. Nicholas fell back on his diapered bottom, his bland expression registering only mild surprise.

But Anneke collapsed in a tangle of long, skinny legs and

flailing arms, her cry of indignation a complete overreaction to what had actually happened.

"Where's Teddy, the worm?" she exclaimed.

"Should have gotten her a dog," Dan muttered, finishing his cookie as Anneke scrabbled around on the floor.

"I lost my worm!" Anneke wailed.

Two words, *lost* and *worm,* galvanized me into action.

I pushed past Dan and snatched Nicholas into my arms before he found Anneke's new pet and inspected it the way he did with all new discoveries. With his fingers, then his mouth.

I quickly scanned the floor. A pink worm should be easy to pick out on the Day-Glo linoleum. "Honey, stop crawling. I see it." I juggled Nicholas, reaching for her arm just as she put her hand down in the wrong place.

And Teddy was no more.

Anneke discovered this the same moment I finally snagged her hand. The wail she let loose would send air force pilots scrambling to their planes.

Dan made it to the murder scene in time to catch his sobbing child in his arms.

"A little speed would have been nice," I muttered, shifting Nicholas's chubby weight on my hip.

"It's just a worm, Leslie."

"That's now squished all over our kitchen floor and your daughter's hand."

Dan inspected Anneke's hand, then wiped it on his shirt. He cuddled Anneke, whose sobs didn't show any sign of shifting to normal.

"Dan, for goodness sakes, wash her hands," I snapped,

raising my voice to be heard above the growing din. *Great, Leslie. Way to motivate him.* I opened my mouth, apology ready to spill out when I heard the door open behind us followed by the thump of shoes and two young girls burst into the house.

"Hey, Uncle Dan!" they both said at the same time.

I looked over my shoulder in time to see the grinning faces of Tabitha, Gloria's daughter, and Allison, Judy's oldest girl. Tabitha was fourteen, Allison thirteen, and to me they were interchangeable. They could be sisters instead of cousins.

"Is your dad at the corrals already?" Dan asked Tabitha, obviously thankful for the interruption.

"He's backing up the trailer with the horses in it," she answered in a tone that made it clear she was Gloria's daughter.

"Then I better get going." I saw an unfamiliar light of pleasure in his eyes as he scrambled to his feet. Dan had been talking all day about the horses Gerrit was delivering, and the sparkle in his eyes left me with a flicker of jealousy.

He handed a still-sniffing Anneke to Tabitha, flashed me a quick smile, and left.

Nicholas let out an angry wail, but Tabitha, still cradling Anneke on her hip, tickled him, distracting him from the departure of his beloved father. I often wondered how Dan got such a huge return on such a small investment of time. I spent precious hours playing with Nicholas, reading to him, and still he resisted my charms. A quick tickle, a brush over his chubby cheeks was all Dan had to bestow on our son and Nicholas was desolate whenever he left.

"So how do you like being on the farm?" Allison asked,

watching Tabitha play with Nicholas and Anneke but making no move to join them.

Time to put on my hearty voice. "It's really beautiful here. So much scenery." So far I wasn't really faking too much. This morning, as I cleaned, every time I glanced out the window, the nearness of the mountains took my breath away. As did the amount. When God made Montana, he didn't skimp on the mountains.

"Didn't you have mountains in Seattle?" Tabitha asked, scrunching her face as Nicholas's chubby hands reached for her long hair.

"We did, but I could only see them out of the upstairs window of our condo." And only if I leaned my head against the window frame to look past the rows of other condos that blocked my view.

"So why didn't you have your own house?" Allison asked, now leaning back against the counter inspecting her nails.

"We were going to buy one—" I stopped the note of self-pity creeping into my voice.

"But you moved here instead," Tabitha said with a quick grin. She got up from the kitchen floor, swung Nicholas into her arms, and held out her hand to Anneke. "Is it okay if I take the kids outside?" she asked. "I thought they might like seeing the horses."

"They might be scared," Allison said. "They're still city kids."

Tabitha simply shrugged Allison's comments away with a grin. "Not anymore. They're farm kids now."

"Give me a few minutes, and I'll come with you," I said.

Tabitha may have allowed Montana to make its hurried

claim on my children, but I knew that the horses and cows Tabitha felt so comfortable around would terrify my children.

"Are you going to help?" Tabitha asked.

"Isn't that what farmers' wives do?" I was going to make the best of our time here, and if working with large, unwieldy creatures was part of it, I could play *Little House on the Prairie*. I hadn't considered helping with the cows until Gloria had called. I don't know if it was the take-charge note in her voice that spurred me on when she said she and Gerrit and the kids were coming or the blanket assumption that I wouldn't be able to help. Pride makes a woman do foolish things.

With a shrug in my direction, Allison followed her cousin out the door, leaving me alone to do what quick preparations I could before the VandeKeeres invaded.

Twenty minutes later I stepped out into the empty yard. I glanced around but could neither hear nor see Allison, Tabitha, or my children. I heard the distant whinny of a horse but couldn't place the direction. Suddenly the rattle of a truck penetrated the stillness and an empty stock trailer came toward me from behind one of the barns. Gloria was driving, and behind her, in the cab of the truck, I saw a jumble of heads.

The truck screeched to a halt and three boys piled out in a tangle of arms and legs and laughter, followed by a barking dog. The boys glanced my way, nodded, and gave me the sheepish smiles of self-conscious teenagers. The dog ignored me.

I racked my brain for the boys' names. Joseph, Douglas, and Nathan. Gloria and Gerrit's boys. During our time in Seattle I had accompanied Dan home once for Christmas and once for a family get-together. All I remembered of the nieces and nephews was a bunch of kids sitting still long enough for the obligatory prayer before the meal, then filling their plates and running off to various rooms in the house.

Just as Gloria turned the truck off, Allison and Tabitha stepped out of one of the older barns on the yard.

The boys had already run off toward the fields, the dog following, its tail waving like a plume, its mouth open like it was smiling at the prospect of moving cows.

"Good morning, Leslie," Gloria said as she got out of the truck. Gloria was a slimmer, more nervous version of Wilma. Pretty in an uptight way. "So. Here you are." She twitched out a smile. "It's good to have you with us. Mom's so happy about that, too."

I almost mouthed those last words along with her. Each time I met Gloria she said precisely the same thing. Like she had written down somewhere, "Things to say when I meet Leslie," and each time I got a sense of her watching me, looking for cracks or possibly the same lewd behavior that my sister exhibited at the wedding.

And now the next thing would be . . . Wait for it . . .

"So how have you and your lovely children been doing?"

Bingo. Okay, these were often the same blank phrases tossed out when people first meet. A conversational equivalent of letting your car run to warm it up. But with Gloria the conversation was always the same phrases in the same order and she always started with, "So,"—pause—"here you are," as if my presence was something she'd have to get used to all over again.

Today she had her long blonde hair tucked under a farmer's cap. She wore coveralls with a pair of gloves hanging out of the back pocket. In spite of the farmer attire, she still managed to look like she was setting some new fashion trend.

I couldn't help but glance down at my clean blue jeans and pale pink jacket.

"Sweet coat, Leslie," Allison said.

I didn't detect any irony in her voice, though I noticed too late that she and Tabitha were wearing faded and worn jackets and jeans.

"What the well-dressed farmer's wife wears," I quipped.

"You won't be doing much," Gloria said, waving her hand at me, dismissing my capabilities with the flick of her wrist. "So you won't have to worry about getting dirty." Another twitchy smile.

Down, hackles.

"I'm a farmer's wife now," I said with a blustery confidence that was ninety-seven percent fake. I still couldn't tell barley from wheat or hay from straw, but I was undaunted. "I can help."

"Well then," was all she said.

"Are the horses unloaded already?" Tabitha asked.

"Dan and Dad are already headed out to gather up the cows. And Oma is getting the needles and medicine ready." Gloria pulled the gloves out of her pocket. "We'd better get going."

"Wilma's here, too?"

"Of course." Gloria frowned. "The cows belong to her."

I nodded. My big attempt at integration struck aside by the reality of ownership. Wilma's cows. Dan and I were simply hired help.

"We'd better get going." Gloria's command became everyone's wish, so we started off. Nicholas babbled as Allison pulled him along in the wagon. Anneke sang. And I had to look back to make sure these happy children were my offspring. My long nursing shifts had left me with the tired and cranky version of my children after they had spent ten hours in day care. My mission had always been to pick them up, feed them, and clean them up before Dan came home, then get ready for another twelve-hour shift at the hospital.

Beside us Gloria and Tabitha chatted about the weather, school, the cows, the farm. At one point Tabitha laughed and dropped her head onto her mother's shoulder.

The little gesture made me feel a tad despondent. Gloria just seemed too good to be true. Like her mom. Inadequate me had been secretly looking for chinks in Gloria's armor that would make me feel less deficient, but so far she seemed well and truly in charge of her world.

"So, what do we do with the cows?" I asked Allison, slipping my hands into the pockets of my "cute" jacket.

"We process them. Give the calves shots for blackleg before we put them out on summer pasture in a few weeks. You never did this before?" Allison's voice suggested that processing cows was something normal people knew all about.

"Honey, the first time I found out that the milk I bought in those nice cardboard containers actually came from a cow, I was physically ill."

Allison released another laugh, which netted us a curious look from Tabitha.

"You've gotta come and see my dad's milking parlor," Tabitha said with a touch of pride as she glanced over at us. "It's so clean you can eat off the floor."

"That might not mean much. I can sometimes eat off my kitchen floor, but that's only because I didn't manage to pick up all the crusts that Nicholas threw off his high chair in the morning."

Tabitha and Allison both laughed. Auntie Leslie. What a cutup.

"I don't believe you're that messy. Auntie Judy always said your place in Seattle was immaculate."

The secondhand praise from my favorite sister-in-law warmed my heart.

"You lived in a condo, didn't you?" Gloria asked.

Judy and Dayton had managed a trip to Seattle to visit us, but Gerrit and Gloria could never get away from their dairy farm long enough to make the trip. So they never saw our place in Seattle. Nor our place in Dallas, or Minneapolis.

"Yes. We were hoping to get a house, but when Dan went broke, that was the end of that dream." I kept my voice detached, breezy, skimming over the soggy ground of disappointment. "I know it bothered Dan . . ."

"It wasn't his fault." Gloria rushed to her brother's defense. But what surprised me more was the anger in her voice. And the flash of accusation in her eyes. Did she think the fault was mine?

I looked ahead, trying not to take this personally. She was simply upset for her brother, that was all.

"Hey, Aunt Leslie, did you ever go see the underground

city in Seattle?" Tabitha asked. "We learned about that in some history class a while back."

Bless you, child, for validating my existence. I told her about the tour I had taken one afternoon when a friend from work and I had finally managed to make a coffee date sans children.

While we talked, we made our way around the shed where the machinery was stored. As we came through a break in a line of trees that surrounded the farm yard it was as if the land opened up in front of us. All I saw was a vast expanse of field with mountains crouching along their edges. No houses or buildings broke the breadth of the vista. My steps faltered as a wave of dizziness washed over me. It still caught me unawares, this endless space. It was as if the world had been sucked empty.

"You okay, Auntie Leslie?"

I flashed her a nervous smile. "So where are the cows?" I asked, pulling in a long, slow breath into my oxygen depleted lungs.

Tabitha pointed past a barbed wire fence that bordered the field.

Against a tree line beyond the fence, I saw the herd of cows moving toward us. A man with shaggy blonde hair anchored by a baseball cap waved a rope as he whistled through his teeth at the cows slowly moving ahead of him.

What made all of this unusual was he was doing this from the back of a dark brown horse . . . and the cowboy was my husband.

Gloria and Allison forged on ahead while I stopped in my tracks to watch. I knew Dan had a horse. Its name was Taffy, and it was part quarter horse, part Morgan. That was information I had absorbed casually without understanding the implications for me and my life, until now.

My husband was an honest-to-goodness cowboy.

One of Gerrit's boys rode up, and soon he and Dan were moving the herd inexorably toward us. The cows and Dan silhouetted against the mountains were truly a calendar-worthy picture. Why hadn't I brought my camera? The picture would make a lovely memory.

"That's good, right?" I asked as my eyes caught Gerrit and the boys moving the herd in our direction. I could feel my heart speed up. "The cows coming at us like that?"

"Yeah. Though one of them could take off for no reason," Tabitha said with a casual shrug. "Cows aren't too smart."

Her words were almost prophetic. As we watched, a cow swung its head to one side, took a few steps, then veered off, running out toward the open field, its calf right on its heels. One of the boys ran toward it to cut it off as another cow followed. Then Dan turned his horse and galloped after the cows, the dog racing alongside of him. The cows turned, but the rest of the herd that had been heading toward us stepped up the pace, and soon they all were running—a lumbering, bellowing group of bovines, calves skittering away from the pack and then returning. All that lay between this thundering herd and us were four feeble-looking strands of barbed wire strung between fence posts that now seemed way too far apart.

"That's not so good," Tabitha said with an air of nonchalance that I envied deeply.

"Okay, I don't like this," I said, not even attempting to

keep the shaky note out of my voice. My fear rose up at their relentless progress, but Gloria and Allison kept going ahead of us, following the fence, and Tabitha, pulling my fragile youngsters, followed them.

"Gates! Open the gates!" It was Dan. Yelling. Loudly.

I'm not your typical submissive wife, but when Dan yelled, it inevitably sent me into action. Trouble was, I had no idea what action to go into.

Gloria and Allison did know and started running. They clambered up and over the wooden fences and disappeared, only to reappear on the other side between the corrals and the cows. Above the bellowing of the cows, I heard the screech of metal as Gloria pushed open one half of a large gate, Allison the other.

The cows saw them and their forward momentum slowed, but only for an instant. Then they veered off in a cloud of hooves and bellows and dust, away from the men and dog behind them and away from the corrals.

Dan yelled, Gerrit waved his arms, and the boys tried to cut them off as the dog raced alongside the cows, but the animals thundered on oblivious to their cries.

I guessed this wasn't the desired effect.

"Dad's gonna be ticked," Tabitha said in a matter-of-fact voice. "Better head over there and see what we can do."

I looked back at Nicholas and Anneke, who had been watching the entire production with wide eyes. "I don't think the kids should get close to this."

"They'll be okay. They'll be on the other side of the corrals," Tabitha said with a shrug.

I didn't share her optimism. Those cows were big and heavy and loud. The boards of the corral didn't look strong enough to hold them back. I had two children here. Which one would I be able to save if the cows burst through the boards?

"Hey, Aunt Leslie, the kids will be fine," Tabitha said, sensing my unease. "Uncle Dan would never let anything bad happen to them." She gave me a crooked grin that was so much like Dan's I felt suddenly like I could trust her.

"Okay. You're the farm girl."

Tabitha punched me lightly on the arm, the ultimate teenage compliment.

Taffy snorted and stamped one hoof as Dan conferred with Gerrit, Gloria, and Wilma, who had joined him outside the gates. The dog lay at Gerrit's feet, his head on his paws, clearly bored. By the time I got there, they had come up with another plan.

Gerrit and Gloria's son Joseph was assigned to gate duty. He was only eight years old and small, even for his age. He would get trampled.

I don't know what got into me. Delusions of grandeur? A desire to show Gloria and now Wilma that I could do this, too?

"I can do the gates," I said with false bravado, quickly, before my brain could catch up with my mouth. "How hard can it be?"

Dan straightened up in the saddle, and his expression made my moment of stupid self-sacrifice all worthwhile. His features softened and he winked at me. "Are you sure?"

"Yeah." I glanced back at Tabitha, who gave me a thumbs-up. "I'm sure."

He told me what I needed to do. As soon as the cows were inside the gates, I was to swing them shut. There were two gates, and they needed to be chained up in the middle where they met. Simple. And Dan assured me that the cows would respect a shut gate. I had to trust him on that. As a backup, he gave me a long flexible stick, covered with woven nylon with four small knotted strands waving from the end. A whip that he assured me the cows would respect as much as the gate. I looked at it, then at him. Okay. Whip. Shut gate. Cows' respect.

I started to feel a little more confident.

Dan gave me another smile, then clucked to his horse, turned it around, and cantered off toward the herd of cows, the dog racing alongside him.

My heart kicked in my chest. That was my husband looking so suave and western. So at ease on the back of the horse, one hand holding the reins, the other resting casually on his thigh. So in charge of his world. So different from the worn and tired man I had seen the past few months. I could fall in love with him all over again.

I hugged the thought close to me. Love hadn't factored into a lot of our interactions back in Seattle. Fear, frustration. And, oh yes, betrayal.

Definitely not one of the five so-called love languages.

So who knew? I thought as I watched my man slash cowboy being all manly and magazine ad-worthy. Who knew what could happen?

Twenty minutes later the cows moved our way again. As

they picked up speed, heading toward the gate, my previous bravado and confidence were replaced by fear that started in my stomach, then spread its icy fingers out to my arms, my legs, my head. I clenched the gate in a death grip, the chill of the metal adding to my ominous feeling that something terrible was about to happen.

C'mon, Leslie, an eight-year-old kid was going to do this.

The cows kept coming, the ground shaking. I was facing death. Dan blurred into the dust-filled distance.

An unwelcome thought pierced my bluster.

We hadn't updated our wills.

Our children would be parceled out among family members. Separated. Would my mother push for guardianship? Would she and Wilma fight over the kids? I could see them already facing each other down, our poor children crying, calling out for their mommy and daddy.

I almost got a lump in my throat. But then the pounding of the cows' hooves grew. I stood perfectly still, trying to make myself insignificant, unthreatening.

The cows got bigger and bigger, noisier and heavier the closer they came, and the only thing that kept me at my post was a larger fear of ridicule and the fact that I was wearing an unsuitable pink jacket. I wanted to prove to Dan, to Gloria, and especially to Wilma that I could do this in spite of my lack of farm experience and fashion sense.

I expected the cows to come in a huge rush, but as soon as they saw the corrals, they slowed down. But the momentum of the herd kept them moving. They pushed past me, a jumble of brown and black bodies, snorting and bellowing their displeasure as they swung large shaggy heads and rolled their eyes in my direction. Heat and steam engulfed me in a bovine sauna. I fumbled with my whip, ready to close the gate that they would respect.

Right.

"Wait, wait!" Dan called out as the herd going past me thinned out. But the cows in the front had seen the end of the line, and spun around, using their large heads to push the cows behind them out of the way, bellowing and snorting and straining against the boards of the corral. They creaked, and I hoped that they would hold the churning herd.

Gerrit whistled and his dog started barking, nipping at the stragglers' heels. A few kicked, but the dog danced out of harm's way and the herd slowly pushed its way into the corrals. The last dawdler trotted past me when I heard Gloria yell, "Shut the gate! Shut the gate!"

That was my cue. I swung one half of the gate closed, wincing at the screeching metal that would surely clue the cows in as to what was coming down.

I ran across the opening to get the other half just as Dan shouted, "Watch that cow!"

I looked up in time to see a large, angry-looking animal turning around. The monster was huge, with buggy, bloodshot eyes. It was ten times my size and coming straight for me.

"Stop it from getting through!" yelled Dan.

He was being crazy, yes? He was making a joke, right?

I stood in the breach, holding the narrow whip he promised they would respect and waving it threateningly even as the renegade cow accelerated toward me.

A hero I was not.

I jumped.

The cow thundered through, then stopped.

From my vantage point behind the gate, I saw the dog scoot out around the cow, face it down. To my shock and surprise, the cow spun around, kicked out behind her, but ran back inside the corrals.

Here was my chance to vindicate myself. Still clinging to the gate, I ran, the opening growing smaller, smaller. The cow turned, faced me again and started coming again as I caught the chain from the other gate. With trembling hands I flung it around, hooking it like Dan had showed me, realizing that me and my pink coat were drawing the cow's attention, hoping, praying, that the cow wouldn't charge.

But it only blinked, shook its head once, as if warning me, then turned and trotted back to join the herd, its moment of rebellion quashed.

My heart thundered in my chest and my arms hung like limp spaghetti. I had overcome. My children weren't motherless. Dan wouldn't have to find someone over the Internet to marry him. I took a long, slow breath as the adrenaline eased.

Dan vaulted off his horse and came running over. "Are you okay?" he asked, all solicitous. He put a dusty hand on my pink jacket, and I didn't even mind.

"I'm fine," I said, wavery with relief.

"You did good," he said, hugging me quickly. "You did fine."

"Way to face that cow down, Aunt Leslie!" Tabitha

shouted from the other side of the corrals. She was holding Nicholas. Anneke stood on the fence beside them, her tiny feet clinging to an opening, her arms hooked over the rough lumber. She was laughing at the cows milling about in the corral below her, showing absolutely no fear. Nicholas waved, grinning a wet, drooly grin.

Nathan, the middle boy, strode over and high-fived me. "Good job, Auntie."

Dan winked at me, then vaulted over the corrals to get ready for the next stage.

I clung to the wooden fence, glancing at the cows. Some stood quietly; others wandered around bellowing for their calves that had gotten separated in the melee. But on my side of the fence, I felt safe. I felt strong. I was woman, hear me roar.

And I was definitely going to walk over and join Wilma, Gloria, and Dan.

As soon as my knees stopped trembling.

Chapter Four

eslie, do you have pastry forks?" Gloria cornered me as soon as I stepped back into the kitchen, face sore from scrubbing and my wet hair pulled into something resembling a rat's tail rather than a ponytail.

When we got back from working the cows, I had ducked out to wash dirt out of my hair and try to create a kinder, gentler Leslie. No mean feat, considering the dust from the cattle caked every inch of my body, inside and out. My "cute" pink jacket was now a sickly gray and my jeans sported a rip in the knee I probably got from clambering up and down the wooden fence. My head rang from the constant bellowing, so I could hardly see straight. Hardly the idyllic afternoon experience I had pictured in my head when Dan first spoke of this adventure.

Gloria had brought extra clothes along and made the transformation from farmer's wife to hostess in less time than it takes to say "lightning change." Her tidy hair and impeccable lipstick put me to shame. *I should take notes,* I thought. Wilma had gone home to change, leaving her alter ego in charge of domestic duties. "We'll need the forks for the cheesecake," Gloria continued.

Ah yes. The cheesecake. Gloria had brought it. Dan's favorite, she had explained as she put it on the kitchen counter.

I took one look at my artfully arranged trans-fat-laden store-bought cookies and discreetly hid them under a cooking-pot lid.

"I thought I saw them when I unpacked." My mind scrambled as I pulled open the utensil drawer. The faint odor of burning cheese rose from an oven overloaded with pizza, but I couldn't shake this mission.

"I looked in there already," Gloria said. "It would be nice to have them."

That comment, plus the fact that I got the pastry forks from Gloria as a fifth-anniversary present, was a surefire recipe for pressure. I dove into the pantry and then the disastrously disorganized odds-and-ends cupboard to no avail.

Coming out empty-handed and desperate, I almost collided with Judy, who had arrived carrying a large crystal bowl full of layers of cake, whipping cream, and chocolate shavings. If I didn't know she loved to bake or that the nearest bakery was half an hour's drive away, I would have guessed she bought it and was trying to pass it off as her own.

"Hey, Sis," she said, handing the bowl to Gloria with a casual gesture. "Dump this wherever."

Judy turned back to me, and her smile shifted. Grew warm and welcoming. "So farmer's wife, now you can add processing calves to your résumé."

"The employers will just snap me up."

"So, what should we do about the pastry forks?"

I stifled a sigh. Persistence, thy name is Gloria.

The door opened again and the kids burst in, enveloping me in another round of hugs and kisses and well-wishes and noise.

And all the while my pizza was overflowing and burning to the bottom of the oven and Gloria's fingers were tapping out her desire for my elusive pastry forks.

This was going to be so-o-o much fun.

Stop dissecting the dessert," Judy said, pulling the large crystal bowl away from Dan, who was mining Judy's trifle for leftover chocolate. We were all gathered in the kitchen digesting the remnants of the various delicious desserts. It was a tight squeeze, but the family insisted that it was cozy.

"I'm making sure I get all the chocolate," Dan protested, pulling the bowl back toward him.

"You poke to your heart's content," Wilma said with a benevolent smile in Dan's direction. "You're probably going to throw it away when you get home anyway, aren't you, Judy?" Wilma asked, lifting an eyebrow that turned the question into a suggestion.

"Gee, Mom, not so sub with the subtext," Judy said with a laugh, as she patted her ample hips.

I was surprised she could be so blasé. Even as my anger rose on her behalf, Judy seemed completely unfazed.

"Dan always did love chocolate," Gloria said with an indulgent smile.

"But he didn't always respect it. Remember when Dan and Cousin Ben had that food fight here on his birthday?" Judy laughed and leaned over the table toward Gloria. "That chocolate cake that you made?"

"It would have turned out if you hadn't distracted me."

Judy dropped her head back and let out a hearty laugh. "Still blaming it on me. I bet you still think I was the one who ate your Halloween candy when really it was Uncle Orest who was always pilfering it when he came over."

"I did catch you with a Hershey bar."

"That was my Hershey bar," Dan said, coming up for air.

Everyone laughed as the conversation splintered, then separated and flowed past again, memories intertwining with conversations about work, kids, and people I had heard only vague mentions of from previous visits. I sat back and let it flit past me. I didn't know the people they talked about and by the time I caught the connection, they were off on another topic. Hard not to feel like a stranger in my own house.

Tabitha and Allison huddled on the floor at one end of the table, their conversation liberally sprinkled with prepositions and exclamations. Near as I could tell, for the past half hour they had been analyzing the latest romance of a mutual friend and hadn't, to my knowledge, come to any conclusion whether they approved or disapproved of the liaison.

Allison bounced Nicholas on her lap, playing peekaboo with him.

The little piker had been a tangle of misery all evening, crying and rubbing his red cheeks against my face when I tried to comfort him, twisting his blankie around his hands when I tried to entertain him. And now he giggled at everything Allison and Tabitha threw at him, charming them with his tenor belly laugh and clapping his chubby hands.

Lovable little turncoat.

And Dan, well, he was looking around at his family, that half-smile of his that never failed to give my heart a little kick, hovering over his well-shaped lips. He looked so content and so at peace that for a quick, sharp moment my envy was bigger than my love for him.

"So, Leslie, when are you going to put the garden in?" Wilma asked.

What? Where did that come from?

"I . . . I didn't plan on gardening," I said, flailing into this new topic like Nicholas waking up from a nap.

"You'll like gardening," Judy said. "Besides, fresh vegetables are so much better than those strip-mined, poor excuses for food that the local co-op tries to pass off," she continued with surprising vehemence.

"Did that nasty co-op turn down your application to sell your vegetables to them again?" Gerrit asked. I guessed this was an ongoing family joke, and I was glad for the deflection away from me and anything botanical.

"Without even giving us any kind of explanation," Judy huffed. She puffed out her lip and blew her bangs out of her face.

"I think they should be happy to get fresher vegetables," Wilma added, obviously put out with a store that wouldn't take produce from her own child. "I'll have to talk to Dennis Verweer."

"No, Mom," Judy answered. "I can take care of this myself."

"Dennis is an old friend of the family."

"Mom, if I find out that you even mentioned the word *produce* and my name in the same sentence in front of Dennis, I won't come to Sunday dinner for two months."

Wilma and Judy's gaze held as I sucked in a breath, amazed at the standoff happening before my very eyes.

"But darling, surely . . ."

"Three months," Judy said, holding up three fingers.

Wilma pressed her lips together, glancing at Dan as if hoping to enlist his support, but Dan was still buried in the trifle.

Full of admiration for Judy's bold move, I kept watching. I knew where I had to go now for "Coping with Wilma and Gloria" advice.

"Hey, Judy," Gloria put in. "Mom's just trying to help."

Judy just smiled and lifted a fourth finger.

"It was merely a suggestion," Wilma said, a grudging note in her voice. Her glance skittered away from her daughter and grazed over me, caught and held. Her eyes narrowed as if warning me not to try this at home. I almost held up my hands in a gesture of surrender. Judy was in a league of her own.

Dan looked up from the trifle and wiped his mouth. "Speaking of gardening, once the crop is in, we could work on ours, Leslie," Dan said with a helpful grin, as if I had been restlessly hovering on the edge of the garden, rake in hand, an avid desire to stake beans burning in my heart. "Wouldn't you like to put a garden in, Anneke?"

"That would be fine," Anneke chirped from his lap, having gravitated from the kids' table, where Tabitha's watchful eye kept everything under control. She laid her head on her father's chest and wrinkled her nose at me. From any other child this could be misconstrued as a taunt. From my Anneke, a sign of deep affection. I took what I could get from her.

I reached over and stroked a delicate strand of hair behind her ear in a moment of motherly connection. Dan caught my glance, and the smile deepened.

He tucked his hand behind my head and lightly stroked my neck with his fingers. Like he used to when we were courting. And like then, a shiver of delightful goose bumps flickered up my spine. I had missed this and welcomed it now.

"Hey, you," he said, his voice dropping to that intimate octave that never failed to elicit a smile from me. My heart warmed to him. He was really trying.

"Hey, yourself."

We had our own highly evolved communication system.

Anneke blinked slowly at me, her imitation of a wink and I winked back at her as Dan smiled at us both.

"So, do you want us to come over and help you with the garden?" Wilma asked, her helpful question pushing a conversational wedge through this quiet moment between me and my husband. Anneke pulled away, making Dan lower his hand from my neck and our little warm family moment cooled.

"We could get some seeds at the co-op. It wouldn't take that long." She had obviously given up on her face-off with Judy, but I didn't have Judy's background or forcefulness. I was still working my way through the maze of family relationships here and trying to find my place. But I resented feeling like I was failing a test I hadn't studied for.

"Might be too early to plant yet," Judy intervened.

"I'm putting my garden in next week," Wilma insisted.

"What's your hurry, Mom?" Judy pushed back. "Lay off the poor city girl. She doesn't know about gardening."

"I've planted a few things," I said, feeling torn between accepting Judy's offhand definition of me and Wilma's push to assimilate me completely into rural life.

"And they all died," Dan said with a light laugh.

"Not right away," I protested.

Wilma and Gloria didn't need to laugh nearly as loud as they did. Judy shook her head at her brother's humor.

"I doubt it's that bad," Judy said.

That's it. In my new will, Judy's getting my diamond earrings.

"I'm good with the greenhouse, but death on house-plants," Judy complained.

And *my opal necklace.*

"I think that's why my houseplants died," I said. "They got jealous and died of spite because I spent more time fussing over patients than I did over them."

"You won't have to worry about that now," Gloria said. "I'm sure you're looking forward to taking time away from your job."

"I liked being a nurse," I said. "I know I'll miss it."

"Yes, but now that you're on the farm, wouldn't you rather stay home and putter around the house?"

"I never perfected the fine art of puttering," I said with my own feeble attempt at a joke.

"Judy could give you a few tips," Dayton said, pulling himself out of his conversation with Gerrit. "Didn't you give a course on that at the ag fair last year?"

"That was pottery." Judy rolled her eyes and turned to me. "You'll have plenty of time to come and visit us if you're home all the time. I could teach you to sew if you want. We could have a lot of fun."

"I don't know about fun," I said slowly. "All that cutting and pinning. I doubt I can be trusted with so many potentially lethal instruments."

"Leslie was the kind of child who ran with scissors," Dan put in, giving me a gentle poke.

"Sewing is a good way to save some money on clothes," Wilma said. "You might want to think about it."

No pressure from the family here. Sewing. Gardening. Who did they think I was? Ma Walton?

"And if you're not going to be working, that is something to consider," Gloria put in. "Farming is a wonderful life, but there isn't always a lot left over when all the bills are paid."

"Great, Gloria," Dan said with forced jocularity. "You're going to make her think we're two checks away from being broke."

"Been there," I muttered. And from the looks of the check we were getting from Wilma each month, we were still only a few dollars from "there."

Dan shot me a hurt look, and I regretted my quick tongue. I reached over to lay my hand on his arm, to recapture the moment we had shared earlier.

"Anneke, can you come to Oma?" Wilma's quiet request

pulled Anneke off Dan's lap and brushed my arm aside and the chance was gone. "Could you get me the Bible?"

Bible? Low-level panic struck again. Was I supposed to have it handy? I knew we had our own around somewhere. Someone from Dan's church had given us one on our wedding day.

Anneke danced toward her grandmother, then stopped, looking puzzled. "What's a Bible, Oma?"

Wilma's eyes cut to Gloria, who lifted her perfectly plucked eyebrows in a "What did you expect?" expression I couldn't help but resent. These two were like the tag team of familial censure.

"It's this book over here, honey," Wilma said, pushing her chair back and picking up a large black book from the countertop. I relaxed. I guess Wilma figured, in this house it was Bring Your Own Bible. "Why don't you bring it to your father, and he can read something out of it for us?"

"That's okay," Dan protested. "Someone else can read."

But it was too late. Anneke, bursting with pride at her own importance, hustled to our end of the table carrying her sacred burden and duty.

Dan bit his lip as he took the heavy book from her, then pulled her onto his lap. "Anything in particular?" he asked as he flipped through the pages, their rustling the only sound in the reverent quiet that had descended the moment he laid the Bible on the table.

Even the teenagers, who had seemed oblivious to what was going on with the adults, became quiet. Everyone seemed to know the unwritten rules, I thought, glancing around the table as people sat back, folded arms across chests, or leaned forward, waiting.

"Read what you like, Dan," Wilma said quietly.

Dan bit his lip, frowning as he paged through the Bible. Then a gentle smile eased over his lips as he stopped. "I've always liked this piece." His hand smoothed over the page like a caress.

"This is from 1 Corinthians 13. I know it's read a lot, but I want to read it again." He cleared his throat, took a slow breath, and started reading.

" 'If I speak in the tongues of men and of angels, but have not love, I am only a resounding gong or a clanging cymbal. . . . It always protects, always trusts, always hopes, always perseveres. Love never fails.' "

I listened to the cadence of the words and caught a tone in Dan's voice I had never heard before. It was gentle, soft, and carried warmth and comfort.

Everyone else seemed to pick up on it as well. The lines in Wilma's forehead eased away; a genuine smile warmed Gloria's face. Judy stared off into the distance as if remembering other Bible readings around this table, in this room.

Even Anneke, my wiggly worm, now leaned against her father, her head on his shoulder, the quiet sound of his voice soothing her restlessness.

I turned my attention back to Dan and what he was reading. " 'And now these three remain: faith, hope and love. But the greatest of these is love.' "

The warmth in Dan's voice pushed the last words deep into my being. More than the words, the tone and timbre of his voice touched me, as if he had become another person right in front of my eyes.

"Thanks, Dan." Wilma's voice sounded like a benediction. "That was lovely. Could you close in prayer?"

I felt nervous for my husband. Reading the Bible was one thing, but praying off the cuff? The only thing resembling a prayer I'd ever heard from Dan was a muttered "Good Lord" when he was especially frustrated with Anneke or Nicholas.

Dan nodded slowly, glanced around the table at everyone but me, then lowered his head. And as he prayed, I got another surprise. His voice filled with an emotion I'd never heard before. I opened my eyes and glanced around the table. Everyone, even the teenagers, had their heads bowed and their eyes closed.

Once again I felt peripheral to a family I couldn't understand.

A pause followed the end of Dan's prayer and then the table erupted into a cacophony of noise and busyness.

I started clearing away the plates, when Judy put her hand on mine. "Don't. The kids can clean up. We'll move to the living room."

The seven adults seated themselves in chairs, on floor pillows, laughing and chatting as they settled in. I perched on the edge of a kitchen chair that had been hauled in, feeling like the cliché homely girl at the prom who people smile patronizingly at but never talk to. The noise coming from the kitchen counterpointed the buzzing talk in the living room.

Judy and Gloria's kids alternately cleaned up and entertained mine.

I shot a yearning glance over my shoulder at the chaos of the kitchen and the kids. Call me immature, but that party seemed like much more fun.

"So, Mom, how are you doing? Really?" Judy asked point-blank during a lull in the conversation. "Keith's been gone two months now. Have you heard from him?"

Wilma shook her head as she toyed with her wedding ring and released a long, slow sigh. "Not a thing. It's like our marriage never even existed." Wilma's voice wavered. The hint of vulnerability softened the starch in my spine I habit-ually felt around her. I grasped that moment of pity I couldn't find when she was her usual pillar of strength. She pressed trembling fingers against her cheeks. "I wish I knew what God is trying to teach me through this."

A heavy silence followed that remark, and I resisted my usual urge to fill it.

Give me a sucking chest wound or a broken arm and I was Mrs. Capable and Efficient.

Broken hearts and questions about God were best left to those with more experience and wisdom.

Gloria patted her mother's shoulder instead. "God will make His purpose clear, Mother. We have to be patient."

"But what are you and Dan going to do about the farm in the meantime?" the ever-practical Judy asked, her elbows resting on her knees man-style. "Let's be honest, Mom. Keith was a worse farmer than he was a stepfather."

"Judy, you shouldn't say that," Gloria protested, glancing

at me as if to gauge my reaction. "Keith did the best he could with what he had."

"Hey, Glor, is it time for your medication or mine?" Judy said in exasperation. "Keith was lazy. Straight up."

"Judy, that isn't humorous," Wilma said, but her tone held an air of resignation.

"I'm dead serious," Judy continued. "Forgive and forget is important, but let's be realistic, Mom. He wasn't treating you well the past few years. And we all know Dan left the farm because of Keith. This isn't classified. I'm sure Leslie knows that he was a lousy stepdad." She glanced at me, singling me out and in a moment of what could be described only as non-inspiration, I gave a lame shrug.

"Now, now, Judy. That'll do." Dayton put his hand on Judy's shoulder in a "down, girl" gesture that netted an angry glare, but when she saw Dayton's smile, she laughed herself and sat back. Dayton turned to Dan. "Now that we've covered the past we're supposed to forget, I'm sure you and Mom have gone over the bank stuff. Why don't you tell us how it's doing?"

Dan's shoulder drifted up as he glanced at Wilma. "Mom has a better handle on the money part than I do right now. I've been concentrating on getting the cows fed and going over the equipment in time for spring seeding."

I felt embarrassed for my husband. Wilma should have brought him up to speed on the farm's finances, but it was as if Wilma had regained control and wasn't going to relinquish it too quickly. Which made me even more convinced that the farm needed to be assessed before Dan did one more minute of work on it.

"I know each of you has your own farm and your own problems to deal with," Wilma said, "but I hoped you could give Dan some advice. He's been away from the farm for a while, and I'm sure he could use the help."

I tried to catch Dan's eye, but the shag carpeting held his intense concentration.

Wilma informed everyone of the farm's financial affairs. Though it seemed the farm was doing well, it hadn't prospered under Keith's tenure. Equipment hadn't been maintained, and land had been mismanaged. Income was steady, but it was down. The farm would need an input of cash before Dan put a crop in. Gerrit recommended a short-term loan. The wheat futures were good, as were cattle prices. With proper and diligent care, the farm looked like it might pull out of its current slump and pay it back.

Which meant that the farm would be worth more at the end of our year than at the beginning. Which came back to the need for an assessment to be done. I waited for Dan to assert himself, but he kept the topics of his conversation limited to putting in the crop and what kind of fertilizer to use.

Suggestions were thrown out on whether to plant barley or wheat. Whether to hay the one quarter or silage it. Should Dan dig a new well or hope for high rainfall to augment the irrigation available from the canals? Gerrit and Dayton launched into a lively discussion about crop yield and water rights and the high cost of fertilizer, spray, and fuel.

Everyone had something to add, some piece of advice to give. The women as well as the men.

Everyone except Miss I Grew Up in an Apartment. Call

me crazy, but I couldn't catch the wave of enthusiasm these people were projecting over inanimate objects. Land. Seeds. Equipment.

"I don't want to borrow money if we don't have to." Wilma twisted her hanky in her hands. "Your father worked too hard to get this farm where it is now. In spite of Keith's lack of care, I know your dad would want Dan to take it over." Wilma gave Dan a maternal glance that held a world of hope and expectation. Which in turn sent a shiver down my spine. Did she know? Had Dan told her?

"But the farm has a value, Mom," Dayton said. "Borrowing isn't a bad thing. Not in long-term planning."

I could feel my heart pushing hard and fast against my chest. Dan wasn't saying anything. His mother assumed we were staying here. This had to be stopped.

"Has anyone done an assessment on the farm lately?" I blurted out.

Blank looks all around, then all eyes focused on me.

"There's never been a need," Gloria said, frowning.

"I'd like to see one done before Dan does any more work here." *There.* It was said and out in the open.

"Why do you want that?" Judy asked, snapping a cracker in half.

I took a deep breath, ignored my husband's warning glance, and plunged in. "I think it's important for us to ascertain the value of the farm at the present moment." *Listen to you, Leslie. You actually used the word* ascertain. "Because Dan will be working on the farm for a while and hopefully increasing the net worth. I would like to make sure he's re-compensed for his work."

And now recompensed. *Aren't you the business whiz?*

"You're drawing a generous wage from the farm,"Wilma said, clearly puzzled where I was going and clearly unaware of what constituted generous. "And you'll be building up equity over the long term."

"Leslie means——" Dan started.

I cut him off at the impasse. Too late. I had the conversational reins now. "What I mean is *when* Dan and I leave"——I made sure to put exactly the right amount of emphasis on *when*——"I want to make sure Dan is paid for the work he's done on this farm. I don't know how much growth there'll be in the year we are here, but Dan is a hard worker and I want to make sure that is recognized."

If it weren't for the shag carpeting in the living room, you could have heard a pin drop. I did hear a whistling intake of breath, then a "well," and without moving my eyes from my fingers, twisted nervously around each other, I knew these ominous sounds had come from Wilma.

I felt myself mentally backpedaling. But I pressed my lips together, holding back any verbal retreat I might be tempted to indulge in. I risked a glance at Dan, who was tapping his fingers against his arm, staring at me.

I've seen a lot of Dan's expressions in our married life, but this boldly assessing look was a new one. And I didn't like it.

"I agree that we should have an assessment done," Dan said, and I slowly felt the tension in my shoulders relax. *Finally.*

"Why?" Gloria asked. "It's going to cost the farm money, and for what purpose?"

"The purpose is to make sure that if the value of the farm goes up because of the work Dan puts in it, that is acknowledged when it's time for us to leave."

Judy's puzzled look glanced off me and onto Dan. "You just got here! Why is Leslie talking about leaving?"

Dan had obviously not prepared them for this. Had he been hoping that once we were here I would change my mind?

I scanned the room. The sisters wouldn't meet my eye. Worse, they were looking at each other, and I certainly didn't have to be a VandeKeere to know what they were thinking.

Our poor brother.

I closed my eyes, sucked in some air, and counted to seven. I couldn't wait 'til ten, but knew I needed more than five.

"Our move here was never meant to be permanent." I focused on Judy, the one sister I felt the most connection with. But her glance was the merest whisper of her eyes over my face, and in that brief moment I caught a shout of disappointment that hurt. I resisted the urge to explain. Dan was supposed to have done all the groundwork, but obviously the sisters knew nothing. His mother, even less.

Retreat in the face of overwhelming odds would not have been cowardly. But fear and pride can make people do undiplomatic things.

"We're only here a year and then we're moving back to Seattle. That was supposed to have been made very clear." *By your precious Dan.*

Dan's arms folded across his chest as he leaned back. Away from me.

"Is she right?" Gloria asked Dan. "Why does she want to go back?"

"We had discussed it," he hedged, lifting his hand in a vague gesture.

Discussed it? We'd drawn up a plan with a timeline. Stay in Harland long enough to get the farm in decent shape to sell. Get Wilma set up, give ourselves a chance to regroup, and make some decisions about what to do when we moved back to Seattle again. I had initially lobbied for six months, but Dan had contended that it wasn't worth the bother if we didn't stay at least a year.

Gloria slipped her arm across Wilma's shoulders, as if protecting her from the heresy of a daughter-in-law who didn't want to live here with the family. If anyone could imagine that. "This is news to us. However, if that is your plan"—her gaze cut to me as if the idea were mine and mine alone—"then we shall have to work within that."

Dan shot me daggers, and I knew we were going to have a "talk" when everyone left.

"For now we still need to decide what to crop," Dayton said, tapping his large fingers on his arm, thankfully bringing the conversation to a manageable, practical topic. "As well, the tractor needs a new engine. I'm sure you can get Uncle Orest to help you put a new one in."

More ideas surfaced, but I understood from the lack of eye contact that I no longer had a part in the conversation. At some unseen signal, Judy got up and brought coffee around and Gloria brought out cream and sugar. The sisters worked in an easy, efficient rhythm.

Me? I sat there. Inadequate hostess. Ungrateful daughter-in-law.

Finally I got up from my chair. "I'll go check on the kids." Eyes swiveled my way, telegraphing unspoken relief.

They wanted me gone. Well, gone I could manage. So I headed out of the room, leaving them to make their decisions without the interloper.

I quietly made my way back up the stairs and slipped into Dan's old bedroom, where Nicholas now held court. He lay curled up on his stomach, his behind in the air, his arms tucked under him like a cat. As I tried to rearrange him into a more comfortable position, he flung his arms out and stiffened. I recognized the first step toward wakefulness and withdrew, pulling his quilt over his shoulders even though I knew in ten minutes he'd shrug it off again.

Thankfully summer was coming and I wouldn't have to worry about how to keep him warm in this drafty old house.

Winter would be another story.

Don't go there yet. One day, one chocolate at a time was the only way I was going to get through this year. The jar sitting beside my bed down the hall whispered to my mind like a siren. *Come eat us. Drown your sorrows in dark chocolate with creamy centers.* If scarfing down the entire contents of the jar would reduce my time here I'd be unwrapping and chomping quicker than you could say "liposuction." But it wouldn't shorten our time here, and it *would* make me sick. I glanced at Nicholas's window but caught only the reflection of light coming through the partially open door behind me. Moving to the window ledge, I looked out at, well, nothing.

Just my ghostly reflection superimposed on a thick, heavy darkness broken only by pinpricks of light from the stars, millions of miles away.

Cue the violins, I thought, turning away. I headed downstairs and bypassed the living room, where the responsible adults were still talking. I joined the kids playing board games in the kitchen. It was cozy, welcoming, and nonjudgmental.

My kind of place.

From: tfroese@hotmail.com

To: lesismore@montana.net

I wouldn't sweat the VandeKeere hegemony. Honey U need to get UR own job. UR own paycheck. Remember that dollhouse we got when the Hardistys down the hall moved out? U were always playing with it, pretending family and house. Don't lose the dream. If U Rn't careful that farm will suck U in and, maybe even suck U dry of money. And what if U don't end up with anything in the end? U were born to be a nurse. Okay, U R a great mother too. And a good wife. But when I see U with patients I just know this is what U R called to be. Think about it. BTW, gotta new man in my life. And no, I'm not going to pull a Mom. He's a nice guy and I'm being careful.

Sultry Sister Sashaying in San Fran

From: lesismore@montana.net
To: tfroese@hotmail.com

Make sure you're careful. Remember, it's marry first, THEN have kids. I would love to go back to work, but my stock in the family isn't real high right now and Dan is happier that I'm home with the kids. I have to confess I am too, but I do have a lot of time on my hands. I love my kids, but I really miss my job. The eternal struggle between kids and purpose beyond these four walls that are starting to close in on me at times. But don't worry about me. I'm okay. Or so Dan keeps telling me. He's managing to keep busy. I'm still working out the whole "shouldn't he feel more guilty" scenario. He apologized and it helped, but since moving here he's been happier, more settled and I'm the one feeling disgruntled. Also haven't heard a thing from Josie back in Seattle. Some friend. At least you write once in a while. So. Write!!

Lugubrious Leslie

Chapter Five

 think the next time you throw stuff like that out in front of my family, we should discuss it first." Dan pulled Anneke's toast out of the toaster and handed it to me to butter and spread.

"We did. Endlessly. One year. That's what you promised me." I turned back to our son, his weaving head struggling to follow the path of the spoon I waved around with my other hand. Hard to hold summit meetings and feed a squirmy toddler his breakfast at the same time.

Nicholas got his plump lips around the spoon and then tried to grab it. "And we also agreed to ask for an assessment on the farm," I said, snatching the spoon from Nicholas's porridge-encrusted hands. I handed Anneke's toast to Dan. "Can you cut this, please?"

"You didn't need to bring the assessment up at the family meeting," Dan muttered, hacking the remnants of her toast into nine small pieces. He handed the plate to Anneke, who grimaced at the mangled bread. No way was she going to eat that. Had I handled her precious peanut-butter toast in such a cavalier manner, I would have had to convene the United Nations Human Rights Tribunal.

Dan glared at me as if the whole subject of the assessment had come from nowhere. Then wiped his knife on the edge of the tablecloth.

I chose to ignore his culinary faux pas. I had bigger issues at stake than bread crumbs and peanut butter on my table-cloth.

"The farm isn't doing as well as we thought. And your mother wants to maintain control." I enunciated each word as if I were talking to Nicholas instead of to my husband. "If we are going to stay, we need to do an assessment and draw up an agreement with your mother so we're covered for the time you put in."

Dan tapped the knife on the table as if preparing for bat-tle. I wished the battle weren't with me. I thought I'd get some momentum from the warm and tender moment we'd shared the other night, but my insistence had precipitated a cooling trend.

"What is your problem with my mother?" he asked. "She's not trying to cheat us."

"I didn't say that. You just need to get compensated for the work you do while you're here." Nicholas jerked his head to the side, his little sausage hands flailing at the spoon as he spat out his mouthful of porridge. Telling me in his usual diplomatic way that he'd had enough of breakfast.

"It looks like we don't trust her," Dan continued, drop-ping the knife with a clatter.

"It's not a matter of trust or greed," I shot back, wiping Nicholas's mouth, then his hands, then everything within reaching and spitting distance. I knew I was being practical. My voice was quiet, my body language nonthreatening. I was a living, breathing ad for Reasonable and Practical Female. So why was Dan drumming his fingers on the table, telegraphing in a stuttering Morse code his disapproval of what I had said?

"Daddy, you cut my toast too small." Anneke shoved her plate back toward him. "Make it bigger."

"Daddy can't make it bigger," he grunted, rearranging the pieces into a bread shape and pushing the plate back at her. "It makes it look like money is more important than helping my mother out."

"Money is important." I lifted the tray up and unbuckled Nicholas from the harness anchoring him to his high chair. "It's the lack of it that got us here in the first place."

"When are you going to get past it? The garage is gone. It's over. We're not going back." Dan stared me down but I couldn't give way.

"Maybe not to the garage, but we are going back to Seattle," I said slowly, clinging to Nicholas like a lifeline. "We decided that."

"Maybe."

Funny how that simple word could send my heart rate into coronary territory. "You don't really mean *maybe*, do you? You mean *when*."

"We were barely hanging on there, Leslie," Dan continued. "Money was tight, and neither of us was happy at work."

I wasn't liking this. Moving to the farm was supposed to give us a reprieve from talking about money. From stressing about how we were going to spend it and where. I watched reruns of *Little House on the Prairie*—I knew how this worked. I made the sacrifice of not going back to work so we could spend our mornings talking farmer talk. Cows and crops and being all close to the land. Facing the elements together as a family and coming out stronger. United. With one purpose. Strong in our relationship and ready to take on our future.

In Seattle.

Instead we were covering the same ground we had for the past two years. Our location had changed, but the view stayed the same.

I lowered my voice, willed my heart to slow, and pressed on. "When we were dating, you told me you could hardly wait to leave this place." I smiled at him, hoping it softened my words. I really didn't want this confrontation. I wanted us to be husband and wife again, not business partners. "In all the times we've moved, you never talked about coming back here."

Dan ran his hands through his hair. He needed it cut, but there hadn't been time. Truth was, I kind of liked the shaggier Dan. Made him look more like an Eddie Bauer model. When he was mechanicking he kept his hair short. He said it was easier to wash.

I'm sure his bilingual secretary would feel the same about his new look. Which made me hold back and temper my words instead of pushing hard and fast. A fragile relationship needed gentle movements. I learned this from working with the cows the other day. Low and slow was the name of the game with skittish prey. Don't bring up subjects he'd assumed had been dealt with. Don't ask too many questions. Just get through this.

Realize that someday we would look back at this time in our life, laugh nervously, and then change the subject.

"That was a while ago, Leslie," Dan said. "And I had other reasons for wanting to leave this place."

"Like your stepfather?" I asked.

"We had the worst kind of fights right here in this very room."

Sort of like we're having now. Although on an emotional level, we were only flirting with the "shock-and-awe" stage.

"Plans change. Life changes," he said with a light sigh. "And if we're both honest, moving here works out for the best for all of us."

"I never had a problem with the moving-out-here part." *Big fat liar.* "I'm having a problem with the staying-here part."

I stifled a flutter of panic at the idea of being home all day, every day. Ever since I started working, I may not always have had time, but I always earned my own way. I had agreed to stay at home while we were here. We would squeak by on Wilma's "fair wage," but if my car broke down or we needed to make a major purchase, we would have to dip into the "Dream Home Fund."

I couldn't let that happen. The DHF had to be protected at all costs. I wasn't going to watch all the sacrifice of time I could have spent with my family sift into the black hole of the farm. The lure of our own home on our own piece of property—a safe place where my kids could play outside with room for toys and running and laughing—a home I could put my own stamp on—this Thomas Kinkade vision kept me going to work, saving money, being cautious and careful. I couldn't sacrifice all of that to help out his mother.

"I know that is a problem for you, Leslie"—he leaned back in his chair, frowning, looking all contemplative and serious—"but with each day I stay here, I feel like I'm seeing things differently. I think it's a clear answer from God for us."

"To what?" I didn't remember asking God any questions.

Dan's gaze flicked from me to the window beside the table. "When Anneke and I went to church last Sunday, the minister talked about how God sometimes closes doors and opens others."

"Losing you, Dan." Nicholas and I hadn't attended church with him, so I couldn't partake in the pastor's insights.

Dan twirled a strand of hair around his finger. "I think that we had doors closed for us in Seattle." He gave me a troubled look. "Maybe they were opened here. Maybe God wants us to be here."

Okay. He was freaking me out now. "Sorry, Dan. The little I know about God? I can't see that someone who flung stars into space and came up with something as complex as the human body, would care whether we live in Seattle or Harland."

"I don't like my crusts." Anneke gave her plate a quick shove, sending it spinning across the table and onto the floor.

Dan ignored her, and I didn't dare take my eyes off him. The discussion was moving in a direction I hadn't practiced for. I was fairly sure he received coaching from his family. As for me . . . a sister whooping it up in San Francisco was hardly a fair competition to Wilma, Gloria, Judy, and assorted cousins, uncles, and aunts. Terra popped in and out of my life via e-mail and the occasional phone call. His family, however, was always here, always present.

"It's called taking care of us. Taking care of our marriage," I said slowly, hoping he didn't hear the rising panic in my voice. "Something we haven't done as diligently in the past as we should have."

Dan stared me as silence rose between us, heavy and threatening. And swirling around us as we faced off was the sibilant hiss of one name. Missssss Bilingual. "I told you before we moved here—that's over," he said, zipping up his vest. He stepped over the pieces of Anneke's toast and strode toward the porch.

Coward, I thought, watching as he jerked his bootlaces tight. I wanted to go out after him and finish this, but for now I was chained to the kitchen by two soft but tyrannical obligations and nine pieces of toast scattered all over my kitchen floor.

"I'm going to be leaving for the auction in an hour," Dan said as he slipped on his coat. "I'll stop by the house to say good-bye."

Thank goodness for the auction. I needed a clothes dryer and Dan needed a few things for the farm. Our old dryer had come brand-new with the condo and died about eleven minutes after the warranty expired and days before we had to move.

I had assumed we would simply head into town and pick up another one once we got here. But I hadn't counted on the Dutch tendencies lying dormant in my husband and only now, in the bosom of his family, revealing themselves. Thankfully, last night Gerrit had told Dan that the neighbor down the road was selling out and having a farm and yard sale so now Dan was going.

I cleaned up Anneke's bread and dropped another piece in the toaster while Nicholas rooted around on the floor for crumbs I had missed.

My kitchen was finally organized and I'd had breakfast with my entire family for eight days in a row—a new record. I should be full of warm, soft, motherly thoughts.

Instead I felt like I was running out of breath.

Toward the end of our time in Seattle, when I worked my crazy twelve-hour shifts and covered any extra ones I could pick up, I would come home in the late morning to the smell of bacon and eggs still lingering in the air. I would feel a twist of sorrow that Dan had been the one to give the kids their breakfast, bonding with them at their best time of the day, singing cute songs and laughing, while I, the ghostly mom, struggled to keep the family and Dan's mechanic business afloat after the Lonnie Dansworth debacle.

Sometimes things that are out of reach become appealing simply because they're unavailable. In my soft and tender dreams, the boy I had a crush on could be both strong and gentle, wise and caring, and spend all his waking hours exuding sensitivity. Reality is a boy who spends most of his waking hours wondering if his hockey team is going to make the playoffs and learning to make interesting noises with his hand and armpit.

My little grimy boy with pablum in his hair and distinct diaper odor was someone I had forgotten in my dream breakfasts. As was the daughter slowly working her way up the emotional scale from scattered periods of grief to a tsunami of hysteria because her toast wasn't coming fast enough and her tummy felt sore, sore, sore. Pre-farm I'd had to deal with only a slice of these family crises, never the whole loaf. It was exhausting and demanded a relentless creativity I'd never had to utilize before.

"You are a little worm, aren't you?" I said, hooking Nicholas around his chubby stomach in frustration and spinning him around to face me. No way was I going to let him ruin my one and only semi-live plant.

"Awwaw du wa," were his eloquent words as wide blue eyes sparkled up at me, kindling a warmth as unexpected as it was welcome. And in spite of the crust edging his mouth and the dirt in his hair and the ever-growing odor from his backside, I pulled his rounded body close to me and kissed a sticky face only a mother could love. I could indulge in the love right now. At home, I would have seen him as another job to squeeze in while I had one eye on the clock. Now, I could see the potential sweetheart that was my adorable Nicholas under the grime and beyond the smell.

Good thing, because right now with Dan? Not so much with feeling the love.

As I washed and wiped, all the while breathing through my mouth, I reminded myself of my promise. I was going to make the best of it. Be proactive. If you can't change it, adjust to it. *Carpe diem.* Seize the day.

I glanced at the clock, a surge of dread grabbing me. I had acres of time to carpe this particular diem. Since Anneke was born, I had been chasing time, trying to catch up to it, to grab hold of it, and make it work for me. After we moved here, it had taken me a surprising amount of time to get the house set up. My kitchen finally looked orderly. The house smelled like artificial lemons.

Now I had time on my hands and I didn't know what to do with it.

Two days after we were done working with the cows, Dan turned his attention to the farm equipment to get it ready in time for spring seeding. And he had been working on them ever since.

A passing glance at the windows gave me an idea. I could take the kids for a walk.

"Shall we get dressed?" I asked Nicholas and Anneke, injecting a note of fake heartiness into my voice. My morning conflict with Dan still churned in my mind. As I brought the kids to the porch, I rehearsed alternate endings and gave myself much wittier dialogue. My intelligence level always rose after our arguments. I would be ready for Dan if the topic came up again tonight. Hopefully it would. Bringing an argument to completion in under twenty-four hours would be a novel concept for Dan and me.

I laid Nicholas down on the porch floor to weave him

into his jacket and pants. Anneke was at the "I-can-do-it-my-self" stage of dressing, which would give me enough time to get Nicholas ready, get dressed myself, file my nails, and maybe read a couple of Shakespeare sonnets.

But I didn't need to stuff her protesting arms into a jacket, her twisting feet into boots, one eye on the relentless clock. No schedule hung over my head like Damocles' sword as it had at home. We didn't need to rush off to day care so I could rush off to work, where I rushed to catch up to a constant influx of patients, then rushed home through snail-paced rush-hour traffic, my thoughts on my waiting children.

So I let Anneke dance around the porch with her mittens on her feet, entertaining her little brother, who was content to sit like a bundled-up Buddha, babbling his incomprehensible jargon while I slowly put on a coat and gloves. I listened to a recitation of a "pome" Anneke had made up about a frog and a ball and laughed with her at the ending. When she graciously allowed me to zip up her coat, I made buzzing noises as I pulled the tab upwards and finished it off with a kiss on her pudgy nose.

"I love you, Mommy," she crowed, grabbing me tightly around the neck.

Her four words shot straight to my heart and wound around it, slowly, holding it as tight as her arms held my neck. *She's mine,* I thought, jealously squeezing her hard. *She belongs to me fully and completely and wholly.* Dan's heart may have wandered for a time, Nicholas may treat my love for him as something to tolerate, but Anneke was purely and wholly my child.

The warmth her declaration kindled in me lasted as long

as it took us to step from the porch outside. A faint breeze sifted through the buildings, snaking up through my jacket when I bent over to put Anneke and Nicholas in their plastic wagon. The resulting chill was a leftover of a nasty winter more than content to stay around like an unwelcome guest who had one more joke in his repertoire.

Beyond the house lay a large open patch of ground bordered by bare, red canes of raspberry bushes on one side and a row of apple trees on the far south end. The garden itself was a clean, neat expanse of black dirt, waiting for planting.

An expanse of dirt that awaited the garden that Dan and his family thought I might want to plant. As if. The closest I got to living things was my mother's single ivy plant, which my sister and I watered with leftover tea and, when we had money to spare, soft drinks.

"Let's go, Mommy." The handle of the wagon shook in my hands. The natives were getting restless. Anneke smiled as she rocked the wagon. Nicholas's heavy coat bunched up at his neck, made his head effectively immobile, but his eyes flitted back and forth, taking everything in. As I watched my two children act utterly content in the cold, I realized how long it had been since I had taken the kids out for something as ordinary as a walk. Since the cow-moving day, I'd been either busy setting up the house or the weather had been too cold.

Smiling myself, I turned around and started down the long driveway toward the road. Anneke burbled snatches of an unfamiliar song—something macabre about God watching a sparrow falling—and then she belted out the chorus: "He loves me, too; He loves me, too; I know He loves me, too." And every now and again Nicholas burbled some unintelligible comment that I chose to translate as "I'm happy."

I sucked in a deep gulp of biting air and turned my eyes toward the road. In spite of a flush of well-being, something nagged at me, scrabbling at the edges of my consciousness. Something eerie and unfamiliar. I paused. Listened. That's when I heard it.

Nothing.

No cars. No horns honking. No airplanes. No people calling out to one another. No music. No neighbors.

I stopped, listening to the great big nothing. Anneke and Nicholas must have sensed my uneasiness, because they grew silent as well.

Emptiness pushed on my ears, pressing deep into my head. I felt the sweep of the wind urging me along over the fields toward the mountains that guarded our valley.

My heart pounded, pushing against my chest. I could hear it as my raspy breath drew in and out, in and out. I thought again of that moment just before I had helped with the cows. The same feeling, but then I wasn't alone. Now it was just me, and my two vulnerable, tiny children lost in this huge emptiness . . .

Don't panic. It's okay.

I breathed slowly, like I often told parents of patients to do.

Easier to be the coach than the coachee, I realized. I got control of my breathing as my heartbeat slowed.

Then, behind me, I heard the slam of a door. A truck starting up. Dan was leaving. And I would be all alone in this vast, quiet nothingness.

I spun around and strode quickly to the shop, the wagon bump-bumping over the washboard ruts in the driveway as I honed in on the truck. Nicholas squealed with pleasure and Anneke laughed as I quickened my pace.

Dan was heading toward the house when he saw us.

"Hey there. I was coming to say good-bye."

"I thought we could go with you." I had the panic under control now so I didn't miss the faint downturn of his mouth. Though I couldn't speak mechanic, I had "Dan" pretty well mastered.

He didn't want us to come.

But Anneke heard "go with you" and with a high-pitched squeal repeated the words, effectively bolstering my faint suggestion.

"Are you sure? It's not going to be that interesting." If it wasn't for the fact that Miss Bilingual had moved to Winnipeg and he had promised me it was over, I would think he was heading out to meet her. He looked that guilty.

"I don't have a lot to do."

Dan adjusted the fit of his ubiquitous billed cap and sighed. "I'll get the car seats."

Moments later we had the kids strapped in and the wagon in the box of the truck. As I climbed into the cab, Dan adjusted the radio, cutting off some country singer mid-sob. Dan never listened to country music at home. But then neither did he let his hair get this long or go out in public without shaving.

I climbed into the truck, feeling like I had accepted a ride with a stranger.

"Are you sure you want to come?" he asked, giving me one more chance before he turned the key in the ignition. "The kids will probably get bored and cranky. These sales go on a long time."

"I like the idea of spending the afternoon together." I wasn't going to let him talk me out of it. Besides, in my current frame of mind I didn't know if I could deal with the strong possibility of a visit from Wilma.

"Okay," he said in the "I-think-you're-crazy" tone that usually set my teeth on edge. But these days I was trying to construct a new and improved Leslie VandeKeere and I let it slip under the radar.

We drove in silence as I stared out at the endless landscape of brown ditches, brown fields, and bare trees, stark and clear against the leaden sky. *This is no different from Seattle this time of the year,* I reminded myself. *Just fewer houses and less traffic. Appreciate it for what it is.*

I was starting to get good at this self-talk, I thought, leaning back in the seat.

Dan cleared his throat, laying his hand on my arm.

"I'm sorry about this morning," he said. "I shouldn't have walked out on you like that."

Usually this was my cue to meet him halfway, acknowledge my part in the argument, then shore up my defenses. But usually I had most of the day or night shift at work to go over the argument and find weaknesses in his statements, and usually I had the help of sympathetic co-workers who faithfully took my side.

But today he had caught me defenseless and rebuttal-less.

"I still think we should do the assessment." Lame reply, but the best I could do on the fly.

Dan looked away. "If I agree, will you be willing to put our money into the farm?"

Marriage was about give and take, but on this I couldn't give. The money from the house was the down payment on the life I needed to return to. On a future that had security and steady, regular income. I didn't dare risk losing any ground on that. Not the way he talked this morning.

"I'm sorry, Dan, but I can't." He held my gaze and I pushed. Had to. "We'll get money from that court case against Lonnie Dansworth, then we'll be okay."

"And if we don't?"

"Then we can use the house money to start up another business and in time, we'll get it back."

"How can you talk about putting the money into a business I don't like, instead of putting it into something I do like?" He looked ahead again, his jaw clenched.

And we're off . . . "Because we agreed we were going back." I could do stubborn too. What I lacked in creativity, I made up for in persistence. Dan, however, was exceeding his usual quota. Of course, he had the rallying support of his family behind him. I was on my own. "We agreed, Dan," I added for artistic impression.

Dan reached over and turned on the radio, filling the cab with wailing guitars and nasal twangs. The conversation was over. And now I had put myself in the unenviable position of being stuck in close proximity to him for the rest of the day.

This was a mistake.

Chapter Six

long snakelike line of pickup trucks—twin metal caterpillars—lined each side of the narrow road leading to the farm sale. As we walked toward the farm's driveway, I wondered where all these people had materialized from. In the twenty-five minutes it had taken us to get here, I had counted maybe twelve yard sites. There were at least eighty vehicles parked along the road.

In the distance, as if in counterpoint to the silence that had risen between Dan and me, a nasal chanting rose and fell, then paused and continued again. After a few minutes I realized the sound came from the auctioneer, his voice carried to us by a faint breeze.

"So, why are there so many people here?" I asked, glancing sidelong at Dan. "Is this a special sale?"

Dan glanced my way, recognizing my conversational peace offering for what it was. Avoidance. But his light shrug told me he was game. "Not really. I remember going with my dad to farm sales every spring. Most of the people are 'lookie loos.' It's something to do and a chance to visit."

I pulled my coat a little closer around me and thought of a hundred other ways to visit that didn't require standing around in cold weather.

"So, why do people have farm sales?"

"This one is an estate sale. Dwayne Harris died about three months ago, and the wife is moving to town 'cause the kids don't want to take over the farm. Been happening a lot lately," Dan said, melancholy edging his voice.

I was about to ask him if Wilma would have an auction sale when we left, but his tone told me he didn't need my happy questions.

We turned into a long, narrow driveway enclosed by trees. The amplified voice of the auctioneer lured us on while chiding the bidders to recognize the deals they were getting. Bargains, folks. Absolute bargains.

The driveway wound for a few hundred feet and then opened up onto a wide yard. A large red barn, the kind that come with farm play sets for kids, held court on one side of the yard, its doors and windows creating a face that looked with bored tolerance at the large group of people milling about in the yard below it. Beside the barn, a large shed, open in the front, held an assortment of machinery.

The house sat across the yard from the barns, an older two-story affair with a large wraparound porch. Brown paint peeled off the siding and a few old pots trailing dead branches and leaves still hung from the beams of the porch. The house looked weary, as if it were ready to move to town as well.

Furniture stood in neat orderly rows on the grass. A couple of couches, one with a matching chair and loveseat, some beds, a dining-room table and chairs.

People looked into boxes, sat on chairs, tried out appliances, inspected items normally secreted in the cupboards of the house behind us but now laid out for anyone who had the least bit of curiosity to look over and comment on.

"I can't believe she's selling this," one woman sniffed, holding up a chipped porcelain dog. "Why not pitch it out?"

Maybe it was a daughter's favorite figurine, I thought as the other woman rolled her eyes.

"Hey, Dan, there you are." A tall, older man wearing a red plaid shirt over a T-shirt strode toward us, waving. Two younger men trailed him. One of them wore a jean jacket, the other a loose hoodie and the oversized pants favored by young city boys trying to look tougher than they really were. I would know. I'd stitched up enough of them.

Both of these clean-cut, strapping young men who didn't look like they would know beer from iced tea had the same sandy blond hair as Dan, and when the one smiled I saw Dan as a teenager. They had to be relatives.

"Why haven't you been by?" the man asked, clapping a large hand on Dan's shoulder. "Auntie Gerda made your favorite pie when she heard you were back, and she's been waiting for you to come and eat it." His dark eyes slid over me, then the kids, then back to Dan. "And you got your family along?"

"Leslie, this is Uncle Orest and my cousins Ben and Jason. This is Leslie and Nicholas and Anneke."

Orest gave me a huge grin and caught my hand in both of his, burying it in a pack of calluses and thick knuckles. "Good to see you, girlie. Heard lots about you."

Which, of course, begged the question, what? But I wasn't going to head down that path and simply smiled, trying not to look too threatening.

Ben and Jason acknowledged me with the imperceptible nod of teenagehood, then turned back to Dan.

"So, you here to check out some deals? I saw a Massey here, like the one Keith used. 'Course, Keith didn't use it much after he blew the head gasket on it." Orest shook his head as if he couldn't understand Keith or his actions. "That man didn't know how to maintain equipment. You ought to check this out. Old man Harris got T-boned with it turning a corner with a load of bales so the body is useless but I bet you could scam the engine off it."

Dan's eyes lit up . . . until he looked my way. "I'm going to check out a few things. Do you want to come or stay here? I can take the kids."

I shrugged. I sensed a mini-family reunion and I would cramp his style. "Go ahead. I'll keep the kids."

He gave me the kind of smile that reminded me why I fell in love with him in the first place, and I knew I had done exactly the right thing. For a change.

"I'll keep an eye out for the dryer." Dan touched my arm lightly, cementing our brief flash of togetherness. Then he and Uncle Orest and his cousins left, deep in discussion about head gaskets, cylinders, and pistons. I knew the terms but hadn't developed the deep affection for them that Dan had or, it seemed, his uncle and now animated cousins did. What was it with men and internal-combustion engines that put a light in their eyes that even lingerie could barely compete with?

In spite of my assurances that I'd be okay, fear nipped at my heart as Dan walked away. I felt trapped in a bubble of strangeness that pushed people away, separated me from the crowd. I tried to smile and make eye contact, but no one seemed to notice or care.

"Mommy, I want out," Anneke called out from her perch.

"No, honey. Stay in the wagon." I couldn't let her go in this strange place. One glance away from her, and she would be gone, lost. And I would be running around, calling out her name, an irresponsible mother full of panic.

No thanks.

"Let me out, let me out, let me out, let me out!" Anneke called out, her voice rising a few decibels with each repetition.

Of course she chose this moment and this place to push.

"No, honey. You stay in the wagon with Nicholas." I kept my voice low and quiet as I concentrated on projecting "be rational" vibes, the only tool available to mothers when their children are spiraling out of control in a public place. I don't know why I tried it here. It didn't work in toy stores, grocery stores, or parks.

And, of course, she started to climb out just as I turned around to warn her. I went to grab her arm and she danced out of reach, and suddenly I was giving the auctioneer competition as irritated eyes turned toward me and my daughter.

"Hey, little girl. I don't think you should wander off." A man blocked her line of flight by crouching down in front of her. Curious, she stopped, sizing him up.

"My mom says I'm not 'posed to talk to strangers," she said primly, as if her mother's feeble pronouncements were the laws that dictated every action of her day, instead of the other way around.

"That's a good thing your mother told you," he said, glancing up at me with brown eyes fringed by thick lashes. His dark hair had a wave that would make a woman as jealous as his eyelashes did, and when he smiled a slow, lazy smile, I caught the faintest flash of a dimple. He wore blue jeans, a leather jacket, and cowboy boots. Something about the combination, the quality, the way he wore the clothes set him apart from all the other men present. Even my Dan. He could have been anywhere between thirty and forty-five and had that self-assured air that both appealed and sent warning signals up my spine.

Axe murderer, I thought instantly as City Leslie kicked in.

"She sounds smart," he said, pushing himself up, his gaze still holding mine. "You've done a good job with her."

Now he was he flirting with me? I glanced down at my farm-wife clothes. No makeup, hair worn in the artfully tousled "mommy ponytail" that looked great on Julia Roberts and sloppy on me, yet, when I looked back at him, I caught the faintest hint of interest. Had to be crazy.

I caught Anneke by the hand to pull her away just as the man held out his own hand.

"I'm sorry, Leslie. I should introduce myself. I'm John Brouwer."

He knew my name. He wasn't flirting with me at all. Fear grabbed my heart with icy fingers.

Stalker, then. Well-dressed stalker. Did he know where we lived? Would we have to move?

"I was talking to your sister-in-law Judy," he continued, "and she told me that you used to work ER in Seattle."

I blinked and stopped edging away from him as reason pulled me off my usual rabbit trail of delusion. "Pardon me?"

"I'm a doctor in the local hospital, so when I heard you were a nurse, I paid attention."

My heart slowed down, and I mentally gave myself a slap on the head. Some animals have a fight-or-flight defense mechanism when they are frightened. Me? I freeze and let my mind dive into the worst possible scenario and *then* I run with it.

I finally took his outstretched hand, regretting the shoulder cramps he must've suffered while I mentally labeled him everything from Lothario to deranged killer. "Sorry. My name is Leslie VandeKeere, but it seems you already know that. And yes, I did work as an ER nurse."

"You must have seen your share of trauma." Now that his status had been downgraded from psycho to physician, I realized how attractive he was.

"The usual," I said with an airy wave of my hand. "Gunshot wounds, stabbings, sometimes a broken arm to keep us on our game."

He nodded and glanced at the kids. "How old is your little one?"

"Nicholas is a year and a half."

"So, when did you go back to work?"

"Pretty much right after he was born."

"Dedicated, then."

"Broke, then."

"And now?"

"Well, I'm trying full-time motherhood on for size." I swung Anneke's hand to remind myself that I was still supposed to be interacting with my children, that they weren't mere accessories.

"And how does it fit?"

"Still working out the wrinkles." *Okay, enough with the metaphors.* "Why do you want to know?"

"Again, I apologize. Not too deft with this head-hunting business," he said, suddenly serious. "When I heard you were an ER nurse, I thought I'd ask. I'm not a stalker, and I'm not trying to come on to you, in case that's what you were thinking . . ."

I dismissed the comment with an airy wave of my hand as if that wasn't even worth consideration.

"But I hope I can talk you into coming to work for us."

Desperate much?

"I've decided to take a hiatus from nursing." I tried to inject a note of heartiness into my voice. "The kids are only young once." And wasn't that profound?

"If you ever change your mind"—he lifted his hands in a "what can I do?" gesture—"I'm sure you know where the hospital is."

Forty-eighth Street, along the main highway going through town as you come to the bottom of the hill heading into Harland.

"Thanks, but I think I'll wait for now." I gave him my best motherly smile, then turned and walked briskly away from temptation. Anneke skipped along beside me, happy to be on the move, and Nicholas was smiling, his cheeks rosy and his eyes bright as his wagon bumped along the frozen ruts in the yard. I couldn't help but smile too, he looked so adorable. How could I even consider going back to work when I had these two precious children to take care of? Surely that should be enough. I was a farmer's wife. I was going to expend my energy on my family.

How? You can't bake or garden, and that cow thing—did you really think you made a difference?

Of course I did. Dan was proud of me. That had to be worth some sacrifice.

If that cow had come out, you would have turned tail and run. Wilma knows you're a fake. Why even bother trying to get her approval?

It's Dan I'm worried about.

You're going to be here a whole year. You're going to need some kind of distraction. And money would help.

I shoved the thoughts into a box, slammed the lid, and quickly went searching for my husband. I was here to maintain our marriage and build it on mutual trust and respect. At least that's what the book *How a Marriage Can Succeed or Fail* said. And because I was campaigning for the Succeed part, I figured I better stick with my plan even if Dan didn't.

I followed the auctioneer's voice and found Dan. He stood with his hands in his coat pockets, his shoulders hunched against the sharp wind that had sprung up. Anneke danced beside me, but as soon as she saw her father, she called out his name and ran to him.

Dan bent down and swooped his little girl up in his arms.

He was talking to Uncle Orest, nodding seriously. As I came alongside, he glanced at me and stopped talking.

That didn't hurt. Not a bit. I forced down my frustration. Dutiful Wife, I thought, Dutiful Wife. If I repeated that enough, it might soak into the part of my brain that doesn't analyze everything trying to make it fit.

"So, what's up for sale now?" I asked. This was the classic "ask open-ended questions" portion of *How a Marriage Can Succeed or Fail.* Chapter Three, page seventeen. The part toward the bottom. I was still trying.

"A couple of terrific appliances up next," the auctioneer said, answering my question. "Brand-new and hardly used."

He led the bidding, starting high and flowing down 'til he caught a bid and away he went. Dan waited and I watched, trying not to get nervous. I knew shopping opportunities would be limited and I really, really needed this dryer.

The bidding was desultory, but steady.

"I think Mrs. Harris had that machine for two months, tops," I heard a woman beside me say as Dan upped his bid. "If it doesn't go much higher, you'll get a deal."

It took me a few moments to realize the woman was talking to me. "She hardly used it. Too cheap, you know. Hung her clothes on the line, spring, summer, fall, and winter." She shot me a conspiratorial wink.

The young woman wore a shabby down-filled jacket over a fitted T-shirt that said "Baby" in pink glittery letters, tucked into snug and faded blue jeans. With her black spiky hair and five earrings marching up each earlobe, she didn't exactly blend.

She rocked on her heels as she glanced at Anneke and Nicholas. "And I'm sure you could use a dryer right about now."

I scrambled for words, trying to figure out what I should or should not say to this complete stranger.

The woman stuck her hand out, grinning at me. "I'm Kathy Greidanus. Married, two kids." She waved her hand vaguely. "We live just a few miles from your place."

She was short and wiry, with quick darting eyes that flicked from me to Dan to Nicholas, still in my arms, to Anneke, crouched by my legs, and finally to me. "So, you got to move into the hallowed home place?" She quirked a laughing half grin at me. "Lucky you."

And in that one gesture underlined by the hint of sarcasm in those two words, I read a lifetime of knowledge of both Harland and its residents.

"I'm Leslie VandeKeere, but of course, you already know that."

Kathy shook my hand and turned to Anneke. "Hey, cutie patootie," she said casually, waggling her fingers.

I peeled Anneke from my leg with one arm, juggling Nicholas with the other, but Anneke froze, staring at Kathy.

"I'm guessing you're Anneke," Kathy continued. "How old are you?"

Anneke rubbed one foot against her ankle, ducking her head slightly. "I'm foah."

"Really? I have a little boy who's 'foah,' too. His name is Cordell. He likes worms and jumping on the trampoline. If you want you can come and jump on it, too." She clucked her tongue against her teeth. "If spring ever comes." She glanced at the auctioneer then at Dan. "Looks like you got yourself a dryer."

I saw Dan nodding and realized I had missed the entire event. I didn't even know how much he had paid for it. It was all so anticlimactic.

"Do you do coffee?" Kathy asked, slipping her hands into the pockets of her jacket and shrugging it up around her neck.

"You mean, like now?" I watched Dan drift away, following the crowd who followed the auctioneer, lured on by the "Bargains, absolute bargains, folks."

"I mean, coffee—like the visiting thing."

I gave her a blank look, and she laughed. I hardly knew her, and she was inviting me over already?

"Let me explain," she said in the patient tone specific to use with especially dense people, misunderstanding my hesitation. "I come over, you make coffee—though for me, you make tea—we sit down at the kitchen table while our kids fight over LEGOS, and we talk about the people we know." With her hands still in her pockets, she pointed at herself. "Me. Kathy. Incurable Gossip."

"I think I got that," I said with a light laugh. "I've done coffee." Not as often as I would have liked. I had a couple of friends in Seattle, mostly co-workers, who had the same hectic juggling schedule I did. Coffee was often a quick cup at the local McDonald's while our kids alternately played at the Play Place or cried for our attention. The topic of conversation never rose above the advantages of cloth over disposable diapers. Or vice versa. Depending on which article we read in what magazine.

"I don't want to overwhelm you," Kathy said, angling me a puzzled look. "Your sisters-in-law said you weren't much of the visiting type. But I'm the kind of person who needs to find out for herself."

I felt a pinch of anger at Dan's sisters for talking about me behind my back, transforming me from a person to a topic of conversation. I'd had enough of "she" and "her" at the family meeting.

"I could come." *Gee, didn't that sound gracious.*

Kathy smiled as if sensing my confusion. She patted me on the arm. "Don't worry about the gossip part. I know how to keep my mouth shut when I have to. I can wait."

"No. That would be great. I don't have a lot of secrets anyhow." I set Nicholas down in the wagon, glad to be relieved of his weight and even gladder he didn't kick up a fuss.

"Good thing. People in this county can sense a secret quicker than an upcoming sale at the Coop."

"Coop? Now you'll have to translate."

"Coming, Sprout?" Kathy held her hand out to Anneke, who, to my immense surprise, took it as Kathy angled her chin toward the crowd and started following. "The Coop is more formally known as the Harland Co-operative started about the same time that Harland was birthed back in the early 1900s. Locals call it The Coop or The Co-op. Make sure you capitalize the 'The' when you're talking to give it and the ancestors the proper respect."

Kathy flashed me another grin.

"It's that important?"

"Oh, very. We may have a bunch of churches in Harland but

we have only one graveyard and one main store, The Coop. Theology may not unite us, but death and shopping do."

I had to laugh. I could like this blunt outspoken character and Anneke, who never went to strangers, tripped alongside her, telling Kathy about her dolls and about Nicholas and how he liked to eat dirt and how his diapers smelled bad, bad, bad. Kathy pulled a face at that and pinched her nose and Anneke giggled.

"Is your husband here?" I asked as we squeezed through the mob gathered around the farm-equipment shed and headed toward Dan. The crowd had thinned out. An aura of intense focus surrounded the remaining group. Clearly I was in the presence of serious buyers.

"He's holding the fort with the kids. It's my afternoon off."

"So you came here?"

"Hey. Out is out. Besides, I picked up some good deals. The tradeoff is that I'm supposed to stick around long enough to find out what the equipment went for. We're not in the market, but Jimmy likes to stay on top of the prices in case we ever are." Kathy pulled a pen and paper out of her pocket, all the while holding on to Anneke's hand and throwing my daughter a question now and again to show that Anneke still had her attention. As I studied her, I knew I was in the presence of a professional mother and wondered if I should take notes myself.

"So, what's that he's selling now?" I asked, daring to expose my ignorance. Kathy seemed totally non-threatening.

"A John Deere 9650 combine. Not in our league, but obviously old Harris had a few pennies or more."

"Not enough to paint the house."

"Dead investment," she said, winking at me. "Lesson number one—farmers tend to see houses as a money drain. If you want the kind of farmhouse that gets featured in *Country Woman,* you have to stake your claim early on in your marriage and defend it against tractors, combines, more land, more pivots, and more livestock."

No problem. I had no intention of creating a farm show home out of the VandeKeere residence.

The auctioneer shouted "Sold!" and moved on to the next item. Bidding shot up quickly but then, just as quickly, stopped. The people here seemed to know exactly how much they would spend before they came. Kathy scribbled the amount down in her book, and as soon as she was done, Anneke reached for her hand.

Nicholas started crying, and I snagged a couple of annoyed glances, even one from my own husband. I may not be able to take charge of my kids, but I could take a hint. "I'll be back," I whispered to Kathy, as if my discretion could offset the angry wails of a little boy who had had enough of auctions.

Kathy shooed me away with a friendly wave. "No worries."

I quickly pulled the wagon away, hoping the vibration of the wheels over the ruts would lull Nicholas into mellowness. Picking him up would only net me his balled-up fists in my face. Public demoralization wasn't something I liked to indulge in.

It took a few minutes, but he finally settled and slowly slumped to one side, his eyes blinking sightlessly. When I was fairly sure he was burrowed deep in sleep, I laid him down in the wagon and returned to Dan's side to continue my role as faithful wife and good mother. I was doing A-okay so far.

Anneke and Kathy still stood beside Dan as Kathy frowned at the auctioneer. "Nineteen five, Nineteen five on the Massey!" I guessed he was coming to the end of the sale. I grimaced at the mangled wreck of the tractor and wondered who in the world would buy that thing. "Going once, twice—" He paused, then pointed to my husband and called out, "Sold to Dan Van-deKeere for nineteen thousand dollars!"

"What?" I couldn't stop my involuntary cry. I turned to Dan, who was writing something down in a book he always had tucked in his shirt pocket. "Don't tell me you just bought that tractor?" I hissed, aware of the people now watching us.

"You were here," he said. But he wouldn't look at me.

"How . . . What . . . Where are you going to get the money for it?" Wilma had been pretty adamant that there wasn't a lot of money available right now for any of what she called "extras."

Dan sighed, dropped the book in his pocket, but still didn't meet my eyes. "From the term deposit."

My heart leapt into my throat, momentarily choking off any words I might have been able to utter. My hands clenched the handle of the wagon. "You mean the Dream Home Fund?"

"It's just a bank account, Leslie," he said. Then he walked away.

But it wasn't "just a bank account." It was part of our future. In Seattle. It was our investment in our life. In *Seattle.*

And with one wave of his hand he had chosen the needs of the farm over that.

From: lesismore@montana.net

To: tfroese@hotmail.com

Dan had planned all along to buy that wreck of a tractor. Had planned all along to use the money from the DHF to pay for it. That's why he looked so guilty when I asked if I could come. Nineteen thousand dollars for something he can't even drive home. Said he was going to take the motor out of this one and drop it in the tractor we have now. Oh yeah. And a dog. My by-the-book, non-impulsive man got a dog at the sale too. I didn't know you could get dogs at auction sales. It belonged to the lady who owned the farm and she decided at the last minute that it would be cruel to take the dog to town with her so she gave it away to whoever wanted it and Dan wanted it. Every time the kids and I go outside, Sasha comes running up to us and jumps around the kids' wagon, her tail spinning like a windmill. Okay, she's not the Golden Lab that was supposed to be gamboling in the yard of The Dream Home, but she is kind of cute. She loves going for walks, so she's been very happy lately. And every time I walk, with each step I repeat, Nineteen Thousand, Nineteen Thousand.

Lunatic Leslie Lenient about the Licking

From: tfroese@hotmail.com

To: lesismore@montana.net

Okay, I'm getting nervous for U. Taking money out of the Dream Home Fund AND getting a dog? That is not playing fair. Sounds to me like U are going to HAVE to get a job.

Think on it seriously, Sweetums. Taking money out of the DHF is a serious breach of ethics. To me that calls for retaliatory methods. Get a job. NOW. BTW what are U going to do with the dog when U leave? Seems kind of cruel to me to get a dog and then bring it back to the city.

Ticked off Terra

From: lesismore@montana.net
To: tfroese@hotmail.com

Sasha will stay with the tractor and our ever-expanding livestock when we leave. Or so Dan told me when I asked him. Yesterday his Aunt Gerda came with Uncle Orest and brought me some chickens. That's live chickens, by the way. Complete with feathers and cluck. Gerda's a very sweet lady who loves to chat and give advice. While Aunt Gerda was here, Wilma stopped by again to see Dan's new tractor. She was excited about it. I'm thinking beauty is in the eye of the beholder. Personally, I'm in the "laminate flooring" camp. For my new house. Which is not going to happen now that Dan has used up fully half of the money. I'm still so mad.

From: tfroese@hotmail.com
To: lesismore@montana.net

Go back to work. U will need $$$ to make up for what Dan spent.

I stood in front of the hospital and wiped my hands on the front of my jacket. Ten minutes till showtime. I could change my mind. I didn't have to take the interview.

It had been seven chocolates since the auction sale. The very next day my anger with Dan sent me here to fill out an application. When I got a phone call to come in, I knew I had started a process I had to see to the end.

I had agonized longer over what to do with my children during the interview than the interview itself. In Seattle the kids were in day care. Here in Harland, it didn't feel right to drop the kids off when they had relatives. But Wilma, Gloria, and Judy all lived in the opposite direction of Harland, farther up the valley from our place. Judy lived the farthest—a twenty-minute drive from our place—but she was my first choice today. I simply couldn't imagine bringing the kids to Gloria or Wilma's and facing their censure.

But if I took the job, I would have to rethink Judy. Soon the greenhouse would be too busy, and she couldn't take the kids regularly.

But could I bring them to day care again?

Second thoughts spun their insidious web, tangling my plans.

Then I thought about staying at home day after day and I felt a moment of panic. Yesterday I had alphabetized my CD collection, then changed my mind and arranged them by category. I knew other mothers filled their time with various activities but I was neither gardener nor baker nor seamstress nor true-blue farmer's wife. I was a nurse. It was what I loved to do.

I closed my eyes and opened the door. I didn't have to take the job if I got it.

⁓

I'm so glad you decided to come in." Sally Richards, head nurse at Harland Hospital, picked up the last of my papers and glanced quickly at her watch. Shift change in fifteen minutes. The atmosphere told me more than the clock did. Tired nurses winding down from their shift had "going home" written all over their faces.

"John told me that he talked to you," she continued, "and I hoped you would come. Some of the ward nurses have been covering in the emergency department, but they certainly don't have your broad area of expertise." Sally tapped the file folder holding my application and test scores and smiled. "You might not see near the drama here that you did in Seattle, but we have our busy times."

"If it's an emergency department, I don't doubt you do." I slowly inhaled the mixed scents of the hospital. Clean linen, waxed floors, the pervasive scent of disinfectant that was the first line of defense against a hospital's biggest enemy—infection.

I missed it. I yearned for it. I wasn't a farmer's wife. This was where I was meant to be.

"I was impressed with the results of your NCLEX scores."

"I test well," I said, a faint nervousness bringing out my flippant side.

"And your résumé is also encouraging." Sally tapped her

fingers lightly. "Though I have to say, I am concerned with how often you've moved around."

"Restless husband," I said apologetically.

"I wish we could offer you full-time employment but in light of the fact that, as you told me, you are only going to be here a year, I would like to offer you a casual position. I am going to be doing another interview in a few days for the full-time position we have advertised."

I didn't let my relief show. Casual sounded pretty good to me. The best of both worlds. I would be home enough to satisfy Dan and gone enough to make me feel like I wasn't losing valuable skills. ER work demanded constant upgrading to stay on top of all the latest technology. But my stomach knotted up as I thought of my kids. I didn't want to bring them to day care, but I couldn't bring them to Judy's. Gloria. Wilma. Gloria. Wilma.

The knot tightened as I tried to imagine bringing the kids there every time I worked. Not only did they live in the opposite direction of Harland, they thought the opposite of me. Mothers should be home with their children twenty-four hours a day. Ditto for farmers' wives. For a moment I wished I had gone to church with Dan the couple of times he'd gone. Maybe I'd dare pray that God would help me figure something out.

"When do you want me to start?" I asked, pushing my worries aside for now. Who knew what would come up?

"Actually, next week Friday would be great. We can start with the basic procedures, standing orders—that kind of thing. I'd like to introduce you to the staff while you're here, but I have an important meeting to attend."

"I understand. I'll be here Friday—early." A brisk handshake and she was off, her feet making only the barest whisper of a sound. I waited a moment, taking in the gleaming floors, appreciating the cleanliness of the place.

A man shuffled past, holding onto his IV pole, his eyes resolutely on the large glass doors at the end of the hallway. Determined face. Square outline jutting through a thin cotton house robe. *Smoker,* I thought sadly.

As I walked slowly past the emergency ward, I caught the palpable change in energy. Nurses tidied beds, restocked shelves. A doctor leaned against the desk of the nurse's station, but instead of trading jokes, his eyes cut to the door. And then I got it. They were waiting.

I heard the faint wail of the ambulance. The doctor shoved off, the nurses stopped, and my own heart started pumping.

Soon, I reminded myself, resisting the urge to pull on a discarded gown and join the action. *Soon I'll be part of this, too.*

From: lesismore@montana.net

To: tfroese@hotmail.com

There are two words I've come to dread: "Coffee" and "time." Transmitted over the small intercom we have hooked up between the house and the garage, those words can send my heart into palpitations of nervous angst. They mean that Uncle Orest and his two sons are accompanying Dan to the house for coffee. This is the signal to boil water to make coffee, put out goodies, and clean up the counter while kicking toys under the couch and trying to catch Nicholas so I can wipe his face. Then I have to put out clean towels in the bathroom and a smile on my face. All this I can do. The weak link in the equation is goodies. These guys go through a bag of cookies faster than you can say trans-fat. Don't know what Dan will do with Uncle Orest when I start working. I guess that will be his worry. Haven't told Dan about the job. I'm waiting for the right time. Not sure when that will be. I'll have to play that one by ear.

Logical Leslie with the Limited Larder

From: tfroese@hotmail.com

To: lesismore@montana.net

Don't do that. U are tone deaf! Dan will get over it. Don't sweat it about the kids. Day care a couple of times a week won't kill them. U R not a farmer's wife and it wasn't fair to Dan to expect U to quit UR job. Nursing is what U love doing. I still remember that nurse kit I gave U for UR birthday. U practically wore that thing out. As for mixed motives, hey. Who does anything out of pure motives these days? U have every right to be angry with Dan for siphoning money off the bank acount. And if mom-in-law thinks that Charles Dickens wages are livin' large, don't blame U for going back to work. Don't apologize for doing what U do best. But U better tell Dan before U put on UR uniform. U know U can't wait for candlelight and wine.

Smart Sibling Sunning in San Fran

From: lesismore@montana.net

To: tfroese@hotmail.com

I'm being such a radical these days. After I had my interview, I called the assessor. I didn't know which real-estate agent to go with so I chose the one with the biggest advertisement. I'm a sucker for ostentation. He came yesterday. Dan tolerated him, and I had no clue what he was supposed to do except come up with a figure at the end of the day that we would file away with the assessment that was done after Dan's father died. I was glad to know it had been done before. I wasn't a flaming radical after all. But the way Dan treated him, I was tempted to put a disclaimer on the bottom of the paper: No animals were harmed during the filing of this assessment.

Leslie the Liability

Chapter Seven

I don't want those cookies," Anneke whined as I dropped a cellophane-wrapped package on her legs. She swatted it away and glared up at me.

"Honey, you don't even know what they taste like," I said, curbing my impatience. Her drama-queen repertoire had been on display all morning. Her blankets were scratchy. She didn't like the cute pink turtleneck I had laid out for her to wear. At coffee time Uncle Orest had teased her and she snapped at him, netting me a reproving glance from Dan. As if Anneke's antics were my jurisdiction and my fault.

"I want Oreos," Anneke announced as I consulted the vast array of cookies before me.

I wasn't about to indulge her. In lieu of me baking we were at minimum going to choose wholesome goodness. She would thank me later when she had strong bones and teeth instead of rickets and dentures and bad knees from overindulgence in trans-fat-crammed snacks.

As I put the package in the buggy, she crossed her arms

and slammed them against her chest, her lower lip dropping in a pout that would make Angelina Jolie jealous.

In *Parenting Plus,* smart parents were told to simply ignore bad behavior. To focus on the good. So I chose to ignore her and focus on Nicholas, batting the bar in front of him with his pudgy hands as he blew happy spit bubbles. He grinned up at me and I bent over to kiss his shining apple cheeks.

"You love Nicholas most," Anneke wailed.

Yes, my dear child, at the moment I do. And the guilt I didn't feel was freeing. I gave Nicholas another kiss.

"I don't like you. I don't, I don't, I don't!" Anneke shouted.

A woman sidled past our cart, casting nervous glances from me to Anneke, who now stood in the cart and rocked it with all the vigor of a frat house boy. I gave the woman a feeble smile as I teetered between ignoring Anneke and simply taking Nicholas out of the cart and walking away.

"Hey, Leslie, how are you?"

I sucked in an embarrassed breath, then turned to face the unfamiliar voice calling my name. Kathy—the woman from the auction a few days ago. Today she wore a loose T-shirt and blue jeans tucked into cowboy boots. Today her hair looked like a hedgehog on steroids.

I discreetly inventoried her grocery cart. Organic juices and yogurt alongside plastic bags filled with lentils, oatmeal, beans, and various nuts. I glanced at my own cartload, which leaned heavily toward the processed-foods section of the store. *At least I'm getting healthy cookies,* I reassured myself.

Kathy glanced at Anneke, unfazed by her antics. She reached behind her and pulled forward a little girl who had been clinging to the back of her legs. The girl's hair covered her eyes in a tangled mess. A ring of brown circled her mouth. She wore a T-shirt with an orange stain down the front and baggy pants that couldn't seem to decide if they were shorts or Capris. "This urchin is Carlene. My youngest. I'm going to make a sign for her that says 'I dress myself,' just so people don't get the wrong idea."

"I see." I wanted to make intelligent conversation, truly I did, but my cart still rocked, Anneke informing me and the entire world of her feelings for me.

"So, how are you managing? It must be hard to come down here," Kathy said, absently stroking Carlene's sticky hair out of her face. She half-turned away from Anneke.

"To the store?" I stole a covert glance at my daughter. To my surprise Anneke had stopped rocking and yelling. She watched Kathy, puzzled.

"No, you nut—to the country. From the city."

Just then a boy slightly older than Anneke hurried over full of self-importance, holding two bags of the self-same cookies I had denied Anneke seconds ago. He dumped them in the cart. "These are the bestest ones I could find."

Kathy stroked his head. "Good job, buddy." She must have noticed my puzzled stare. "Cordell is my cookie and cereal expert. One week he gets to pick which cookies we're going to have, the next, it's cereal."

"That's cute." So I *was* wrong in denying Anneke a chance to pick out her own cookies. Why didn't kids come with a manual? How was a mother supposed to wing it through the myriad of decisions required every day?

"So, how is the dryer working out for you?"

I pulled my attention back to her. "Good. Though I did get the helpful suggestion that if I hang my clothes outside they'll dry faster." Wilma generously gave me this comment, accompanied by her usual patronizing smile.

Kathy clucked her disapproval of Wilma's household hints. "I call that cultural warfare and a direct insult to those of us who prefer to aid the cause of global warming by chucking our clothes in the dryer and enduring the thrill of shrinkage through ever-changing heat settings."

This woman was my new best friend. "Not to mention the fact that our overuse of natural resources will spur the government to increase corporate subsidies to companies seeking alternative energy sources," I countered.

Kathy clapped a hand on my shoulder. "Lady, you are speaking my language. I think you should come over for coffee."

I had told Dan I was coming right back, but I figured it wouldn't do Dan any harm to wonder where I was for a while. Maybe he would miss me and worry about me and when I came back he would enfold me in his arms and tell me that he treasured me and that he was wrong and that we would move back to Seattle as soon as possible.

Or maybe he wouldn't even notice. He and his uncle had their heads buried in the bowels of the tractor ever since the auction sale.

"Sounds like a great idea," I said, giving Kathy a quick grin.

Kathy's house was only a few miles out of the way on my

way home, situated close to the Interstate where the valley was wide open and more populated. As the mailboxes flitted past, I read the names. Brouwer, VandeKam, Huttinga, Flikkema, VanDyke. I sensed a pattern here. Pretty much pretty Dutch. Then we came to Greidanus and I followed Kathy down the driveway to her house. Kathy's yard and home surprised me. From her lackadaisical attitude and tough demeanor I expected something less, well, froufrou.

The house was an older scaled-down Victorian—white with green gingerbread trim. It looked like the kind of place a grandmother with an apron would inhabit. Flower beds lined the sidewalk, tulips and lilies poking up through tidily cultivated dirt.

She must have caught my expression as I followed her up the walk, holding Anneke's hand, Nicholas resting on my hip.

"You seem surprised," Kathy said, juggling her groceries and Carlene's clinging hand as she pulled open the wooden screen door.

I knew I couldn't fake it with her and at the same time knew I didn't have to. "I didn't take you for the flowers-and-gardening type."

"It's the hair," she sighed dramatically, as she held the door open with one foot, motioning with her head for me to go in. "I should wear it long and loose, and drape myself in Eddie Bauer socks, Birkenstocks, and L. L. Bean clothes, too." She slipped her boots off on the bootjack and strode into the house. "I've been accused of giving people mixed messages, but hey, in a place like Harland with so much tradition, it never hurts to keep people guessing."

"Well, you had me on the run."

And as my eyes took in our indoor surroundings, I had another surprise. Dishes sat in precarious stacks on a small, old-fashioned countertop. The table, pushed against a long wooden bench, held a pile of bread crusts and beside it an opened pot of peanut butter with the knife still in it. A jumble of clothes lay in a heap on one of the chairs. A plaque above the table caught my eye: "Condition of kitchen variable. Hundreds of people have eaten here and gone on to lead normal lives."

Kathy dropped her plastic bags by a large floor-to-ceiling cupboard and waved her hand in the direction of her kitchen. "Housekeeping and me—not friends. Barely nodding acquaintances." She pulled open the door as Cordell and Carlene heaved cans and boxes out of the bags and put them away.

"Hey, Nicholas and Anneke, you want to help?" she asked my children, whose mouths hung open in wonder at the freedom these children enjoyed.

She didn't have to ask my daughter twice. In seconds Anneke dug into bags asking where things went and putting them away like she was handling the Crown Jewels.

Nicholas had been squirming to get off my lap from the moment I sat down with him. I looked at the floor, then at the fun the kids were having and set him on the floor in the middle of bags and groceries and kids.

"You put this one away, Mommy." Anneke pushed a can in my hand.

Cordell pulled out a bag of boxes of raisins with a gleeful

yelp. "Let's make a raisin-box tower." He ripped the bag open and spilled the boxes out onto the floor. Kathy didn't even blink.

"Yay, a tower," Anneke called out, though she didn't have the first clue what to do.

"Here, Anneke," Kathy said pulling the plastic bag out of Nicholas's reach with one hand while showing Anneke what to do with the other. "You have to be really careful when you pile them up so they don't fall. Carlene, you help Anneke. Here, Nicholas, here's some boxes for you."

"I've been had," I said to Kathy as I helped Anneke balance a box on yet another tower. "All this time I've been spending a fortune on educational toys when fun and games were right in front of me in the form of boxed raisins."

"Welcome to Groceries R Us." We made a couple more towers and then Kathy clapped her hands. "Okay, Cordell, Carlene, Anneke, let's put the boxes away. You go to the playroom and keep yourselves busy for a while," Kathy said in a tone suggesting that no protest would be forthcoming. And none was. When they were done, Cordell picked up Nicholas as if he had been doing this all his life and carted him down the hallway, Carlene and Anneke trailing along behind him. I looked at Kathy with new eyes. And wonder. How did she do this so effortlessly? An artist, that's what she was.

"Close your mouth," Kathy said with a quick laugh. "You look like a fish."

"I feel like a fish. Out of water. Every time I want Anneke to do something, I feel like I have to convene a tribal council, and even then I'm always afraid she'll vote me out of the house."

"Show No Fear is the first rule of parenting." Kathy pulled a kettle off the stove. "So, I heard that you're an RN."

"Heard? From whom?"

"Wilma and Gloria were talking about it at Coffee Break. I was surprised when they said you didn't want to go back to work."

When did I ever talk about not going back to work in front of Wilma and Gloria? The last conversation we had that even touched upon me working had to do with them assuming I would sooner be digging in the garden than starting IV's.

"You look confused," Kathy said.

I pulled myself away from thoughts of work and Wilma. "Sorry, I'm a little lost . . ."

"I should explain. Coffee Break is the women's Bible study that's held at the church. There's programs for the little ones and a nursery that run while the moms are busy. You should come."

"First major obstacles—Bible and study. Don't do either. And if Wilma and Gloria go . . ." I stopped myself just in time. Kathy didn't need to know my struggles with my in-laws.

Kathy glanced over her shoulder at me while she arranged muffins on a plate. "I take it you don't get along with Wilma?" Her tilted smile and saucy wink accompanied by the faint sparkle in her eyes were a clue that she knew precisely how I got along with Wilma. Not. But I was trying to be charitable and discreet. I didn't need anything I said held against me at the next convening of the VandeKeere family.

"We have our difficulties," I said carefully. "But she's had hers, as well. What with Keith taking off and all."

Kathy snorted. "Honey, that was the best thing that happened to her. Keith was a lazy no-good . . ." She stopped and tapped her fingers on her lips. "And here I said I wasn't going to gossip."

"But it still must be hard for her," I said, determined to be compassionate.

"Not so hard now that her favorite child is back. And I'm sure she's happy about you toiling alongside Dan, supporting him and keeping the home happy and healthy."

Was she being sarcastic?

I didn't know Kathy that well and wasn't sure of her place in the community nor her position on the working mother/stay-at-home mother debate. So I went with the ever-popular and seldom out of style, vague. "I'm sorry. What do you mean?"

"Don't worry, Leslie. I know exactly what you're up against with Wilma. She has an old-fashioned view of motherhood and marriage." Kathy turned back to the now-whistling kettle and poured the steaming water into a teapot and brought everything to the table. "So, why don't you go back to work? And if I'm being way too nosy, you can tell me to back off," Kathy said, suddenly serious now. "My husband says I don't always know when to leave things be. And he's right, but my need to know outstrips my need to be discreet."

I laughed at her blunt honesty and then thought of my now sadly depleted DHF and the tractor that Dan and his uncle, even as Kathy put cups in front of me, were fixing up.

"I've actually done that already," I said, choosing my words carefully. "I'll be starting on Friday."

Kathy sat back, her hands cradling her cup of tea. "But what are you going to do with the kids?"

"I thought about the day care in town."

She pulled a face. "Don't do that, Leslie. If you need a babysitter, I'll gladly help out. My place is right on the way to town."

I waited, letting the words sink in. "I work shifts."

"That's okay."

I wanted to jump up and accept her generous offer right away but couldn't escape the guilt over not asking Wilma or Gloria first.

I heard the kids playing and turned toward the window. Anneke and Carlene shrieking with laughter and running across the fenced-in yard, Nicholas pouring sand over his feet in the sandbox, supervised by the cookie expert. My heart ached to see my kids playing in a yard with other kids. The one friend I had, Josie, didn't have kids. I went on play-dates with other mothers, but didn't get much advice from other women. Raising the kids was, to me, like driving a car with very, very dim headlights. I could see only the next thing I had to do. Long term, much harder to figure out.

Ever since the kids were born, I'd felt as if Dan and I were two rank amateurs experimenting with fragile substances. My mother was who knows where and Terra, a single woman, could only cheerlead from the sidelines. Friends at work offered advice, but it never seemed applicable. Now, here was a person I barely knew but felt an inexplicable connection to, offering to help me with the crucial job of raising my kids.

I'm not a sentimental person, but that was definitely a choked-throat moment.

"Thanks for the offer, Kathy. I might take you up on it," I said.

"You do that." She took a sip of tea. "Now, tell me all about Seattle. I've always wanted to go but never had the chance."

From: tfroese@hotmail.com

To: lesismore@montana.net

U better tell Dan pretty quick about job or UR going to be in huge doo doo. Gotta run. Big date. Keep U posted.

Tra, la, la Terra

Chapter Eight

hy?"

The simple question hung between us, edged with anger.

"Because . . ." I could see him stiffen at my standard reply even as the words *tractor, tractor, tractor* echoed in my subconscious and buried even below that, Missssss Bilingual. Right as I might have been, I wasn't ready to play that card yet. "I tried the cows thing, Dan. But I'm not a cow person, horses give me the screaming willies, the chickens give me the creeps. The dog is the only animal I feel comfortable around. I don't know the difference between a cultivator and a combine, and frankly, I don't care. I do know ACLS, how to deal with a stroke victim, and how to assess a burn. I'm comfortable in a hospital emergency department, and there have been days since I've moved here that I wish I was back there. Where I know what I'm doing." I clamped my lips together to stem the tide of my run-on babbling. I wanted him to understand. Needed him to understand.

"I want to go back to work because it's the only place I feel like I belong," I said, stumbling my way through this new situation. "I feel like I should have had my passport stamped before we came here." I drew in a breath, juggling my words awkwardly. I considered bringing up the tractor again and the money Dan had drained out of our house account and the way his mother controlled each penny that came into this household. But that would take us nowhere. After all, technically half of our house money was his. If honesty was my new tack, then I had to lay out the rest of my reasons. "I don't feel like I belong here."

"We had farms in Washington, too, remember?" I could see he was trying to be patient, but he was using up his quota. Fast.

"I never had to live on them. Nor did I have to try to fit into a place that was unfamiliar to me. And there's another thing. This Christian thing and going to church stuff you've been talking about lately. That's not us. It's not what I signed on for when we got married." I was gaining momentum and from the faintly sheepish look on his face, I knew I was also gaining ground. And though I wasn't a farmer's wife, I remembered a few things I picked up from working with the cows. I kept my distance, off and to the side, but maintained pressure. "If you're going to be honest with yourself and me, it's new for you, too. You never went to church in Seattle."

His silence underlined the rightness of my cause. But I knew I couldn't claim victory yet. I gently pushed on while I still had his attention and while he was still in a good mood instead of on the run.

"So, here I am. Pagan. City person. And everything is new and different and confusing here." When I saw Dan fidget I caught myself. "So I walk into the hospital and I hear the clank of med carts and I get a whiff of hospital cafeteria and I hear the bleep of monitors . . . and for the first time since I came here, I relax. I'm in a familiar place. I'm home."

Dan screwed up his face, obviously trying hard to understand. "So, it's not just about the money?"

"That's part of it." I looked him directly in the eye. "We were going to keep the Fund separate, but that changed, didn't it?"

"Leslie, you know why . . ." Dan's lips became two white lines.

"I know you tried to tell me about cash flow and how you access the line of credit, but really it comes down to your mother controlling the farm money, doesn't it?"

"She's had a rough couple of months. I can't expect her to just hand it all over to me. Especially if, as you keep saying, we're only here for a year."

Once again I was caught between the reality of Wilma's humiliating situation and what I had to deal with on a day-to-day basis with her. Hard to feel sympathy when each comment directed my way reminded me that I wasn't really a part of this family.

"If she's going to hand over the cropping and the managing of the farm, I think she could go one step further. And partly because she won't and because the fund is emptier than I like . . ." I hurried through that dreaded but necessary territory of the discussion and plowed on, "I'm going back to work. But even more important, when I came into the hospital, I wasn't reminded that I don't know the difference between hay and straw, between heifers and bulls . . ."

"Steers," Dan corrected.

"See? That."

"But you're learning."

"I don't want to learn——" and then I clamped my mouth shut before I let myself trot down the——by now——old, tired road of "this place isn't permanent."

"That's the trouble. You don't even give it a chance."

"What are you talking about? I'm giving it a year."

"Give it time, Leslie," Dan urged. "You'll come to love the animals, the wide open spaces. Don't you like being home with the kids?"

Direct hit on the guilt zone. "I do. And I wouldn't be working full-time. But . . ." I dug down, searching for a word, a phrase that would connect. "I don't want my kids to grow up like I did. They're going to have the best life I can give them and if it means working, so be it."

"You don't think I can provide for us?" The hurt in his voice was almost my undoing. I knew what losing the business had done to his pride.

"I think you can. And you have." I paused, trying to find the best way to say what I needed to say. "Dan, we were in Seattle two years, before that Dallas for eighteen months. Before that it was Minneapolis. We've spent a lot of years moving from place to place. This is just another stopover."

Right then Anneke pushed Nicholas into the kitchen and

abandoned him in the box while she climbed up on her father's lap. Nicholas let out a wail of disapproval, which I responded to in record time.

"When do you want to start?" Dan asked, the faint tone of resignation in his voice showing me that while he had accepted it, he still didn't like it.

Here came the next tricky part. I shifted Nicholas on my hip, holding him close to me like a chubby shield. "This Friday." I kept my response short and fast, like a quick needle jab, hoping the speed would eradicate the pain.

"What?" He stared at me, open-mouthed.

Or not.

"How did you get that so fast?" Dan asked, the anger in his voice vying with the puzzlement on his face. "Don't you have to take tests?"

"I did that the day before. I wanted to be sure before I told you." I could see him still puzzling this through and went on the defensive. "I'm not a stay-at-home wife. You knew that all along. I wasn't in Seattle, and I'm not so sure I can be here." I conveniently left out the fact that I had come here willing to take a chance. It was the family meeting, his mother, his sister, the cows, and of course, the tractor that had chipped away at those intentions.

"My sisters manage. My mother managed."

Low blow.

He looked at me then, and I felt a chill begin deep in my being. "We moved here to help my mother out, to support her. The family needed us. That's why we came."

"My working won't change that."

"What are you going to do with the kids? Obviously you haven't asked my sisters or they would have let me know."

"I've got that covered already," I said quickly. "Kathy Greidanus is going to be taking care of Anneke and Ben."

"Why not my mother? Or Judy? Or Gloria?"

"Your mom has enough to deal with, and neither Judy nor Gloria are on the way to work."

"Did you even ask them?"

"Kathy offered first. Plus she has young kids for Anneke and Ben to play with."

"Mom isn't going to be happy about this."

"Kathy is right on the way to work. Judy lives fifteen minutes the other way . . ."

"She's going to ask me why you didn't."

". . . And I don't want to add another three quarters of an hour of driving to the kids' day."

"I could take care of the kids once in a while."

"You'll be busy with the field work."

Dan waited a beat, then ran his fingers through his hair. "And what about our marriage? Wasn't coming to the farm about that, too?"

The chill spread to my hands and feet. Since that one major blowup back home when I had come back from work early and Dan had shown up late smelling like perfume, Miss Bilingual remained She Who Must Not Be Named. To give her a name would be to give her a place in our life. I wasn't going to cede one second of my time to her. When Dan started confessing, I cut him off. I didn't want details. I didn't want my imagination creating pictures that would forever waver between us. So we referred to her only obliquely.

"What about our marriage, Dan? What about sticking up for each other and putting each other first? When you used the money from our fund for the tractor, you showed me pretty clearly where what I wanted stood in your life." I clung to Nicholas and thankfully, for once, he didn't protest. I needed an ally and wasn't fussy as to shape, size, or mental ability.

"Leslie, I need that tractor for the farm . . ."

"If that was the case, you should have asked your mother for the money."

Dan's angry glance cut away and I knew I had scored a direct hit.

But I didn't want to be keeping score, to be shown I was right. But I had to keep the vision or it was going to blur and once again I was going to lose myself.

"You chose the farm over me, Dan."

His gaze swung back to me. "No. It's not always about you, Leslie. It's not always about choosing one over the other. Sometimes it's about doing the very next thing that's right in front of you. Sometimes it's about making the best of where you are right now instead of always looking ten years into the future."

Our gazes locked. I turned away first. Maybe I was too caught up in what lay ahead, but if people didn't have goals, didn't have plans, they were vulnerable. You had to take care of your life. No one else was going to do that for you.

"Okay. I'm not going to say anything more about your

job," Dan said, conceding that point. "But could you do me a favor? Could you at least try to make the best of being here?"

Considering I had ruined one of my favorite jackets "making the best of it," his request seemed a tad unfair. But I wanted peace in our home. I didn't want Dan and I to be carping and fighting.

This skirmish was over, and though nothing concrete had been resolved, at least he was resigned to my working.

"I came here with the intention of making the best of it, Dan. This is part of how I intend to do it."

Dan sighed, got up. "Let's go outside, honey." Dan said to Anneke holding out his hand to her. Obviously this conversation's shelf life had expired.

Anneke hopped alongside him, chattering about the dog and the chickens, each word, each step carrying them both farther away from me.

Nicholas saw them go and spun around, twisting away from me toward his father and sister. His deafening wails exploded when the screen door slapped shut behind them.

"I know exactly how you feel," I muttered as I tried to console him.

But he wasn't having any of me, either. I finally resorted to bribing him with some forbidden chocolate chips and set him in the high chair, freeing myself to get lost in the soothing motions of folding laundry.

"It will be fine," I said to the empty house. "He'll get used to it. His sisters will get used to it. His mother . . ." That one was a stumper. I doubted Wilma would get used to it. But that didn't matter. It would all work out.

From: lesismore@montana.net
To: tfroese@hotmail.com

I got rhythm. In my life that is. Dan is busy in the fields. We don't talk about my work though he doesn't seem to mind the extra money in the account. He's still upset with me, but I'm busy enough in the house and at work that I can ignore it. And I have a wonderful babysitter. She loves my kids and she's one of those casual mothers who makes raising kids look as effortless as riding a bicycle. Something I never quite got a handle on, either. Remember how many times I skinned my knees?

Loopy Leslie Loving Her Life

From: tfroese@hotmail.com
To: lesismore@montana.net

That church thing Dan goes to. That's not some kind of cult is it? U won't have to pledge UR kids to it or wear funny hats? Can't go with the flow if U are going to join a cult.

Terra

It was time. I had found all kinds of excuses to put it off, but I had run out. The windows sparkled, the counters gleamed. The beds were made, and the floors were tidied. My immaculate house was a small penance for working the day before and enjoying it so much.

It was time. I looked outside. Sunshine. Warm, friendly sunshine.

I didn't need to put bulky coats and boots on the kids, which meant Nicholas could walk on his own. I slipped a light coat on, picked up the pail of burnt cookies that didn't make the grade, and braced myself to face my nemesis.

The warmth of the sun surrounded us as I closed the door of the porch behind us. I released a lungful of stale air welcoming the change in scenery. I automatically glanced around, wondering who saw us, then caught myself mid-silliness. There were no neighbors twitching aside curtains to see what I was doing. No one watching us.

Though we'd already been on the farm four weeks, (twenty-eight chocolates' worth), I still had to get used to the fact that, if I so desired, I could run outside naked and no one would be the wiser. That was unless Uncle Orest stopped by or Wilma made a sudden stop on her way to town or Bradley VandeKamp, the neighbor, decided to borrow Dan's harrows.

Today, stillness reigned over the yard. Dan was at his mother's house fixing a clogged drain and partly as penance for our fight the other day and partly because Dan had to leave so early this morning, I had volunteered our services to do "chores."

Nicholas didn't want to go in the wagon, so I left it behind, and as we started walking down the sidewalk, Sasha came bounding up, her mouth open, tongue hanging out, a doggy grin on her fuzzy face.

"Oh, Sasha, I love you." Anneke grabbed the dog by the

neck and buried her face in the matted fur. Nicholas leaned toward Sasha, but I kept his hand in mine. One swipe of Sasha's tail would knock Nicholas on his padded bottom. Usually, Nicholas was in his wagon and Sasha's puzzling canine brain saw the plastic conveyance as a peril and walked wide, suspicious circles around it.

My worries were groundless. Sasha sat quietly while Nicholas petted her head, her tail slowly making a half circle in the dirt of the driveway. Anneke urged her brother on. "Pet the doggy, Nicholas. Nice doggy."

"Doggy," Nicholas said, his hand batting Sasha on the head. "Doggy."

My mouth fell open. He was talking. Speaking. Articulating. My amazement was replaced with laughter. His first word was *doggy*? Not *Mommy* or *Daddy*?

"Mommy, Nicholas said *doggy*," Anneke exclaimed, clapping her hands. "Oh, good Nicholas. Good boy," she said, full of maternal pride.

"Hey, little boy," I said, bending down to pet Sasha as well. "This is a doggy, isn't it?" I pointed to myself. "And I am a mommy."

Nicholas gave me a blank stare, turned back to Sasha. "Doggy," he squealed, grabbing Sasha's ear and tugging it, knocking over my pail.

I gathered up the cookies, then herded the kids toward the chicken barn. "Hey, kids, let's go. We have work to do."

Sasha sniffed the ground where the cookies had spilled and snorfed up the crumbs I had missed.

I held Nicholas's hand to give him some stability as we

slowly made our way toward the barn. A light spring breeze sifted through the cottonwood trees, rustling the leaves that were now full green. A crow mocked us from the branches, then flew away. Overhead an eagle circled lazily. I watched its progress, pointing it out to the kids.

In Seattle the sky often hung low—either cloudy or rainy or foggy. Often I was so focused on the car in front of me as I lurched through rush-hour traffic, wipers slapping time, I didn't spend much time contemplating the bits and pieces of nature I could see.

This was educational for my children, I thought, looking around the yard that had slowly morphed from dull brown to soft emerald. I hoped they would remember this.

A few cows lined the fence behind the barn, studying our slow progress, their bovine features benign and dumb-looking. I couldn't understand why cattle ranching seemed such a romantic pursuit. Cows were big, large, and, well, dumb. They took up a lot of space and ate a lot of food. Dan was still feeding them while he waited for the pasture to grow up enough to put them out.

And if cows were lacking in the intelligence department, the chickens we were going to feed rated well below them.

I understood why cigarette companies didn't film commercials about chicken farmers. No pictures of manly men striding through a chicken barn while rugged music played in the background. Chickens were flighty, smelly, and their stupidity had no romantic overtones.

Once upon a time, in some flight of fancy I'd had, gathering eggs brought to mind a hazy picture of plump, contented brown chickens pecking pastorally on the ground while my children and I frolicked amongst them, plucking eggs from soft, straw-lined nests.

I tugged open the door to the chicken coop. Squawks and the muffled thud of flapping wings as the startled chickens took flight shattered that daydream. I sneezed, batting away fluttering feathers, trying to find the chicken feeder in the half light of the chicken coop.

"No frolicking today, kids," I warned as I dropped the cookies on the straw-covered ground. The chickens at least liked my baking. They usually gobbled up my hapless attempts at the culinary arts, magically transforming them into eggs that I would use for my next attempt. Which would probably end up back here, thus completing the cycle of life.

I shook some pelleted chicken feed into the feeder, then turned to deal with the most complex part of the operation.

Three chickens crouched in the boxes, wings spread over their bounty, glowering at me with beady eyes as they clucked out a warning. Dan had shown the kids and me how to gently slip a hand under their bodies to pull the still warm eggs from under them. He hadn't even flinched when a chicken jabbed the back of his hand with its beak. Not for me. Bravery wasn't my middle name. Actually it was Annie, but I tried not to advertise that fact.

"The chickens are too noisy," Anneke said, wrinkling her nose in distaste. "And very, very stinky."

"I agree, honey." I eyed the still-nesting chickens. If I made a mad dash I might be able to pull off a daring egg retrieval and save myself from being called a wuss. I know Dan would laugh if I told him, he would tell his family and they would laugh, and I would, once again, look like the silly city girl I was.

Let's see. Pride, wuss, pride, wuss.

Nah. *Wuss* was fine with me.

We beat a quick retreat from the chicken coop, closed the door behind us, our onerous task for the day partially completed. Sasha, who had been sitting guard, bounded to her feet, her tail telegraphing her pleasure.

Anneke scampered ahead of me, Sasha loping alongside her. Taffy, Dan's horse, whinnied hopefully at us.

I didn't have anything for her, but she appreciated our attention nonetheless. Nicholas petted her head, then saw the cows grazing in the pasture and pointed one pudgy hand. "Cow. Cow."

I laughed and gave him a quick hug. "You little stinker. You'll say *doggy* and *cow* but not *Mom*."

He looked up at me and blinked, his hand still pointing away. "Cow. Cow."

"Mommy. Try it," I encouraged. "Mommy."

"Cow."

Well, maybe in his mind they were one and the same thing.

We wandered along the fence line as Anneke plucked some dandelions. I let the peace of the scene wash over me, thankful that the open spaces no longer intimidated me. Maybe, by the time I left, I would love this as much as Dan did. Maybe we would come back more often. If he didn't determine that Seattle wasn't good enough and decide to move across the country again. We really needed to get that Dream Home so we could put down some roots.

By the time we got back to the house, Nicholas was rubbing his eyes and ears. If Anneke could be kept occupied for a while, I might have a chance to send my sister another e-mail, maybe even read another chapter in a book I had gotten from Judy.

As I hung up the kids' coats, the jangling of the phone pierced the quiet. I glanced at the clock as I ran to answer it.

"Leslie, just thought I'd call." Gloria. Her precise words, spoken with such scrupulous caring, shriveled the faint hope that it might be someone interesting or fun. One of my friends from Seattle apologizing for not answering my e-mails, my sister maybe, or even a telemarketer asking for donations.

"I heard you started working. And that Kathy Greidanus is taking care of your children."

Nothing like coming out swinging. "I met her in the store one day and she offered." I tucked the phone under my chin as I lifted Nicholas into his high chair. *Thank goodness for cordless phones,* I thought as I started buttering bread.

"Do you think that's wise?"

"I'm sorry . . ." Peanut butter for Nicholas. Just jam for Her Majesty. No clue what she was talking about for Gloria.

Gloria's silence beat on my ears, but I wasn't going to break it. The veiled anger in her voice got my back up. I just wished I knew what had gotten her knickers in such a twist.

"I realize that you feel the need to work, but I'm just a bit worried about Dan," she said. "He's going to be starting field work in a few days. What is he going to do about supper?"

Supper? The man didn't have two hands to feed himself?

"He made his own lunches before."

"Do you think that's fair?"

"Sorry. You lost me." I deftly cut up the kids' bread. Nine pieces for Anneke, cut off the crusts for Nicholas.

"Out here in the country we farm wives bring supper out to our husbands when they are working in the fields. They put in long days and can't come home for a warm meal. I don't mean to sound nosy . . ."

But you are.

". . . but how are you going to do that if you're working? And, I would like to come back to my original point, why is Kathy Greidanus taking care of Nicholas and Anneke? Didn't you think of asking us? Mom and I talked about it. We could easily do it, as well."

I dropped into the nearest chair and rubbed my forehead. How to work through this? Sure, Gloria was Dan's sister and the children's aunt. But the kids didn't know her any better than they knew Kathy. And I liked Kathy. And she was supportive of my working. And the kids liked it at her place.

When I picked them up after work yesterday, Kathy had Nicholas on her hip and gave him a kiss before she handed him over. Knowing that he was loved and cared for made his protest at me taking him away worth the moments of self-doubt I'd had about working.

Dan still resented my going to work, but once I laid out my reasons, he gave grudging approval of my bringing them to Kathy's place. I wasn't used to making my decisions by committee. I thought that I would have earned some Good Mother points simply by finding a wholesome alternative to day care.

"I'm sorry I didn't consult you, Gloria . . ." *Big, fat liar* . . . "But Kathy volunteered. My children are used to her and I don't think I should change that now. Besides, she's right on the way to town."

"I would be willing to come and pick the kids up," Gloria said. "We're not that far away."

And with that she offered me an immediate out. "Thanks, but I don't want to run the kids around that much. Besides, I'll be working shift work and it won't always be convenient. Thanks for the offer, though."

Nicholas threw the last of his bread on the floor, signaling the end of his lunch.

"I gotta go, Gloria. The kids need their nap." And I needed to regroup. "Thanks for calling." I hung up before she could say anything more.

I cleaned up the kids, changed Nicholas, and by the time his eyes were drifting closed, the phone rang again. This time I checked the call display. *Wilma.*

I had used up all my energy on Gloria, so I let it ring. When she called again, I let it ring again. And one more time.

Chapter Nine

told her that if she doesn't take her medicine the voices will start and people will think she's crazy." Darlene Anderson rolled her eyes as if to say "you know what I mean," then angled her head toward the middle-aged woman she was escorting to an empty cubicle. "Then she started running a fever and I don't know what's causing what."

The woman in question wore a pink hat with a bedraggled feather, a man's woolen vest over a stained white shirt, and a long sweeping velvet skirt. As we settled her on the bed, she kept whispering about a gig she was late for, her fingers twisting around each other. Her cheeks flamed, her eyes were glassy, and I could feel from her arm that she was burning up.

Darlene was slightly more lucid. Emphasis on *slightly*. In the time it took us to walk from the reception area to the emergency department, she had been chattering steadily about the VandeKeere family, how low the river was, the shameful movie being shown in town, and horoscopes.

She finally lowered her voice and drew me to one side as

she glanced sidelong at the woman now settling onto the bed. "I brought her in for the fever, but you know she's right cuckoo, don't you?"

"The correct term is *schizophrenic*," I said primly.

"Whatever." Darlene dismissed the terminology with a flip of her hand. "Doesn't change the fact that she thinks she's a concert pianist." Darlene sighed. "Absolutely nuts. Thinks she has to go out tonight to play in New York."

It was a Thursday evening. I had drawn the afternoon/ evening shift this week, grateful once again for my wonderful babysitter. Kathy gladly took the children this afternoon, promising to feed them supper and bring them home when Dan was done with fieldwork. I knew they would be all cleaned up and read to and cuddled and snuggled. I had felt a moment of jealousy when I first thought of her taking them out of the bathtub all slippery and wet and drying them off, then reading to them. But when I came into the hospital and felt the energy of the place, my emotions balanced out.

I don't know how I managed all the juggling I had to do with day care and Dan's work before. It wasn't pleasant, but somehow we coped. I would have a hard time going back to that.

"And what is your association with Mrs. Tebo?" I asked, trying to find my way around this bombastic and rude yet caring woman as I started a chart for Mrs. Tebo.

"Oh, nothing at all. I help her once in a while. Come and clean her house. She throws a fit, but honestly—it's a pigsty." Darlene sighed heavily. "Just doesn't take care of herself. I found her today sitting stark naked in the bathtub. She was shivering even though she was burning up. Silly woman."

I cringed, glancing over at Mrs. Tebo, who, thankfully, was oblivious to all this chatter.

"These old people," Darlene continued. "Hard to take care of. Just like that Mr. Mast. He's a stubborn old coot. Just won't take his insulin. I suppose you need to take her history again." Darlene glanced at the chart. "I don't know why you can't use what you had before."

"It's procedure." I ignored her complaints and got the particulars on Rena Tebo via Darlene and a few muttered responses from Rena herself.

Once I got the woman's sad and all-too-familiar history down, I pulled out the blood-pressure cuff.

"Here. I'll need to help you with that," Darlene said, scurrying over as fast as her formidable bulk would allow her. Amazingly, she didn't knock anything over as she bent to lift Rena's chin up. "The nice lady is going to take your blood pressure, okay?" she yelled, as if Rena were two miles away instead of two inches.

Rena just blinked and stared.

As I put on the cuff and started up the machine, I caught Darlene inspecting me. "You don't go to church with your Dan, do you?"

I blinked a moment, surprised at the question, though after spending even these few minutes with Darlene, the boldness shouldn't have been a shocker.

"No. I don't."

"Why not?"

I ignored her as I noted the blood pressure and took Rena's temperature. Through the roof.

"I prefer not to," was all I could muster. My focus was Rena Tebo right now, not my faith life.

"You should. Be good for you." Darlene nodded, her chins jiggling as if underscoring her comment. "You need to know that God is in control. Especially when those really bad cases come in the hospital."

I thought of the multiple motor vehicle accident earlier this week that had resulted in three deaths—a mother and her two children. I was so relieved I had missed it. Judy had gone to school with the mother and was heartbroken. She and Dan were going to the funeral tomorrow. But I was staying home with my children, blocking my life out into compartments. Work. Home. They didn't intersect. I couldn't allow it or I would constantly be seeing Dan or Anneke or Nicholas on the stretchers that came in.

"I'm sure God has enough people to occupy His time. He won't miss me," I said, thinking I was so smart and glib, hoping I could get her to stop prying into my life. Who was the nurse here after all? Who was in charge?

"He's missing you now," Darlene said with a knowing look. "Like the one sheep missing from the ninety-nine. He goes after them because He cares."

Sheep? Ninety-nine? What in the world was she talking about?

I shrugged lightly, then moved on to things I did know about. "Dr. Brouwer will want to listen to Rena's chest. Do you think you can get her to put on this gown or at least take some layers off?"

Darlene waved me off. "Not a problem. And don't forget.

God is waiting. He wants you to know what your only comfort in life and death is."

I supposed she wanted that to sound comforting, but it sounded more ominous than reassuring.

"Rena Tebo?" Dr. Brouwer sighed as he finished what he was doing and clipped his pen in his pocket. "That's the second time this week. Medicaid is going to give me grief over this one. What is it this time?"

"Elevated temp and b.p. Some question as to what medications she's taken. I've got her ready for you. A Darlene Anderson brought her in."

To my surprise, Dr. Brouwer laughed. "She's a character, isn't she? I don't know how many of the town's down-and-outers she's tucked under her wing, but it's quite a few. Good thing she's got large wings."

"Darlene is . . . interesting," I conceded.

To my surprise, Rena was in a gown by the time we got back. Still muttering and still complaining, but in a gown.

Dr. Brouwer checked her over, then pulled out a prescription pad and scribbled something on it. "She'll need to take these twice a day for ten days," he said, handing it to Darlene.

Darlene nodded slowly, looking over the piece of paper as if she could decipher Dr. Brouwer's handwriting. I knew *I* couldn't.

Dr. Brouwer talked about ongoing care and follow-up but Darlene waved him off.

"I know how this works," she said decisively, tucking the prescription into a pocket of her sagging sweater. "I've got it under control."

"I don't doubt you do," he said quietly.

We left Darlene chattering to Rena and as soon as they were out of earshot, Dr. Brouwer started laughing again. "I imagine you've seen all kinds in Seattle. But I doubt you've seen too many like Darlene."

"Not too many," I agreed. Darlene was a puzzling combination of generous and strange, but in my mind the generosity won out over the rest. Someone willing to cart around a schizophrenic woman and keep tabs on an elderly diabetic man was high up in my books—in spite of her questions about church.

"So, what did you do with your kids?" Dr. Brouwer asked, obviously not in a hurry to go. His shift had been over for ten minutes and still he hung around, looking like he wanted to chat, something I had to get used to. In the emergency department in Seattle, there was no time for small talk. The smallest it ever got was "You ready for a break?" or "What are you doing this weekend?" usually thrown out as we passed each other in the hallway.

"I took them to a babysitter."

Dr. Brouwer had been gone on vacation when I started and only now, after three weeks of work had our shifts intersected.

"Who?"

"Kathy Greidanus." I didn't know whether to finish charting or fully engage in chitchat. I picked up Rena's chart and Dr. Brouwer followed me to the nurses' station.

"Remind me how old your kids are?" Dr. Brouwer asked, leaning against the chest-high divider that separated the desk from the rest of the department.

"Nicholas is one and a half, and my daughter is four," I murmured. Why was he still hanging around? Most doctors I knew stayed beyond their shift only in case of a pressing emergency or if they were coming down off a tense code. And then they didn't make with the yik yak—they kept busy, trying to corral their stress into the farthest corner of their mind where they could handle it.

"Nicholas being the little boy who was with you at the auction," Dr. Brouwer continued, settling in for a chat. "And what's your daughter's name?"

"Anneke." Usually I would have brushed off such a blatant and rather clumsy effort at getting to know me. But it had been a quiet evening so far on the ward and I was in a good mood. Our little family had eaten breakfast together today and, as my peace offering, I tried to make French toast. Though it wasn't completely done in spots, it wasn't burnt, either. We'd sat down together and talked in complete sentences. Dan told me what he was going to do that day—fix the air-seeder and work up the back fields—and I told him my evening work schedule. Nothing new about my job, whereas Dan's created a steady stream of jargon that was as foreign to me as the church talk he currently indulged in during coffee times with Uncle Orest. *Irrigation, no till, wheat and barley, heat units, desiccation, redemption, reconciliation,* and *offerings.*

"How are you coping with the move from city to farm? It must be a bit hard to get used to." He leaned in, not enough to invade my personal space but enough that I caught the barest whiff of cologne . . . and interest.

"I've had some adjusting to do." My foray into and hasty retreat from cow-moving territory and egg gathering came to mind. "But the countryside is beautiful, and that helps."

His smile slowly transformed his face. Very easy on the eyes. Why hadn't some single woman snapped this man up yet?

"I love it here. I can't imagine moving into the city." He shifted his weight so both his elbows were on the counter. "I've been hearing good things about your work." Deeper smile. Dimples even.

Pause. Freeze frame. Was I being overly sensitive, or had he made a subtle shift from getting to know me to making a move on me?

Me—with two kids and stretch marks? *Right, Leslie.*

I didn't know how to reply to the compliment or the perceived move, so I made do with an awkward but brief "thank you." Then quickly concentrated on finishing Rena Tebo's chart.

"I'm sure your mother-in-law is happy to have Dan back here with her."

"She is. She's been lonely, as well." *Very good comment, Leslie. Shows sensitivity and caring.*

"Not surprising. Being alone can be difficult." He paused as if for effect, and again I felt myself floundering. Was this a cue for me to express my sympathy?

"Wilma's not the easiest person to be around," he continued. "I imagine it's been difficult for you to establish boundaries." Then he leaned closer, his eye contact lasting a hairsbreadth too long.

He *was* coming on to me.

I had to blink a moment, as if to refocus my eyes. I wasn't used to this kind of attention. I savored the pleasant thought for a brief, fluttery moment.

"Boundaries are important," I said with a meaningful tone to my voice. I casually brushed a nonexistent strand of hair away with my left hand, making sure the diamond on my wedding band caught the light.

"I know I'm probably overstepping my own boundaries here—"

I'll say.

"—but I want you to know that I understand what you have to deal with as far as Wilma is concerned. I grew up here and I know her family. Gloria and I went to school together. We used to hang out, and I got a sharp taste of what Wilma could be like. Very controlling. Very manipulative." He paused a moment as if to let this sink in. Which it did once I got over the "I-hung-out-with-Gloria" part. Harland wasn't that big, I reasoned. If Dr. Brouwer grew up here then of course he would know most of the people here. Including Gloria and the rest of the VandeKeeres.

And Dr. Brouwer was the first person I had met who called Wilma for what she was without qualifiers and excuses. I felt the burden I had been carrying slip off my shoulders. I wasn't evil incarnate. I wasn't a paranoid scheming daughter-in-law. I was right about Wilma. His words were like rain on parched ground.

In one corner of my conscience I heard a faint warning.

This is gossip.

Maybe, but it's also the truth.

She's Dan's mother, and he loves her.

Well, yeah, but his mother doesn't love me. And no one seems to get that.

"Thanks for that," I breathed.

"Don't worry. I know exactly what you're dealing with." He let his smile deepen, paused another moment, then pushed away from the desk. "I should go," he sighed. "You take care."

He held my gaze a split second longer. A compatriot who knew. I smiled back, and it was as if we now shared a subtle bond.

And when he left, I couldn't help but sneak a quick glance at myself in the glass panel beside me. My features were juxtaposed over a fire hose but I could make out the faint flush on my cheeks and a heightened sparkle in my eye.

You've still got it, I thought, winking at myself.

———

You have time for tea?" Kathy asked when I stepped onto the porch that afternoon after work.

I was falling into a rhythm. Thanks to a couple of nurses who preferred working evenings and a hospital that preferred eight-hour shifts to twelve, I was able to work day shifts. Which meant I often dropped the kids off and picked them up myself.

"The kids are in the playroom," she continued. "Nicholas had a long nap this afternoon, so he's not going to be ready for bed when you get home."

Most of the time our chats moved from the doorway to

the porch to the stairs and finally to her kitchen table if I had
time.

"I'd love a cup." Dan was seeding on the higher land.
Wilma had called me at work and informed me that since I
was too busy working, she would make sure Dan got a warm
meal for once. All of this was delivered with a subtle re-
proach that made me feel guilty, which then made me resent
feeling guilty, which, in turn, I felt even more guilty about.
She was technically doing a good deed, and I should be grateful. Something else she made sure I realized as I struggled to
untangle the confusing emotions she raised in me. So, for
now as far as feeding Dan was concerned, I was off the hook.

Kathy waved me in. "Always time for a friend."

Friend. I liked the sound of that. I kicked off my work
shoes, wiggled my tired toes, and relished the feel of the cool
floor on my hot feet as I strolled into her kitchen.

Today Kathy looked like a G-rated version of Daisy Duke
with a pair of old blue jeans cut off at mid thigh and an oversized
cotton shirt tied at the waist. "So, how was work?" she asked.

"Busy," I said with a sigh. "Today was national 'I've-been-sick
for-two-weeks-and-now-I-demand-immediate-care' day."

"I didn't see that on the calendar. Is that a holiday?"

"Only for doctors. We couldn't scare one up for love or
money. Finally, long-suffering Dr. John showed up. He's just
great."

"Dr. John? You mean Dr. Brouwer?"

"Yeah." Dr. John had informed me with a conspiratorial
smile, that though he would have preferred I call him simply
John, he realized the necessity of maintaining professional-

ism, so could I please call him Dr. John. I did, simply because of all the doctors in the hospital, he was by far the easiest to work with. Always friendly and smiling and helpful.

"Are you sure that's a good idea?" Kathy studied me with a frown of uncertainty on her face.

"What subliminal message are you sending me?" I asked.

"Nothing." The frown melted away, replaced by an uneasy smile which, I sensed, had something to do with my casual use of Dr. John's name.

"How were the kids?" I didn't want to talk about Dr. John. Right now he was an ally, and I didn't want to analyze the relationship.

"The kids were great. Anneke helped Jimmy and me plant a garden, and Nicholas played with Cordell and Carlene."

"You put in a garden with four kids watching? How did you find the time?"

"Are you kidding? Look around and smell the toast burning, honey." Kathy's wave encompassed plates from dinner stacked on the counter and an overturned box of cat food in one corner of the kitchen. "Gardening vs. Cleaning House. Guess which one triumphed?"

"The dilemma of the ages," I said.

"So, next couple of days off. Whatcha goin' to do?" Kathy set the mugs on the table, brushed a cat off her chair, and plopped down.

I didn't want to tell her that I was going to clean my house. Not when my elbows now rested on a table covered with crumbs of cookie, grains of sugar, and a little pile of powdered coffee creamer.

"I don't know. Hang out. Read. Work on my unhealthy cancer-causing tan while Dan goes to church and try not to let the collective pressure of his family pull me into going as well."

Kathy nodded and I felt a subtle shift in the atmosphere.

"Don't tell me you think I should go?"

"Okay, I won't." She shrugged then took a sip of her tea.

"It doesn't make sense, you know. I never went before."

Still she said nothing.

"It would just be hypocritical. Right? So, don't pressure me, okay?"

"You're the one who brought it up. Now, and just about every time I talk to you."

"My guilty conscience prods me to justify my absence." I flashed her a quick smile to show her my humorous side.

"So, come and you won't feel guilty anymore. There's not a lot going on in Harland, after all. The theater usually has second-run movies, and we don't have much else going on. Church is kind of the only show in town."

"I've discovered that," I said with a grin. "First time ever I heard an advertisement for church on the radio. Seemed almost sacrilegious."

"What could it hurt to come? You could test out Pascal's Wager."

"You've read Blaise Pascal?"

Kathy placed a hand on her heart and affected an injured tone. "Some of us here in Harland have an edjumacation, you know. Yes, I've read Blaise Pascal. I took two years of a liberal arts degree before I met Jimmy and moved back to Harland."

I wanted to ask her more about what made her come

back here but couldn't abandon Pascal just yet. "So tell me about the wager. Though wagering, I understood, was a distinctly non-Christian thing to do."

"Only if you do it for money," Kathy said with a wink. "It goes like this: If you believe, and God exists, you will be rewarded in the afterlife. If you do not believe, and He exists, you will be punished for your disbelief. If He does not exist, you have lost nothing either way."

I had to make a mental shift to ponder that one. "Okay. So, believing God exists is a 'cover-your-angles' philosophy."

I glanced outside again. Anneke was running from Cordell, shrieking. Nicholas toddled after a butterfly, his hands in the air, followed by Carlene, who dragged a teddy bear over the grass. As I watched the kids, I considered what Kathy told me. I've always thought of my children as mini-miracles. When they were babies, I used to marvel at the perfection of their fingernails, their ears, eyes, tiny toes.

"You know, if I'm honest with myself, I can't completely dismiss God . . . or a god," I mused, voicing thoughts I had never spoken aloud to anyone. Not even Dan. "I know enough about human anatomy to be consistently amazed at how complex and intricate it is. How fragile and yet how strong."

"So, why not start finding out a bit more about Him by going to church?"

I tested that suggestion a moment. It couldn't really hurt to go. It would ease the guilt I felt lying in bed while Dan got himself and Anneke ready. Goodness knows, I had enough guilt already.

"I suppose I could," I said reluctantly.

"It would ease the tension between you and Wilma and the rest of the family."

"Is that a good reason?"

"Good enough. Church is a great place to be."

Kathy had the same look on her face that I saw on Judy's when she talked about church. That peace called to a deeply hidden yearning that surfaced in my own life between bouts of hectic activity. It always caught me at odd times. Once I was kneeling on the living-room floor, phone tucked under my ear as I juggled shifts with another nurse, folded Nicholas's diapers, and tried to ignore the rustling pages of newspapers that Dan dropped on the floor beside his chair. Anneke called from her bedroom for her fifth drink of water and Nicholas protested his incarceration with intermittent shrieks. When my conversation with my nursing friend was over, I hung up the phone, looked around my house, and a whisper of "Is this all there is?" invaded the edges of my mind.

Trouble was, I never knew precisely what else there was or how to find it.

"The only time I've been in church were the few Christmas services we attended when we came here. I'm sure it was a shock to dear Wilma and the sisters to discover that they'd been harboring a perfect, or imperfect, heathen in their midst." I tossed the words out with a flippant air to cover the faint hurt I still felt at their censure.

"I know they're not perfect, but they do care."

"You're not allowed to defend them," I said with a pained note in my voice. "You're my ally in the battle against the VandeKeere machine."

Kathy laughed again. "Okay, I know you are having severe Wilma issues. If it's any comfort, you're not the only one. But even she has her good points."

Kathy poured me another cup of tea, and I didn't protest. In spite of the faint squirmies Kathy's defense of the Vande-Keeres gave me and her admonishment to go to church, I wasn't ready to end the conversation.

"Judy can be a lot of fun—" Kathy added.

"Judy's great," I said, taking the mug. "She and Dayton were the only ones who came and visited us when we lived in Seattle."

"Judy is a sweetheart. But you know, Gloria is the kind of person you want in your corner when you're stuck."

First Wilma, now Gloria? "I can see that I'm not going to get anywhere with you right now. You are obviously in the VandeKeere cheering section."

"Hey, I'm trying to make your life here in Harland easier for you and Dan's family. Besides, they're good people— warts and all."

"I appreciate the help. I do." I gave my tea an extra-vigorous stir. "But we're not going to be here long enough for it to matter."

"So. All the more reason to try to get along with Dan's sisters. And one of the best ways to do that for now is to have one of them over."

I frowned. "What do you mean?"

"What we're doing now? This is called visiting. Sometimes it happens at your house. Then you get to be the hostess. What you should do is try that. Start small and start easy.

Invite Judy over and practice on her. Then, when you're really good at it, you can graduate to Gloria and Wilma."

I gave her a "duh" look. "Thanks for the step-by-step instructions."

"I thought breaking it down would make it more under-standable."

"It would make Dan happy," I conceded.

"And a happy Dan is easier to live with. It'll make your time here easier."

She mentioned that so casually. "And it doesn't bother you that I'm only going to be here for a short while?"

"Why should it? It's your life. Harland isn't heaven, though I know most people here would disagree with me on that point. Besides, you're a city girl. I don't blame you for wanting to go back."

"Well, not right away." A defensive note crept into my voice.

"But someday. And once you've mastered the Vande-Keeres, you can move on to other women around here. You'll find out there's an interesting mix of people in this community. At Coffee Break, for instance."

"I'll think about it." I wanted to keep the one-step-at-a-time concept. To avoid leaps and bounds into the bonds of community.

"For now, think about the inviting Judy thing. I know she looked forward to having you and Dan move back home."

I nodded, seeing the wisdom in her advice. Family harmony was a good thing to aim for.

As for church, also a small thing to do for family peace. Besides, it would give me a chance to dress up.

Chapter Ten

untie Judy is here," Anneke called out from her look-out point upstairs, just as Sasha started barking.

Thank goodness for a long driveway and Sasha's early warning system. I had a chance to give the kitchen a quick look over. A plate lined with toast crumbs tilted toward the kitchen sink. Quick. I didn't have much time. Rinse it off. *Where's the tea towel?*

All right, then, a quick swipe across the stomach of my clean T-shirt would have to do.

Everything else passed nervous inspection. Coffee brewing, cups out, cookies on the plate. House clean and tidy. Leslie VandeKeere, ready to entertain.

Judy's delight at my invitation made me feel like I had done a Boy Scout–worthy good deed. I actually looked forward to the visit.

I called for Anneke, already thundering down the stairs, and caught Nicholas before he crawled into the kitchen. Anneke's steps never slowed on her way out the door. "Auntie

Judy, Auntie Judy!" she yelled, even though Auntie Judy couldn't hear a thing.

Nicholas's hair was a tangle of curls. I had been more focused on the floor than my son, so I gave him a quick finger comb and wiped a smear of jam from his cheek. He swung his head away from me and pushed at my chest, but I held on. One of these days he would clue into the fact that I was his actual mother.

Anneke was already skipping on the back step by the time Nicholas and I stepped out of the house. The rain shower last night had washed the world clean, and I took a moment to inhale the fresh warm scent. Earthy and, yes, inviting. A bluebird swooped past, and I watched its flight, flashes of blue against the green trees. That bird had been hanging around the house for a couple of days now, fluttering against the windows, desperately trying to get in. Dan had set up an old birdhouse, but the bluebird seemed more interested in ours.

I heard the mocking squawk of a magpie and laughed as it swooped across the yard, out of reach of Sasha, who was trying to bring it to ground.

A perfect day for a visit.

As Judy parked the minivan, my heart filled with anticipation. Finally a chance to talk to her on her own and get to know her better.

Then the front and back passenger doors opened and my fragile expectation was squashed flatter than a mosquito. I took a deep breath, pulled out a smile, and walked down the steps to meet Judy, Gloria, and Wilma.

"Hope you don't mind that I brought Mom and Gloria

along," Judy said as they came up the walk. "They weren't busy today and wanted to come, too."

I did mind, but it was too late for that. How was I supposed to get to know any one family member when they always came en masse?

"That's great. Glad you could come," I said, shifting Nicholas more comfortably on my hip as they came up the walk. But he was already leaning away from me toward our company.

Wilma headed the line and easily caught Nicholas in her arms. She gave me a Stepford smile and once again I felt eclipsed.

I knew Nicholas wasn't exactly bonded to me. I knew that guilt was woven into my relationship with a child I hadn't wanted in the first place. But I was working on it. And that he would still prefer Wilma to me was a small sting every time.

I wanted one small part of my life where I shone brighter, where I had an ally. I thought of Dr. John and got a warm feeling. He knew. He understood. I wasn't alone in this.

I invited them in. The house that had looked fine for Judy now took on an ominously dirty note when I saw it through the combined eyes of Gloria and Wilma. I saw a line of dust edging the carpet, a discarded shoe lying behind a door— things I had missed when I was cleaning for Judy.

"I'm surprised you put the couch here, Leslie. Wasn't it along the wall when you moved?" Wilma asked.

In our apartment in Seattle, I had the couch tucked away in a darkened corner of the living room. I viewed windows as strictly an economic version of electricity. To be used but not faced.

When we came here, Dan, a creature of habit, automatically relegated the couch to the corner. And me, wife of the creature of habit, left it. Then, a few days after the family meeting, as I was dusting, I heard nothing. Two children under the age of four not making noise are usually cause for concern. So I stopped to listen. I detected the rumbling of a box of blocks emptying onto the floor above me and relaxed.

Then I looked out the window.

We had been in the house two days and I had treated these multipaned pieces of glass the same way I had at home. Their sole function was letting light in. But this time I really looked.

First thing I noticed was that they needed washing. Then I saw the bare apple tree in the yard and the empty flower garden beyond the window, and then, as if for the first time, I saw the slowly rolling hills and the rugged mountains, snow stabbing into crevices and crowning their peaks. And I felt awed and amazed that this calendar-worthy view was ours for the looking any time of any day.

It took me about twenty minutes, but I moved that heavy couch so I could look out those windows whenever I had the chance to sit down.

"I always liked the view out this window," Wilma said quietly as I put out coffee and cookies.

I saw her dreamy expression, the faint smile threatening to crack the bright red polish of her lips.

And for the first time since I met her, I felt an affinity to her.

She let the smile come to fruition, then blinked and the moment vanished. As I offered her my lopsided cookies that had originally been for Judy's eyes only, I saw by her forced smile that the old Wilma had returned.

I wanted the other woman to make an appearance again. I could learn to like that Wilma.

"You've been baking. Good for you," Gloria said with approval as Anneke wiggled her way onto my chair. Anneke blew kisses at Nicholas, who had switched allegiances to Judy and now sat on her lap, toying with the buttons on her faded and worn cardigan.

"Yes. I thought I would give it a try," I said apologetically. For a moment I felt like a traitor for baking Kathy's cookie recipe instead of Gloria's. "They didn't turn out that great, though. They look more like dog doo than cookies."

Wilma's faint gasp and Gloria's suddenly pinched eyebrows signaled my mistake. Not only had I used mild emergency-department words in the house, I had performed the nefarious deed in front of the combined decorum of Gloria and Wilma.

Judy laughed. "As long as they don't taste like dog doo we should be okay."

"Judy, let's leave outside language, outside," Wilma's reprimand, safely delivered to her daughter, ricocheted off her and toward me. Which was probably their initial intended target.

"Oh, c'mon, Mom. We're on a farm, for goodness sake," Judy said with a shake of her head. She took one of the offending cookies, bit it, and winked at me. "Like I said, they taste great."

"Thanks a lot," I said in a small voice, hoping that by keeping a low vocal profile I'd escape causing further offense.

"Hey, did you hear about Belinda Ivor? I heard she broke her wrist," Judy leaned back in the chair with her cup balanced precariously on her lap.

Wilma perched on the edge of the couch and took a careful sip of her coffee, leaving only a hint of lipstick behind. "She and Connor have four children, don't they?"

"I think the oldest is in the same grade as my Paul," Judy said, laughing. "He's a pill. He ran away from home once because Belinda made him eat cauliflower. Didn't come home until he heard the coyotes howling and got scared."

"Remember at the Christmas program? How he hopped around at the back like a rabbit?" Gloria laughed. "Aunt Gerda had the hardest time not laughing."

I wanted to say something about Aunt Gerda and the chickens she brought us to try to make some connection to the discussion, but lost the momentum as they moved on to names that I knew nothing of, so I sipped my coffee, smiled appropriately, and kept my mouth shut. Gloria and Wilma passed over a few more names and stories while Judy ate another cookie and entertained Nicholas.

I sat and smiled, and let Anneke have small sips of my coffee, feeling like a stranger in my own home as I wondered how listening to Gloria and Wilma chitchat about complete strangers would help me get to know Dan's family. I was going to have words with my dear friend Kathy over her stellar suggestion.

"Hey, we didn't come here to bore Leslie to death," Judy said finally, pulling herself out of the chair and swinging Nicholas up into her arms. "I don't want those plants to sit in the van much longer, so I figure we should get at it."

"Plants? Get at it?" I asked.

Judy smiled at my confusion. "We came to help you plant the garden."

"But I don't—"

"Don't worry, city girl," Judy said, gathering up the empty mugs and plate. "We'll help you through this step by step."

I didn't want a garden. I had no intention of adding extra responsibility to my life. Plants needed watering, talking, caring. I had a hard enough time keeping up with Dan and the kids, let alone some plants that would only wither and die under my watch.

"You don't have to worry about the seeds and stuff," Judy threw over her shoulder as she set the dishes in the kitchen sink. "We brought everything you need."

"I'm not much of a gardener," I said. *Actually, I'm not anything of a gardener.*

"It's not a difficult thing to learn," Wilma said, rising from the couch. "You might even enjoy it."

So I followed them outside. Gloria took charge of Nicholas, and Anneke pranced alongside Judy, prattling away to everyone about the chickens and Sasha and how Mommy was afraid to get the eggs.

Harland, Montana. Where secrets go to die.

As I watched Gloria and Wilma laugh at Anneke then exchange some more chitchat, I felt a twinge of envy at their relationship. In spite of their feelings toward me, I wished, for a moment, that I could have a bit of what they shared. Bonding with my mother, when she was around, had meant letting us finish the beer in her bottles or sit quietly with her while she watched *Wheel of Fortune*.

"Mom, you can put out the bedding plants in the raised bed," Judy called as she set a tray full of green, lush plants on the edge of a long box, framed with wooden timber and filled with dirt. The last time I saw that box weeds had taken it over. Dan must have been busy here. "Leslie, you can work with Gloria and me in the garden, putting in seeds."

"Sure." How hard could putting in seeds be?

Actually, very hard.

Carrots went in only one eighth of an inch deep and had to be carefully tapped into a furrow from the package so that only a few seeds came out at a time. Nicholas grabbed my arm and I dumped half a package in one spot.

Beans were spaced an inch apart and covered with dirt— but not too much or they wouldn't get the proper moisture and not too little or they would dry out.

Peas, corn, beets, and potatoes also had specific rules. I gave up trying to remember the regulations and instead dumbly did whatever Judy and Gloria told me to do. I was getting real good at that.

"Last row," Judy said as we moved a long string, the heat of the sun now beating on my unprotected head. "This is great, isn't it? Being outside and working in the garden. I just love it."

I wiped a trickle of sweat from my forehead and glanced

at the dirt lining my fingernails. My back was sore, and my thighs ached from crouching down. "Yeah. Great fun," I responded with forced enthusiasm. This was an entirely new project for me and, thankfully, not one I would have to repeat.

"Just think, in a couple of months you'll be eating your own vegetables," Judy said, looking over the rows we had already put in.

I had been so busy bending, dropping, covering, tamping, and trying to keep Nicholas from sticking bean seeds up his nose, that I hadn't had a chance to see what we had done.

Stakes holding the empty packages marked the rows of tamped-down dirt. As I looked over the large space of ground still empty and bare, I tried to imagine plants coming up.

"That's a lot of garden," I said hesitantly, wondering if I would know what to do with the plants once they made an appearance.

"Well, thankfully Mom kept the garden area pretty weed-free. As long as Dan didn't throw a huge load of manure on it, you shouldn't have to battle too many weeds," Gloria said, catching up to me and Judy. "It will be fun to can and freeze your own homegrown vegetables. I have a great pickle recipe you can use."

Can? Freeze? Weeds? Pickle?

I thought of the long rows of vegetables laid in artful arrangements in the coolers of the grocery stores. Seemed to me that putting in an extra hour at work, then buying what I needed for the month, was a better use of my time. But I smiled and nodded, like bringing in the bounty of a garden was a longing that occupied all my waking hours.

"There. All the bedding plants are in," Wilma said, brushing the dirt off her hands. "Anneke helped me so nicely."

Anneke squirmed with pride. "I want to do this again tomorrow."

"We only need to do it once, sweetheart," Wilma said, brushing Anneke's damp hair back from her face.

"What did you plant, Wilma?" I asked weakly.

"Cabbages, tomatoes, cauliflower, and some peppers for fun," Wilma said.

Fun? She had some crazy sense of humor, my mother-in-law did.

"I like the garden," Anneke said with satisfaction.

"Soon the plants will be coming up, and you can help Mommy and Daddy weed them," Gloria said with the same enthusiasm other mothers use telling their kids about a water park.

"Can I help, Mommy?" Anneke asked, swinging Wilma's hand.

"Of course you can. Maybe you can help Mommy figure out which is a weed and which is an important plant," I said, trying to turn the joke onto myself.

"I have a foolproof method," Judy said, surveying the garden with pride. "You give the plant a tug. If it's hard to pull out, it's a weed. If it comes out easy, then it's an important plant."

"Well, in spite of everything, that went well." Gloria brushed the dirt off her pants, and, big surprise, it all sifted off. She caught Nicholas, whose mouth was a huge smear of brown.

"He's been eating dirt," I said, trying to keep the panic out of my voice. Dirt and who knows what else.

"He'll be fine," Judy said, pulling out a Kleenex from her pocket and wiping his mouth. "It's good for him."

The last time I checked the Good Health Eating Guide, dirt wasn't on the food pyramid.

"The ground has extra moisture," Judy said. "Something we haven't seen in a while."

"It will be a good year." Wilma smiled down at Anneke as she spoke, and in the expression on her face and the soft tone of her voice, I caught an echo of the emotion I had seen a few hours ago.

In those unguarded moments I caught a glimpse of the Wilma that I knew Dan loved. And I wished she would show that self more often to me so that I could learn, as well.

"So, Leslie, I hope you can keep the garden weed-free. You need to work at it regularly, you know." Wilma's comment dampened the faint spark of warmth I had felt.

"I guess all I can say is that I'll try."

"Do, or do not. There is no try," Judy said in a female imitation of Yoda as she dropped an arm around my shoulders, waggling her eyebrows at me. "So, cookies have you left? Hungry are we."

"I have to get back to the farm," Gloria said, glancing pointedly at her watch. "Sorry."

Judy gave me a look of regret. "Maybe some other time?"

"For sure. I'll see if I can scare up an even scarier cookie recipe." I dragged my gaze away from Judy and included Wilma and Gloria in the invitation. "Come again," I added weakly.

———

I took a bite of my toast, caught Nicholas before he climbed out of his high chair, poured Anneke a cup of milk, and picked up a piece of gummed-over toast that Nicholas threw on the floor all without missing a beat. Extreme mothering, not for the fainthearted.

"I don't want my egg." Anneke wiped her mouth with her sweater cuff and pulled a nose at the boiled egg she had insisted on minutes ago.

"You asked me for it, now you have to eat it," I said, proud of the firm tone of my voice. The sound of a mother not to be trifled with.

She gave me a suspicious look, as if wondering where the body of her other mother was. The one she could push around. I gave Anneke a knowing smirk. I had been watching Kathy. Getting pointers. Anneke's life, as she knew it, was changing.

Dan sat hunched over some farm journal. Thanks to the rain of last night, the fields were too wet to work yet, so he was biding his time over breakfast. I had to work one shift tonight, then the blessed peace of an entire weekend off lay ahead. I had bought a fun game that I wanted to play with Anneke tomorrow. I needed to mend some of Nicholas's pants. Maybe we could do something wild and crazy like take the long trip to Bozeman. Dan's birthday was coming up. I couldn't bake a cake. I couldn't knit him slippers. But shopping for that hard-to-buy-for person on my list I could do with my credit card tied behind my back.

My mind flitted over the past week and caught on an errant thought that had been hanging around ever since Darlene's visit with Rena Tebo.

"Dan?"

"Hmm?"

"What would someone mean when they say they know where only comfort in life and death is?"

"And you want to know this because . . ."

"A lady named Darlene mentioned it. Is that some kind of local saying?" I asked, glancing sidelong at Nicholas. He was straining at the harness that clipped him to his high chair. "Down!" he demanded.

If he gained one more inch, gravity would fulfill that succinct demand.

Dan slowly scratched his chin, his fingers rasping lightly over his whiskers as he stared off into the middle distance. "No. It's the first question and answer of the Heidelberg Catechism," Dan said as I got up to stop Nicholas before he became emergency-department material. There was nothing lamer than coming in to work when you didn't have to work.

"And what is that?" I grunted as I managed to get Nicholas back into his chair long enough to unclip him.

"The Catechism? It's, well, teachings. Of our church. Of course, other churches use it, as well," Dan mused, leaning back in his chair, folding his arms over his chest.

I lifted Nicholas out of his high chair and tried to wipe his face as he fought to pull away. I managed a few swipes before giving up and setting him on the ground. Prisoner in Cell Block Nine was free. He scurried as fast as his pudgy hands and dimpled knees could carry him toward his father.

Dan snapped his fingers as Anneke quickly wormed her way onto his lap and then taunted Nicholas. "I remember now. I think it goes, 'That I am not my own but belong body and something or other in life and death to my faithful savior Jesus Christ.'" He stopped there, frowning. "Then something about blood. And that's all I remember," he said seriously, a note of regret in his voice as he looked from his children to me.

"And just when I think you can't surprise me anymore," I said with forced humor. Right before my eyes, my husband had transformed from Dan the mechanic-slash-farmer to Dan the theologian.

"Mr. DeWaal made us repeat that answer again and again until we knew it cold," Dan said, resting his chin on Anneke's head, a gentle smile playing over his lips. "Except I can't remember the rest of it. That question and answer is like a basic confession of everything I believe."

My heart hitched as I watched Dan hold his children and talk about what he believed, an unfamiliar note of yearning in his voice.

He cut his gaze in my direction, then smiled my favorite crooked smile that signaled he had something funny to share. I was ready for a lighter topic of conversation.

"I remember one girl I really liked. I was only twelve, I think. It was one of those innocent boy-girl things. Then one day at supper, Gloria was teasing me and she asked me if this girl knew what her only comfort was. We laughed about it, and it got to be a bit of a joke."

"Gloria and teasing. Not a combination that flies off the top of your head," I said before I had a chance to filter the words.

But to my surprise Dan didn't even catch it. He still had that thoughtful look on his face. "When I was dating you, Gloria asked me the same question. I laughed it off then, too."

"But you went out with me anyway." I smiled to cover up the momentary hurt I felt.

This was his cue to get up and give me a hug and tell me he loved me exactly the way I was. The same thing he would do whenever I made one of my "fat" comments.

He held Anneke and Nicholas, his expression serious as he looked away.

And a faint misgiving began edging around the periphery of my paranoid mind. The same misgivings that had taken hold the first time he talked about coming back to Harland. To family that I knew didn't approve of me. Was it happening already?

Did Dan regret marrying me?

I stacked the bowls on top of each other, then the plates, retreating into the busyness of dishes and cleaning up. *Don't think that. It's this place. He's in the house he grew up in—of course, some of the traditions and ideas he grew up with are going to come back. Haunt him.*

"Leslie, would you consider coming to church with me?"

Dan's question slipped past the noise of cutlery on china. He shifted Nicholas on his lap and flashed me an uncertain look. "I know you always said you don't do church. But I wonder if you would reconsider."

"You didn't used to go, either," I said, still not sure I wanted to make the commitment now that Sunday loomed. "I wouldn't know what to do."

"It isn't brain surgery, Leslie."

"Brain surgery I've assisted on. I've never been to church."

"Anneke likes going to church, don't you?"

Pulling offspring into battles to reinforce arguments was playing dirty.

Anneke nodded vigorously, her hair bouncing on her shoulders. "I sing songs in church. And have a story and a snack."

"Would you do me a favor and think about it?" Dan asked as he lowered a wiggling Nicholas to the ground.

Nicholas padded past me. Thankful for the distraction, I bent over to pick him up and give him a motherly shnoozle, but he thrust my hand aside. A gentle blow that was a direct hit in the Mommy zone. I hadn't been around the past few days, and this was his punishment on the one day I was home.

I looked from a son who was growing more disconnected to me to a husband who was pushing me in unfamiliar directions. I had thought I had things under control. I had a plan. Stay here. Work. Save money. Stay minimally involved so as to make reentry into our real life easier.

However, the ground of my plans was shifting, disorienting me. I didn't know what was expected anymore. I looked at Dan, wondering where our relationship was moving. Or drifting. The longer he stayed here, the more he sounded like the rest of his family.

"I'll think about it." This was a change in strategy and I had to retreat to reformulate my battle plan. "Do you want me to take the kids to Kathy's tonight or can you keep them?"

Dan considered. "I'll take care of them. What do you want me to feed them?"

I thought of the empty day he had ahead and tried not to resent the fact that meals were still my department. "There's a few leftovers in the fridge."

"Sure. I can do it."

Dan gave Anneke a kiss before he left. My world was ordered for the next twenty-four hours. I had hoped to ask him to come in this afternoon so I could grab a nap, but figured I was already pushing things with my supper request. I hoped it would be a quiet night at work.

But as I washed kids and cleaned house, I couldn't get Dan's request off my mind. Nor his recitation of that catechism slipping so easily off his tongue.

Coming to Montana had caused him to shed a disguise. Hard not to feel disoriented and unsure in the face of this "other Dan." The Dan, I was sure, his family preferred to see.

I can't go to church. It's not who I am.

What could it hurt? Maybe just my pride?

And what would my sister say? She was the one who thought Dan's church was some kind of cult.

Well, I hadn't been feeling strong lately. Dan and I had reached some sort of détente, but it was as if we had reverted to the side-by-side living we had made for ourselves back in Seattle. If going to church could fix that, the price wasn't too onerous.

Chapter Eleven

s her dress okay?" I asked Dan as I leaned across the backseat of the truck and reclipped the barrette in Anneke's hair. "Not too fussy?" Asking Dan was a waste of breath. He was no arbiter of fashion, but I was shooting in the dark here. No fashion or parenting magazines had any hints on what the well-dressed toddler wears for worship, so I was winging it. Though he had taken Anneke before, what she wore didn't concern me as much until this Sunday. I was along now and would see firsthand any reaction to her outfit.

Dan gave Anneke a cursory glance in his rearview mirror. "She looks fine, Leslie."

I smoothed a hand over Anneke's gleaming hair.

Anneke, check.

I noticed a piece of toast crumb hovering at the corner of Nicholas's mouth. A quick swipe with my finger got rid of it before he could spin his head away. His dampened hair still held comb tracks and his apple cheeks shone with health and vitality. His gray cord pants were still clean, his yellow shirt tucked in and crisp.

Nicholas, check.

I pulled down the visor and took a few extra seconds to check my lipstick, tuck a strand of hair back into place. Was the lipstick too much? Did women even wear makeup to church?

Me, not so check.

"Is there something special going on today?" I asked as Dan maneuvered the truck between two minivans. "There seem to be a lot of people here."

"The parking lot is only half full yet. Last time Anneke and I came, we were late and there were even more vehicles."

The nervous fluttering in my stomach grew. Though I was in Harland at least three times a week for work, my drive never took me past the church. The only time I saw this many vehicles in one place at a time was at the mall.

I had thought churchgoing was out of fashion. At least that was the impression I got from the occasional magazine article that bothered to deal with the churchgoing segment of the population. Obviously the families exiting the vehicles were misinformed.

Dan got out of the truck and swung Nicholas out of his car seat. As I helped Anneke, my eyes were drawn to the church building. My stomach twisted and spun.

The church stood on the edge of town, the highest ground for many miles. Beyond the church and the houses tucked around it, looking away from town, I saw open fields and all around mountains sharply angled against a blue sky. God's house nestled in nature's cathedral.

The church was white, solid, with angled roofs and rows of stained-glass windows. From outside, it was hard to see the pattern. They were meant to be viewed from the inside, to let the light shine through them into the church. I knew the building had been put up in the heyday of the twenties, when prosperity was on everyone's lips and in everyone's bank account. It replaced an older, smaller version that Dutch immigrants had put up at the turn of the century. It bespoke solidity, community, and the unchanging nature of faith in Harland. Dan's family had been a part of it since the very beginning.

I reached out and blindly caught Dan's hand. He squeezed back, squared his shoulders, and we started walking toward our now-shared destiny. I guessed from the faint film of dampness on Dan's hand that he was as nervous about bringing me as I was about coming. I wanted to tell him that I wouldn't mess up, but we were already approaching the church and I could feel waves of reverence lapping at our feet, drawing us in.

We went slowly up the steps into the main foyer of the church. I caught buzzing conversation, a few heads turned our way, polite smiles, some frowns.

Don't look at your dress. It's fine. I forced my lips into a smile and held on.

A bank of boxes filled the back wall, each box labeled with a name. When I saw how many VandeKeeres there were, I felt the weight and history of Dan's family and community. Dan's father and grandfather had stood in this entrance waiting to go into the sanctuary beyond the large oak doors. I was walking across the floor that had been trod by Dan's ancestors and now his aunts, uncles, cousins, mother, sisters, friends, neighbors, classmates. A family . . . a community . . . , some now buried in the cemetery down the road from the church, some still very much alive, all anchoring him to this place. The sheer volume of his family, the community, the size of this building—I couldn't begin a tug of war with such an impressive arsenal.

Who wouldn't be feeling a tad jumpy right about now?

At the entrance to the sanctuary, a young couple handed out papers to the congregants. I got one along with a polite smile. But as the woman looked at Dan, her smile shifted and her eyes crinkled with pleasure. "Hey, Danny. You coming to Mom and Dad's open house?" She looked from Dan to me. "Is this your wife?"

"Leslie, this is Barry and Lorna Nichols," Dan said, introducing us. "My cousins."

"From Uncle Orest and Aunt Gerda?" See? I could do the Harland connect-the-dots thing.

"No. My parents are Tenie and Jeff Smith."

Huh?

"Sorry," Lorna said, laying a friendly hand on my shoulder. "My mom is a sister to Dennis and Orest. She married a Nichols."

Spin went my head. "Okay." I'd have to get Dan to draw up a family tree so I could be ready for the next family confrontation. I thought Lorna said something about an open house? I was about to ask her but she bent over and shook

Anneke's hand. She looked up at me. "Your girl is such a little VandeKeere. And this little boy—why, he looks exactly
like Gloria's oldest."

Okay, wasn't staking a Harland claim on Anneke enough?
Couldn't she at least give me Nicholas, who, I knew from my
single baby picture, was a miniature me?

"Wilma's sitting with Judy and Dayton and their kids, but
I can see there's space for your family," Lorna continued,
glancing through the double doors to the sanctuary, of which
I had, until now, caught only a quick glimpse.

Anneke tugged on my hand. "I want to see Grandma," she
whined. Her voice caught Dan's attention, and he quickly
ended the discourse on crops and spray he and Barry had
been having, and escorted me and Anneke down one of the
aisles of the church. As we walked, I caught snatches of conversation, whiffs of perfume, and scores of unfamiliar faces
bathed by diffused lighting filtering through the large
stained-glass windows. I didn't know what to take in first—
the people, the windows, the ceiling, the large pipe organ in
the front of the church.

A symphony of light and color overwhelmed me, combined with smells and people all gathered in one place for an
event that had nothing to do with celebrities or sports. I
caught a sense of anticipation and community. I could see
from the heads bent toward each other, the gentle murmur-
ing of conversation all around us, that these people knew
each other. From the quick smiles that people gave me and
Dan as we passed, they all knew us, as well.

Community, I thought. I had never really been a part of

any group of people other than work, and that was a fractured group at best. But as we made our way toward the front, I caught a glimpse of Delores. Though she was half-turned away from me, her voice carried like a mess sergeant's. I saw another couple that had come into my department. I had my own little connections, I thought as we came to the pew where Wilma and her children were sitting.

As Dan stepped into the pew, his mother looked at him, then past him to me. The pleasure that lit up her face made all the agonizing over my decision to come worthwhile.

Nicholas promptly wiggled his way onto Wilma's lap and granted her his most beguiling smile. My brief flash of resentment may not have been the most suitable emotion, considering my surroundings, but why did he always play the charmer with her?

Judy leaned forward in her seat and blew a kiss at her brother and waved at me.

Anneke sat between Dan and me, the toes of her best black shoes tapping out her happiness against each other.

I settled in, my gaze flitting from the gold and silver lines etched on the pale pink and silver painted pipes of the massive pipe organ to the intricate patterns in the stained-glass windows to the plasterwork on the ceiling to the antique wooden pews curved in a semicircle facing the front.

I saw age and beauty mingling with the reality that this had all been here longer than I had, longer than Dan's parents had, longer than his grandparents had. *A heritage,* I thought wistfully. A bedrock of history I had no experience with.

Dan had been baptized in this church, had grown up

surrounded by these walls, these people. Though I had heard the stories and felt the weight of his legacy at the farm, this church—this unique community—brought into startling clarity the stability of Dan's past life.

And his present life?

Did I dare dwell on that? "Give it time," Dan was fond of saying lately as if the depletion of my chocolate account was buying us the peace and stability we had been looking for since we got married.

Slowly the empty spaces around us filled and people greeted Dan and Wilma, smiling at me and Anneke and Nicholas, who blithely ignored them all.

It was as if everyone knew Dan, and by extension, knew me and our kids and where we had come from and what Dan had done in Seattle, how Dan's business had failed thanks to that man who had cheated us out of all that money.

My smile hid a swift flash of fear. If they knew this much about us in the short time we were here, how much would they know in a few more months? My weight? Our bank account balance? Where I hid the chocolates so the kids couldn't find them?

"Leslie, how's the garden?" Judy asked, leaning past Wilma and Dan.

I gave her a careful smile. Once Wilma and Judy and Gloria left on that fateful day, I thought it best if I simply let nature take its course in the garden department. Nature had a better handle on what to do with all those seeds than I did. I had no idea what condition a garden was supposed to be at by this stage. "It's . . . growing."

"Well, that's what gardens are supposed to do," Judy said, adding a quick wink to her comment, which made me feel even more uneasy. She knew I hadn't even so much as pulled a weed.

Just then a group of kids walked to the front of the church and picked up the various guitars that were set out on the stage. I recognized Tabitha as she sat at the electric piano. She glanced our way with a self-conscious grin. A young man settled himself behind a drum set that had been hidden by a screen. Everyone turned to Tabitha. She nodded once.

And music the likes of which I never thought a person would hear in church started up. It filled the building with pounding rhythm. A screen rolled down from the front and words flashed onto it from a projector somewhere in the building.

I wonder what John Calvin's impression of this would be, I thought as I rose to my feet with the rest of the congregation. Everyone started singing, Anneke and Dan singing right along.

Of the gathered people, it seemed only Nicholas and I didn't know this song.

I kept my eyes on the screen, listening intently, determined to make my own spot in this place, however temporary it might be. Amazingly enough, the melody was simple and the words easy to sing, and by the third verse I caught right up.

At the end of the song, I chanced a sidelong glance down the row. Wilma's benevolent expression was a pale imitation of the one she usually lavished on her beloved offspring, but hey, I took it for a cautious peace offering.

I think I can do this, I thought as we settled into our pews after the third song.

The minister came to the front. He was a middle-aged man, slender with thinning blonde hair and wire-rimmed glasses. He had a friendly smile and I noticed him glance our way, then hold my gaze. For a terrified moment I thought he was going to "out" me and make me stand up and introduce myself. Then his eyes moved on and I breathed a sigh of relief.

As he read from the Bible, I became distracted by Anneke squirming onto my lap, fiddling with my necklace, then wiggling off again. But when the minister was finished reading, he said, "This is God's Holy Word," with an authority that caught my attention.

He then clasped the sides of the podium and looked around again, smiling. He started talking about what he had just read. About God as invincible. As raw power whose spoken word created life. "Yet," the minister said, "His greatest victory was when He became weak and vulnerable. When He kept all the angels, that would have leapt to do His bidding, at bay. He overcame darkness by letting His light be snuffed out."

I tried to follow along, but he was kind of losing me with the light thing.

"When Jesus hung on the cross, when He gave up His life, He became a powerful force that broke the power of Satan forever. It was His weakness, His letting go because of His great love for us, that gave us our greatest strength. We, too, must learn, in love, to let go." I glanced sidelong at Dan, his chin resting on Anneke's head. She had slipped into his lap during the service and now had her head tucked into Dan's neck, her hair falling over her face.

Let go. Become weak. Foreign concepts to me.

"Before giving us everything, before giving us all His love, all His grace, all His peace, God requires everything. All our love, all our lives, all the things that we scramble so hard to achieve. All we have is from Him; to return it to Him is an act of faith. Of falling gracelessly into the arms of grace. Of letting God's love hold us up."

I closed my eyes as his words wound around my soul. Falling into the arms of grace. These poetic words touched a hunger buried deep in my soul. Grace. Falling. Letting go. It sounded so easy. So peaceful. I liked the idea of God's love holding me up.

But that would mean letting go. Letting God take control.

Be careful, Leslie.

I heard Terra's voice of warning like a clear bell sounding, dangerous waters ahead.

I was pulled back to reality. I couldn't give this God what He demanded. Everything? Dan? My children? My dreams and plans?

Something inside me closed, fist hard.

I concentrated on my hands, letting my mind slip away to other things. The housecleaning I had been putting off and should have been doing that morning. The laundry that was piling up. And I should really weed the garden.

Soon he was finished and we started singing a song that

had an older tune. The words were vaguely familiar. I think I'd heard them on the Christian radio station I listened to from time to time on my way to or from work. It was about the Father's love. Vast. Beyond measure.

I sang along but couldn't connect with the words. In my mind I was already driving home, planning the work I had to do yet.

But as I looked at Dan, I caught a glimpse of that hunger I'd seen on his face before, and I felt like he was slipping away from me again.

From: tfroese@hotmail.com

To: lesismore@montana.net

U know where I stand on this whole weakness thing. Don't become like Mom—blaming everyone else—weak and afraid. I told U church was 4 weak people. Doesn't this prove that? U are woman, hear U roar. Hear me roar. U need to come and see me. Cut loose. Be my sis again.

Terrible Tempting Terra

Chapter Twelve

Wilma came and picked the kids up?" I held my cell phone and stared out at the parking lot where Kathy was supposed to have been in a few minutes with my kids. I had looked forward all week to taking them shopping for Dan's birthday. Last year Dan and I were so busy keeping our heads above water that his birthday simply floated by, one more casualty of trying to keep things going. This year things were going to be different. I was even going to attempt the impossible. Dan's favorite chocolate layer cake.

"When did she do that?"

"Earlier today. She sounded like she ran it past you." Kathy's voice had a note of surrender. "She said she wanted to take the kids shopping."

My heart downshifted. Shopping. Right. Way to steal my thunder, Wilma. "She didn't tell me a thing." Had I said something on Sunday that gave her carte blanche to push her way further into our lives? Maybe she assumed we were now best friends? I pressed down my anger as I leaned against the cold brick wall of the hospital. "Then I guess I get to drive home all alone."

"Sorry about that. Next time I'll let you know."

"I'm hoping there won't be a next time."

"Hey, it's the kids' grandma. It's no big deal." Kathy sounded reasonable until she heard my sigh. "I know I'm supposed to be on your side, but at the same time I don't want to always be putting down your mother-in-law. She isn't the easiest person to like, but I know I need to remind myself that God loves her, too."

Anneke's song of the month bounced into my head. ". . . He loves me, too; He loves me, too; I know He loves me, too." God loved Anneke. God loved Wilma. What about me?

"She has her good points—" Kathy continued. "It's just that she has a take-charge attitude." She paused. "Actually a kind of take-over attitude."

I felt abandoned. Just when I thought I had an ally in Kathy, she stood up for my nemesis mother-in-law. These were not the rules we had been playing by up until now. I had understood that Kathy didn't like Wilma so, ipso facto, she would be my sounding board on all things Wilma.

"You don't need to always put her down," I conceded, "but in the VandeKeere family she's still the odds-on favorite. I really could use someone on my side."

"Don't worry, I still like you the bestest."

"And you'll invite me to your birthday party and not her?"

"She won't even get a candy bag," Kathy said, with a light laugh. "Are you going to stop by for some tea?"

"No. I should go home and pretend to be a responsible and loving mother, instead of a moneygrubbing health-care professional," I said. "That's code for nurse, by the way."

"Don't talk like that, Leslie. You are a loving mother. But you're also trained to be a nurse. Doing that honors God as much as if you stayed home every day with the kids."

Honors God? Didn't getting paid for what I did negate the honor of the work?

"Thanks for the vote of confidence," I said. "I'll take you up on the tea another day."

"I'll hold you to that," she said. Then I hung up, pushed myself away from the wall.

In spite of my momentary pique with Wilma, I did appreciate the peaceful drive home. I also couldn't help reviewing what Kathy had said about not always wanting to put Wilma down. I knew I put Kathy in an awkward position with my reversion to childhood tactics.

As a kid, whenever I came to a new school, I picked out one girl and slowly felt her out. Then, as soon as I knew which girls she didn't like, they became my enemies, too. It was how I cemented the relationship. When you changed schools as often as most people change their minds, this desperate alignment became a means of self-preservation.

Somehow I had to figure out a way to get along with Wilma. I recognized the gentle reprimand in Kathy's words, and the adult part of me knew she was right. Surely I could find a way to make peace with Wilma or at least learn to tolerate her in the short time we were going to be here.

As I drove, I caught myself looking up toward the mountains

again. One more turn in the road and I would come to the top of a hill. I slowed down, and even though I'd seen it over a dozen times by now, each time the play of the sun over the valley brought out different features. The sky was a clear Montana blue, wide open and beckoning. I slowed as I crested the rise and pulled over to the side of the road.

If this was a calendar picture hanging up in the hospital in Seattle, I would have stopped, taken a second look, and wondered what it would be like to live there.

Well, I was *there*. Right now. I thought of my family waiting for me back home, of Wilma who could so easily get under my skin. I thought of learning to like where I was. Right now I was making a memory. Why not store these moments up to treasure later on? Sure, living here was not my dream, but there were things I could take away from here, things I could appreciate.

I sighed, remembering my mother's frequent moves. In each place, Terra and I had tried to find the positives. Too many moves to too many dingy apartments and bleak neighborhoods had worn down that skill. As a teenager, after enduring yet another school, yet another round of trying to fit in, I had promised myself with Scarlett O'Hara intensity that when I grew up, never again. Without the "God-is-my-witness" part. God hadn't been a part of my life then, though between Dan, Kathy, and church, He was slowly making inroads on my life now.

I stacked my hands on the steering wheel and rested my chin on them looking over the valley, watching the shadows of the clouds scudding across the valley floor. If I squinted, I could see our yard. Our barns. Our house. I thought of Dan and the kids waiting, but in spite of my eagerness to see Nicholas and Anneke, I slowed, letting the moment imprint on my mind.

A vagrant thought, ethereal as smoke, drifted through my mind. Home. My family waited for me there. At home.

It's not your dream home.

It wasn't that, but I had to concede it was a lovely stopping place.

Does it have to be temporary?

I stifled that thought. I wasn't ready to let go of the dream that had kept me going through so many years.

Letting go is not always a bad thing.

The sermon from Sunday came back to me again as it had the past few days. Letting go. Becoming weak and vulnerable. These were the polar opposites of the lessons Terra and I had ingrained in each other from the time we were young. We had to be strong to survive, to keep going. I'd had to be strong to make it through nurses' training. To hold down two jobs.

And what are you holding on for now? Why does it have to be Seattle?

Anxiety pricked at me like a mosquito. Of course it had to be Seattle. I couldn't stay here. I'd have to share Dan with Wilma and Gloria.

But Dan is much happier here. The kids love it here, too.

But I didn't. Did I?

The question buzzed and wouldn't leave.

A car slowed as it drove by, the driver a young man whom I vaguely recognized as the son of one of the neighbors. He looked at me, his eyebrows raised in question as he pointed at the hood of my car. I smiled my reassurance and shook my head, circling my finger and thumb in a gesture to show I was okay.

He nodded, waved, and drove off.

Neighborly of him. Nice to know that if something was truly wrong with me I could count on someone stopping. I put the car in gear and coasted down the hill toward home.

Fifteen minutes later, I parked by the garage and turned the car off.

As I got out, I saw Nicholas bobbing and weaving toward me from the direction of the garden, something long and dark trailing from his chubby hands, Sasha right beside him.

The smile in my heart reached my mouth at the same time Dan caught our boy around the waist. Dan spun him around and tossed him up in the air, then caught him and planted a kiss on his grubby cheek as the dog danced around them both, his tail sweeping back and forth. Dan tucked Nicholas close in a man-hug. When he turned and saw me, I caught a glint of pure, unadulterated happiness in his eyes.

My husband stood there a moment, looking as solidly planted in the earth as the trees behind him, as the hills rising behind them toward the mountains.

I felt a twinge of envy. He belonged here. Was a part of this. It was in his upbringing, in his blood and bones. If this were a movie, the wind machine would start up now, blowing his hair away from his features as he stared off into the distance, music swelling, creating a mood of triumph, of dominance. A man. His son. His dog. His land.

"Mommy, Mommy, Mommy!" Anneke ran past Dan toward me, her arms outstretched in welcome. I met her halfway and was almost bowled over by her onslaught.

As her warm, sticky arms tangled themselves around my neck, I stole another look at Dan to anchor myself in reality. No music and no wind. Just my husband with his crinkly smile, faint white lines emanating from the corners of his eyes. It was as if each week here sloughed off some of the desperation that had haunted his eyes those last months in Seattle when he struggled to hold on to the business. Each day brought some new life to his face.

Good-looking guy, I thought, my heart giving that funny little lift it used to when we were first married. Before the kids came into our lives. Before life and necessity and circumstances had thrust us apart. *My husband.*

"Mommy, you have to come and see the garden," Anneke announced, catching hold of my face and leaning away from me.

I passed Dan, then on a whim, held back a moment, leaned toward him, and managed an ungainly kiss hello that landed somewhere on the region of his left cheek. Dan caught me by the back of my neck, his fingers tangling in my hair as he steadied my head.

He looked deep into my eyes, then lowered his head and caught my mouth with his. His lips were warm, tasting lightly of salt and promising further intimacy.

He pulled away and he laid his forehead against mine, his blue eyes laser bright. "Hey there, sweetheart. How was work?"

That single question granted me absolution and acceptance of my job, and I resisted Anneke's tugging long enough to catch him by the shoulder and give him another quick kiss. "Work was good, but it's so good to be home."

His smile deepened, connecting with me on a deeper level.

"Mommy, come on. You have to see."

I reluctantly drew away from my husband, drawn inexorably by the pull of a child who presumed to be the center of her world and who would brook no competition.

"Come and see!" she called out as Dan fell into step beside us. He shifted Nicholas and laid his arm over my shoulder, as if anchoring me to the adult world and his own life.

A pile of wilted green plants lay in the top corner of the garden, harvested, I presumed, from between the rows.

"See, Mommy? See?" Anneke, still holding tight to my hand, leaned away from me, pulling me onward. "See the plants?"

I did. As I bent down to inspect a row of rounded stalks pushing themselves through the crumbling dirt, a sense of wonder overtook me. Only a few weeks ago Judy, Gloria, and I had dropped hard white seeds into the ground in neat orderly rows. I knew that for things to grow seeds needed to be planted, but knowing it in your mind and actually seeing the results was another story.

"They came up," I said, touching one that was uncurling.

"And see the corn, Mommy?" Anneke, my impatient guide, pulled me farther along. One row over, tiny blades of what looked like grass were coming up. The carrots were a pale fuzz of green discernible only if you put your head level with the ground, which I had to do, according to Anneke. The crinkly leaves of the potatoes were making an appearance as were the fat, round leaves of the cucumbers.

"I need to put up a pea fence," Dan said as we stopped by a double row of plants. "They need something to climb up. Otherwise they sprawl all over the garden."

I glanced at him, then back at the garden, wonder spiraling through me. All these little miracles came from the few packages that Judy and Gloria had brought. And this was only the beginning.

"How long before the plants start producing?" I asked, bending down to touch a pea plant already sending out tiny tendrils of green.

"About six to eight weeks," Dan said. "Depending on how much moisture we give them and what kind of season we have. We're lucky we had enough moisture to start off with. That doesn't happen every year."

I glanced up at him, the damp coolness of the dirt giving way to the heat from the sun overhead. "This is amazing. I've never had a garden before."

Dan pulled me to my feet. "You might not think it's so amazing when you have to start picking beans."

I heard the faint humor in his voice and on impulse hooked my arm around his waist. "I'm glad we did this."

"Trust me, hon," he said, adding an extra squeeze to his one-armed hug. "Once you've tasted fresh vegetables, you'll be putting in a garden every year."

I looked back over the huge expanse that had been

planted, leaning into Dan, enjoying this moment of closeness. This huge garden would never fit in a city backyard, I thought with a moment of regret.

"I want to eat, Mommy," Anneke said, grabbing my hand and swinging it. "I'm hungry."

"Sure, honey. Let's go make supper." This time I was prepared. I was going to make an awesome supper. I had chicken defrosting in the fridge. All the ingredients for a stir-fry recipe that Kathy solemnly promised me was Leslie-proof.

"You don't need to worry about supper," Dan said as we walked up to the house. "Mom brought a casserole when she brought the kids."

Blink. *Think.* My stomach dropped a bit as my little moment of triumph slipped away.

"She thought we might like some home cooking for a change," Dan added.

Dan's cute smile didn't even approach canceling the innuendo of that particular statement.

"I was going to do home cooking," I said, disappointment putting a note of petulance in my voice. First she takes away my shopping trip. Now my supper? Nuts.

"Well, maybe tomorrow."

All that was missing from this conversation was a patronizing pat on the head. *There, there, Leslie. Be a big girl now.*

My previous pique with his mother bobbed to the surface. "Why did she pick up the kids from Kathy's place to go shopping without asking me?"

"She asked me," Dan said curtly. Dan gave me one of his patented, slightly exaggerated shrugs, shorthand for "You're overreacting, and I can't reason with you right now so I'll ignore you until you can act more mature."

"Don't do that, Dan," I said. "I hate it when you do that."

"Do what?" He gave me a tired look.

"Brush aside what I think is a problem."

"Les, there's no problem. Anneke and Nicholas happen to be my mother's grandkids. Nothing wrong with her taking them out to buy a few things." He yanked open the door and let the kids and me go in, then let it slam shut behind him.

"There is a problem if I, the mother, am not consulted." I sat down with Nicholas and pulled his dirty jacket off.

Dan's face grew grim. "But, I, the father, was." He turned to Anneke. "Here, baby. Put your boots on the boot rack." He hung up her coat. "I wish you didn't have these issues with my mother. She's just trying to help."

I couldn't think of what to say. First Kathy, now Dan. I was trying to like Wilma. But she balked me at every turn. As a woman and mother, I expected Wilma to know the unwritten rules of mother- and wifehood. Uninvited movement into another's territory was considered either a hostile move or an insult. Close friendship or illnesses nigh unto death were the only time these rules didn't apply, neither of which were the case here. "How is taking the kids shopping helping?" I had looked forward to helping them pick something special out for Dan and I had been robbed of it now.

"Well, you don't seem to have time."

Warning, warning. No-win situation approaching. "I'm working, Dan."

"You don't have to. At least not as often as you do."

"You don't seem to mind that half of my paycheck goes into our bank account." And away I went, flailing down the slippery slope of finances.

"And the other half?"

I gave him a narrowed look as I slipped Nicholas's other boot off his foot and dropped it on the porch floor. "The other half is for our house fund. The one that got severely depleted when you bought the tractor."

"We already discussed that, Leslie."

I gently pulled Nicholas's coat off, trying to ease away my growing frustration. I felt as if I were fighting an unstoppable foe. His farm. His family. His community. "I know that. But the house was for us. For our family."

"And saving for that house, that future, means you're gone all the time." If ever there was a red-flag word, *all* was it.

"I don't work *all* the time." I spoke quietly, but my teeth were clenched. I thought he had accepted that.

"Not here. But back in Seattle you'd be back to full-time work. At least here we get to see you during the day. Admit it, Leslie. Moving could be just what we need."

"Like we need your mother breathing down our neck all the time?" Encroaching on my territory. Taking my kids shopping for their father's gifts.

I wondered what she bought Dan. Would she know that I hoped to give him some decent pajamas? A Swiss Army knife?

"She's trying to help."

"Dan, she's trying to control you." I dropped Nicholas's other boot on the floor with a muffled thump as it hit his jacket.

Dan picked up Nicholas's boots and handed them to Anneke, who dutifully put them away. "And what are you trying to do?" He snatched Nicholas's coat from the floor.

"I'm trying to put our marriage back together."

Dan's eyebrows snapped together. "You're not going to forgive me for that, are you?"

"I have forgiven you, and I want our marriage to work . . ." My sentence trailed off as the truth of what he said previously struck me. Maybe I hadn't forgiven him as readily as I said. It had been a large hurt and betrayal. Another woman encroaching on my territory.

"I'm not as strong as you, Leslie. I need help and support. And I feel like I'm getting that here. I'm tired of moving around. I'm tired of trying to find out who I really am."

"So, when we go back to Seattle, we can stay there. Settle down."

"We can stay here."

He spoke so quietly, I almost didn't hear him. His words underlined what had gone through my own mind just up on the hill.

"Oh, Nicholas, look at you," I said in a shaky voice as I brushed the dirt off his clothes and Dan's suggestion out of my head.

Dan swung Anneke in his arms and without a backward glance, strode out of the porch into the kitchen.

Nicholas declared his independence and elected to walk on his own. So I followed more slowly. Had he really said "stay here"?

Dan already had a tablecloth on the table by the time I came into the kitchen. Anneke crouched by the cupboard pulling plates out and setting them on the floor. Nicholas scooted over to her and started slapping his dirty hands on the plates, which initiated a skirmish settled as quickly as it began when Nicholas beaned Anneke on the head with a plate.

By the time I had the kids settled and Nicholas changed, supper was on the table.

Food trumped discussion, so we ate quietly, limiting our conversation to "pass the salt" tacking on belated "pleases" and admonitions to the kids to eat. The homemade casserole was hot, spicy, and creamily delicious. Nicholas decided to eat it by osmosis—mashing food into his face and hair.

When we were done I got up, but Dan put his hand on my arm. "Gloria gave me this children's story Bible," he continued. "I thought we could read to the kids at suppertime."

What could I say to that? Gloria had given, and Dan had taken. But Dan's comment about wanting control, though thrown out randomly had stuck as firmly as the pasta now decorating Nicholas's hair. This home was Dan's as much as mine. If he wanted to read some story Bible, then I could go along with it. Nothing wrong with teaching the kids morals, I figured.

Dan beckoned to Anneke who scooted over to her father and his lap. Dan set a worn, dog-eared book on the table in front of them and opened it to the first page. "In the beginning, God made the heavens and the earth . . ."

Once upon a time, I thought, irreverently. But in spite of my slightly cynical bent, I caught myself listening. Getting caught up in the simple language of the story that, I knew, was ages old. It was still around. It had lasted through generations. *Might be worth paying attention to,* I thought as Nicholas crawled out of his high chair and wiggled his way onto my lap.

As Dan read, his voice grew softer and the Leslie-induced frown on his forehead slipped away. Anneke leaned forward, engrossed in the colored pictures.

This must be what Dan's youth was like, I thought, glancing around the kitchen as the sun slipped below the horizon, drawing the dark across the sky. The kitchen growing cozy, safe, secure. His father reading, his sisters sitting around the table, his mother maybe holding Dan on her lap like I held Nicholas now.

My baby rubbed his face with one hand but lay quietly in my arms, a warm package of little boy wrapped up in stained overalls and T-shirt. It didn't seem that long ago that he was just a tiny bundle of flannelette. Now his head lay pillowed on my shoulder, his dimpled feet, minus the socks he had pulled off, rested easily on my knees. I nuzzled Nicholas's head, inhaling the smells of little boy and food laced with a hint of dirty diaper. I glanced at Anneke pretending to read along, her bow-shaped lips forming the words after Dan.

He closed the book, then moved directly into a short prayer. When he said "Amen," Nicholas repeated it. I couldn't say anything, but I had lots to think about.

‹═══›

C'mon, honey. Wake up." I shook Nicholas gently, preparing myself for a full-scale onslaught. This early in the morning the only light came from the glow of a Winnie-the-Pooh night-light. I heard the hiss and spit of rain on the windows.

Anneke sat on the bed across the room scratching her tummy. When we first moved into the house, I gave each of the kids their own room, thinking I was doing Anneke a huge favor. Anneke—who always complained that Nicholas was manhandling her Barbies, that Nicholas cried too loud, that Nicholas smelled bad, bad, bad—was now sharing with the same little brother because she couldn't handle the bounty of a room all to herself.

"I'm tired, Mommy," Anneke sniffed, letting her hands drop to her sides. "I don't want to go."

"I know you don't," I said, gently commiserating with her like the parenting magazines told me to. "I understand that you're tired and that you would probably sooner stay here, but we have to get going or Mommy's going to be late for work." Oh, very well done. Verbalize the child's frustration to show that you understand; then tell her what's going to happen anyway. This seemed like a lot of work but, apprentice that I was, I was always rooting around in parenting magazines. The magazines should come with a warning, "serving suggestion only," just so a mother doesn't get fooled into thinking her children might actually resemble the perfection of the perfectly posed child on the cover.

"I want you to stay home," Anneke grumbled as Nicholas started twisting like a snake, his face scrunched into deep lines of disapproval.

"Warning, warning. Move alert to code red. Boy is waking up," I heard a voice still raspy with sleep say with a chuckle.

I glanced over my shoulder at Dan, standing in the doorway scratching his stomach. Like father like daughter. His hair was a tangle of blond that still needed cutting, his chin shadowed with whiskers, and his ragged pajama bottoms hung just below his waist. He really needed new pj's.

But it was his smile that caught my attention. That slightly crooked lift of his lips that signaled that all was well with his world. It was this smile that first attracted me to him the first time I saw him with his friends. It was the same smile he had when I walked down the aisle toward him. A smile I saw more frequently.

I felt the low-level pull of attraction and in spite of Nicholas, now squirming under my restraining hand, grunting his displeasure, and preparing for a full-scale assault on our senses, I couldn't look away from my handsome husband.

He moved toward me, lowered his head, and dropped a warm kiss on the nape of my neck. Guaranteed to create happy shivers down my spine. His warm hand caressed my back and rubbed a gentle circle. "How did you sleep?" he asked, brushing another kiss over my forehead.

"I slept good."

A gust of wind threw raindrops against the window. "It's raining. Unbelievable," he said, a trace of awe in his voice. He walked to the window and placed his hand against the cold pane, as if touching the water that now ran down the glass outside.

He turned to me, his smile taking on a note of fun. "I have a great idea. Take the kids to our bed. We'll all cuddle together for a while."

I felt the pull of deep temptation and for a moment imagined myself and the kids curled up together, a little nest of a family all warm and cozy while outside the rain came down.

He caught my hesitation and looked from Nicholas to Anneke, then blinked as if realization finally dawned. "You working today?"

I nodded.

"I thought you had it off."

"I did, but yesterday Roberta called, frantic. She needed to switch with someone and couldn't find a replacement."

Dan's face slipped into displeasure, taking with it my faint moment of happiness. "But we were going to Aunt Tenie and Uncle Jeff's open house today."

Surely I wasn't going *that* crazy? "I didn't know anything about that." I barely knew anything about his Aunt Tenie and Uncle Jeff other than they were connected to him through the young couple we met at church.

"They mailed us an invitation. I was looking forward to introducing you to more of the relatives."

"I don't remember getting an invitation."

He sighed, pressed his lips together, and nodded. A long-suffering nod. My least favorite nod. "Obviously not important, is it?"

I turned away from the no-win discussion as my mind raced over the past few weeks. The junk mail consortium hadn't been alerted as to our whereabouts, so we hadn't received any offers for low-interest credit cards or Publishers Clearing House prizes. Yet.

I wouldn't have missed addressed mail. Would I? Was I slowly going crazy living out here? But if I knew I was going crazy, then I wasn't crazy. Was I?

I picked up the now-squirming boy throwing his head around in frustration. "No up, no up," he grumped. I managed to make it to the bathroom, get the diaper off, and get the majority of the mess cleaned up before Nicholas started thrashing in earnest.

While I performed my diaper-changing calisthenics, Dan silently hovered in the doorway, waves of disapproval crashing over me as his young son made his own similar disapproval clearly known. Nicholas flailed his arms, one little fist connecting solidly with my arm, a fat foot thumping me in the stomach as he screamed.

"Leave those poor kids at home today," Dan shouted. "I'll take them to the anniversary party myself."

I cringed as I thought of Dan showing up sans spouse. I imagined Wilma's and Gloria's surreptitiously exchanged glances, then sighs. That Leslie.

As Nicholas's screams stabbed repeatedly through my Nicholas Defense System, I also imagined driving twenty minutes to Kathy's house with this thirty-five-pound bundle of fury and dropping him off. "You sure you don't mind?" I asked.

Dan's long-suffering look normally would get my hackles up, but with Nicholas still screaming and the anniversary party coming up, I was at his mercy.

"Just wanted to make sure." I raised my voice so he could hear, then manhandled Nicholas back to his bed, his haven. But he wasn't that easily pacified. I had pulled him from his beloved sleeping place and he wasn't going to let me off without a fine.

He screamed some more, but then grabbed his blankie and pulled it toward him, rubbing it over his face with jerky movements as his sobs decreased in intensity.

"I'm going back to bed," Dan said, still holding Anneke. "I'll hold the fort and keep the family intact. You go to work and make your money." He yawned, a jaw-cracking, slow yawn, and then slouched back to our bed, Anneke's head tucked into his neck.

His comment, delivered so casually, pierced me with its barbs. It wasn't just about the money. I worked so we could have a future. I worked so I could keep up my skills. I worked because it was as much a part of me as farming was for him.

But neither he, nor his family, seemed to recognize or understand that.

I heard Nicholas ramping down his anger, Anneke's muffled giggle, Dan's deep voice teasing her.

A few moments ago, I had wanted to cuddle in bed with my husband and my daughter. Now all I wanted was to get to the hospital as soon as possible. Keep the family intact indeed. As if his one day of babysitting was worth more than the dozens of days I had already spent with the kids. Dan was the kind of man who would take out the garbage once and give the impression he had just cleaned the entire house.

I slipped out and almost tripped over Sasha, who lay huddled against the door. She jumped up, her mouth open in a happy, doggy smile, her tail waving a welcome greeting. I took a moment to pet her. At least someone in this house loved me today.

She followed me to the car looking hopeful, then, when she realized there was no trip in the offing, her tail slowed down, her head drooped, and disconsolate she trotted back to the house, dropped down in the lee of the overhang, and stared morosely at me.

"I know how you feel," I muttered as I shivered in the car, waiting for it to warm up.

I glanced up at the house. The lone square of light from our bedroom winked out, cutting me off, and as I drove away, I imagined Dan and Anneke cocooned in a pile of blankets as they drifted off to sleep.

And me? Well, I was off to work to make that money that Dan so quickly denigrated but didn't seem to mind when it showed up in our checking account. I didn't understand why going to work labeled me greedy and why holding on to the bank account simply labeled his mother cautious.

I got angrier as I drove. Thankfully I didn't have to navigate past snail-paced tractors pulling huge implements or fuel trucks that took up half the road. The quiet roads still surprised me. In Seattle, driving to work meant scooting between hundreds of cars, wondering why all these people were on the road, juggling through radio stations to avoid depressing news, and worrying about what the owners of all these cars were going to do when the oil ran out.

I've always been good at multitasking.

But now my commute was quiet and, because my anger always manifested itself physically—in this case via my foot on the accelerator—short. Which meant I had almost an hour to kill before the sun came up and my shift started.

I got some coffee at the staff cafeteria and picked up a muffin for breakfast, looking forward to a few moments of absolute peace. One other nurse dawdled over a newspaper and didn't even look up as I passed.

An empty table called out to me and as I dropped into the chair, I yanked the paper off my muffin, anger with Dan battling with guilt that I would miss his family get-together. Other than Wilma and Gloria, the few members of the extended VandeKeere family I had met were friendly and pleasant. I hadn't met Dan's Grandma VandeKeere. She lived in Bozeman, over an hour's drive away. She would probably have attended the party, and I would have liked to meet her.

I had a grandma of my own stashed away somewhere. My mother lost her when she turned eighteen and was pregnant with Terra and hadn't bothered to go looking for her again.

Once in a while Dan would ask me about my family. I kept telling him there wasn't much to say, which was true. He never really understood. Now, as we were spending more and more time in the bosom of his family, I knew he never really would.

As for our own family, I was getting nervous. Dan had taken to glaring at me each evening as I unwrapped another chocolate. One less chocolate, one less day on the farm. Every week created some new shift in our relationship. I wasn't sure if we were shifting closer together or if Dan was slowly being sucked into his family and away from me.

Not thinking about that right now, I warned myself. I pulled a pen and notebook from my purse. My dream book had all the details of Dan and my dream home. The size, the number of rooms, the style of the cupboards, the brand of siding, the colors of the paint. Sometimes I rearranged the house plan, moved the rooms, added features that I found in home and gardening magazines.

I flipped through the book, coming to the back section. The finances. I examined the final figure Dan and I had estimated our house would cost us. My heart sunk as the dream wavered. Was I being realistic? Would we ever be able to afford it? And if not, then what?

Stay here. The phantom thought reared its head again.

"You busy?"

Dr. John. Yay. Distraction.

"Do you live in the hospital?" I asked, closing my dream book. "Weren't you on call last night?"

"Just finished and needed some down time. I don't like going home. House is too empty."

He sounded so lonely I felt a flash of pity. "How was last night?"

"Steady, though I managed to get some sleep about four o'clock." He brought me up to speed on a few of the cases even though Roberta would be giving me a rundown at changeover. "Amelia Castelman brought her baby in again. Poor thing is going downhill, but she won't let me refer her to either a pediatrician or a social worker. I was tempted to keep the baby in the hospital so we could feed her, but I didn't have a strong enough reason and Amelia wouldn't allow it."

Amelia's baby's chart was long and illustrious, as was Amelia's. Single mother, living on welfare. Her little girl was borderline malnourished and, we were sure, handicapped. But Amelia wouldn't let us refer her to a specialist. Social Services had gotten involved, but again, their hands were tied. Not enough evidence.

It broke my heart. Each time that baby came in I wanted to kidnap her and bring her home.

That's why I didn't read the papers. Why read about misery abroad when enough of it came through the doors of the hospital?

"All in all another night in Harland." Dr. John rubbed his chin, his whiskers dark against his skin. I thought of Dan's whiskers. Mentally compared the two. Then wondered why I did. Married women shouldn't be comparing their husbands to attractive men. It wasn't fair. I got to see Dan in sickness and in health, in dirty clothes with grease under his fingernails and first thing in the morning when both his hair and his mood stuck up in all directions.

Dr. John's smile made his eyes crinkle with warmth. "You're looking lovely this morning."

After my fiasco this morning, his compliment was like gourmet chocolate. Smooth and soothing and easy to take. "Thanks," I said, the kindness in his voice making me feel trembly. "Not feeling too lovely."

"Why not? Your in-laws making you feel inferior?" John covered my hand with his.

I clung to the sympathetic connection, feeling like I had an ally. "I missed an anniversary party today that I knew nothing about. Big problem."

"Was it a VandeKeere function? Sorry, my dear, you are in it deep," he teased.

"I can just imagine what Wilma and Gloria will say," I groaned, shaking my head. "Or look like." I could picture perfect Gloria with her perfect figure, clothes, and hair. Which usually made me perfectly envious. Which I didn't want to be because envy of Gloria meant she had something I wanted, which meant she had something over me, which meant I was lacking.

Jealousy. Not as easy as it looks.

"You don't want their life," Dr. John said quietly. "All that pressure to keep up the facade. I'm sure Gloria spends hours getting the eye shadow right."

This comment struck me as a little harsh, but at the same time I felt a niggling satisfaction that someone somewhere didn't see perfection in Gloria. "I guess I won't be asking her for makeup tips."

"You don't need makeup tips from anyone," Dr. John said. He leaned a little closer, smiled just a little deeper, his hand squeezed just a little tighter. "Especially not from someone like Gloria. You are a very beautiful woman, in your own right."

He's coming on to you.

I knew that, but I let myself linger in the light of his appreciation for a little longer. The insecure part of me welcomed his flattery, his attention. Like eating that extra piece of cake you know you shouldn't. This morning I needed the boost.

He yawned, and rubbed his eyes with his other hand. Lines of weariness etched his face.

"You'd better go home," I said, feeling a moment's sympathy for him. "You look exhausted."

His smile warmed my heart. "I am tired. But it's nice to sit with you a minute."

You're playing with fire.

This time I listened and slowly drew my hand away from his. Then I checked the clock. "Time to go." I stood as Dr. John pushed himself up with a sigh. He was so tired, he almost swayed into me. I had to take a quick step to avoid him.

"Sorry about that," he said. "Exhaustion makes me clumsy."

"That's okay," I assured him, but as I walked away, I couldn't resist a glance over my shoulder.

And he was watching me! His scrutiny made me uncomfortable, but I am a weak woman, and the second glance from him was as tangible as a touch.

From: tfroese@hotmail.com

To: lesismore@montana.net

I wouldn't fuss over the Dr. John thing. Sounds like U can use a friend. As for Dan, U need to set some boundaries, sister. Dan is changing the rules and U shouldn't put up with it. Sure, Montana is beautiful, but so is Seattle. Do U really think U'd manage to survive there? BTW I'm probably going to be moving up there. Lost my job here. Boss was a jerk, so it's all good. So U have to move back, little sis. Be like old times again.

From: lesismore@montana.net
To: tfroese@hotmail.com

I don't know what I want anymore, Terra. Josie, my last friend from Seattle, hasn't been returning my calls or my e-mails. I feel like I'm slowly losing my identity, my husband, my family. I'm getting confused. Dan and I have been living past each other the past few days. Judy called—said she was sorry I missed the party. I felt bad for letting her down. Gloria phoned too. Said she had forgotten to tell me about the party. Said she was sorry. I felt like hanging up on her.

Chapter Thirteen

oberta just called. She's going to be about half an hour late. Had another emergency at home," Arlene said, leaning against the partition that gave me some privacy from the rest of the ward.

I felt a stab of annoyance with Roberta but knew that it could as easily have been me trying to find a babysitter.

"Lucky for her, things are pretty quiet for a Friday night," Arlene continued.

I looked up at the receptionist, horrified. "Are you asking for trouble?"

Arlene shot me a puzzled look.

"You never, never say that out loud." I gave her a stern look, hoping that by warning her I had possibly staved off disaster. The same thought had crept around the edges of my mind, taunting it, but I knew better than to give it even a whisper of attention for fear it would create its own energy. "Every time someone says that, things go haywire."

She laughed. "Sorry. I was just making conversation."

I was about to reply, when I heard the roar of a car pulling up to the entrance, tires screeching and horn blasting.

"Like I said," I muttered as she left to see what the problem was. I got up to prep a room just as the doors swooshed open and the unbridled sobbing of three teenage girls filled the entrance. I couldn't help the faint uptick of my heart, the little adrenaline rush that prepared me to face this so-far unknown.

"She's not talking. She's really sick," I heard the girls wail.

I strode quickly out to the reception area and repressed a sigh at the typical Friday-night sight that greeted me.

A boy who didn't look old enough to drive half-carried, half-pulled a young girl whose long blonde hair hung in a stringy mat over her face. Her head hung almost to her stomach; her bare feet dragged over the floor. She wore standard-issue low-cut blue jeans and a skimpy T-shirt, her clothing almost identical to that of her two friends, who were sobbing and hugging each other.

The sour stench of regurgitated alcohol and food rolled ahead of her, and I tried not to sigh. I could handle blood a lot better than vomit.

Arlene glanced up at me. "Guess you've got work to do. I've paged Dr. John. He'll be here right away." Arlene called one of the girls aside to get what information she could. Her next step was the unenviable job of calling the young girl's parents.

The young man turned to me, desperation in his eyes. "I don't know what happened. We were at a party."

I glanced at the girl's stained blue jeans, the vomit streaking her T-shirt and clothes. And as I brushed her hair aside, my heart skipped its next beat.

Tabitha. Dan's niece and Gloria's pride and joy.

Her pert little face and beautiful shining hair were smeared with dirt and vomit, her head lolling to one side, like a doll with a broken neck.

"What's your name?" I asked the boy.

"Deke," he answered.

"Help me get her on this bed, Deke." I glanced over at the hysterical girls and chose the most lucid one. "You come with me. The rest of you go back to the reception area."

"She's not going to die, is she?" the other girl sobbed, weaving as she stood.

"Go wait in reception," I snapped. I didn't have time for hand-holding.

Once we got Tabitha into bed, I propped her up so she wouldn't choke, then brushed her sticky hair away from her mouth and checked her breathing.

"What happened?" I asked Deke as I pulled open both eyelids. Pupils normally dilated, thank goodness. I slipped up her sleeve to check her blood pressure. Her icy skin made my own heart rate jump. *Possible hypothermia.* I needed to start an IV, but I needed more information first.

To my surprise, my hands were trembling as I pressed the button to inflate the b.p. cuff. I had never had to work on someone I knew so well, and it created an extra tension.

"We were at a party and then, well . . . I don't know," his voice trailed off, guilt emanating from him in waves.

"You do know. Tell me." My don't-mess-with-me nurse voice was colored with an edge of ticked-off-auntie.

"Well, we had some liquor there."

"How much did she have to drink?" I asked, my glance ticking from Deke to the girl. "Did she have any drugs?"

"Do you remember, Cassie?" Deke asked the girl, who steadfastly refused to look at me.

"Don't mess with me, kids," I said sternly as the machine read off her b.p. I clipped an oxymeter to her finger and turned back to Cassie. "I don't care what you did. I'm not going to report you to the police, but I need to know exactly what happened so that I do the right thing for Tabitha. We don't have a lot of time here."

Cassie turned wide eyes to me. "Are you going to tell my mom?"

"Right now that's not important. What else did Tabitha have to drink?"

I glanced at the monitor. Steady and normal. Heart rate slightly decreased.

"No drugs. Right, Cassie? She didn't have any drugs. And she only downed one cooler. I swear."

"Don't swear—tell the truth," I said as I glanced down at Tabitha, hating the way she smelled and looked.

The scenario was so cheap. So common. "She had way more than one cooler," I said.

"Okay. Maybe it was more," Deke relented. I started a chart, scribbled a few notes.

Standing orders in this case were to start an IV to rehydrate and dilute the alcohol, so I prepped the site and started the drip. Cassie wavered at the sight.

I checked Tabitha's oxygen levels, her heart rate, put my hand to her cheek as I double-checked her physical appearance.

"How much more and how quickly did she drink it?" I pressed as soon as I got Tabitha hooked up. I caught another quick consultation between Deke and Cassie and resisted the urge to grab the young girl by the shirt and shake the information out of her. My niece lay on the bed between us, with who knows what kind of alcohol cocktail spinning through her veins, and these two were trying to protect themselves.

But if I pushed too hard, they would clam up, and if Tabitha had taken drugs, this would be a whole different scenario. I doubted it, based on her appearance, but it was too early to rule anything out.

Deke started. "She might have had a couple of coolers. I think." Another quick "cover-for-me" glance to Cassie.

"And some Jack Daniel's," Cassie added sullenly.

I heard Dr. John's welcome voice, then he whisked the curtain aside. He glanced at Tabitha, then at Cassie and Deke. Now that the doctor was here, the atmosphere became more serious.

"How long has she been like this?" Dr. John asked, glancing at the chart, then stepping between Deke and the bed to have a closer look at Tabitha. He took a moment to glance at me. Smile. I felt a flush of warmth, then pulled myself back. *Focus.*

I gave a succinct rundown of what I already knew and how Tabitha was responding, my voice clipped as I struggled with my anger with these kids.

My niece reeked of alcohol and bodily fluids, and I wanted nothing more than to strip her down and wash her up. Clean away the filth that dirtied her body and my image of her. But we had procedures to follow, and we still had to get what information we could from these teenagers.

"Has Arlene contacted her parents yet?"

"I believe so." How often had I wondered what kind of parents would let their kids go wild like this? Even after I met the parents, their protestations of their child never having done something like this before would, at times, strike me as false or naïve in the extreme.

But now I saw what kind of parents Tabitha had. I'm sure Gerrit and Gloria did their best. They probably didn't know every detail of her life.

Dr. John examined her, then scribbled some orders on the chart. "I'd like to keep her overnight. I'm concerned about her alcohol level."

I adjusted Tabitha's shirt, pulling it up around her shoulder. Sweet, loving Tabitha who happily carted my kids around had been hanging around with a guy who reeked of alcohol himself, sporting a ring in his eyebrow and a tattoo on his neck, gravity fighting with his skinny hips for his baggy blue jeans, his T-shirt ripped and stained.

What would Gloria think?

I felt a flash of guilt and shame for her. Getting blindingly drunk with Deke and Cassie on a Friday night was hardly on Gloria's wish list for her daughter.

"You kids should go," Dr. John said as he signed off the orders on the chart. Then he caught Deke by the shoulder. "Don't even think about driving, kiddo. You smell like you're way over the limit."

"I only had a couple of beers . . ." His gaze flicked toward me, then back at Dr. John and held up his hands in surrender. "Okay, okay. I'll get a cab."

Dr. John sighed. "Fourteen. What possesses these kids to be so incredibly dumb?"

I wanted to defend Tabitha. To explain how sweet and sensible she could be.

"We'll keep her overnight." He stripped off his gloves and glanced at Tabitha and sighed heavily. "I'm sure Gloria is not going to be impressed." I got a conspiratorial look and as he passed, a faint brush of his warm hand over my back, right between my shoulder blades. "Thanks, Leslie," he said quietly, his hand coming to rest on my shoulder. "I'm beat and I'm heading home. Dr. Williams is on call the rest of the night." He smiled at me, tightened his hand. "I'll see you tomorrow."

I swallowed at the promise in his voice and couldn't help a quick glance over my shoulder as he left. He was looking at me as well. A flush warmed my face as I turned back to the work at hand.

I got a basin of warm water and started cleaning what I could of Tabitha's face. Other than monitoring her vital signs and keeping her hydrated to dilute the alcohol, there wasn't much else we could do. Arlene would notify one of the ward nurses to come and get her, but for now I wanted to get her clean. To remove the mess that coagulated on her face. I didn't want the ward nurses seeing my niece like this.

Normally I wouldn't know the kids who came in like this at night. Normally I would clean up and when I got home, tell Dan how incredibly stupid some kids would be.

Could I tell him about tonight?

I did what I could, then stayed by her side, doing my

charting while I waited for the ward nurses. I didn't want to leave her alone, and so far no one else needed my help.

Then a sound of hurrying feet and I heard someone call out, "Where's my girl? Where's Tabitha?"

I stepped outside of the cubicle and came face-to-face with Gloria. She blanched, stared at me a moment, then rushed past me to her daughter.

I decided to give them a few moments' peace and returned to my desk. I felt surreal as I made notations I'd made countless times before. But the person I wrote the information on wasn't an unknown person I could create my own scenarios around. This was a sweet young girl who sang in church, who had a cute smile and a cheerful attitude. This was my niece.

"Leslie," Arlene popped her head over my desk, her face flushed. "Got a lady here with chest pain."

I ran to the reception area in time to see a young woman supporting an older woman who had her hand pressed against her chest.

"It's my mother. She's been complaining about her chest," the younger woman said, her frantic gaze flickering from me to Arlene.

I felt an uptick of adrenaline. *Possible heart attack?*

"I'll need you to answer some questions," the clerk said to the younger woman, pulling her aside to the admissions desk. I grabbed a wheelchair and put the older woman in it. I recognized her as the woman who had the auction.

"Dr. Williams is on call now. Get him right away," I said to Arlene. "Then get the lab. I'll need an ECG stat and a cardiac workup." I left Arlene still asking some questions of the younger woman.

As I wheeled toward the trauma room, the usual questions came back to me like riding a bike.

"When did the pain start, Mrs.——"

"Harris. Margaret Harris. I was, well . . ." She hesitated as I helped her into bed.

"Were you working? Resting?"

"I was getting up to get some coffee."

"How did it feel?"

"Like a cow landed on my chest." She stopped. Breathed again, as if making sure she still could. "I couldn't get any air. My left arm tingled. I thought I was going to throw up." Another grimace of pain flitted over her face.

Sounded like classic cardiac symptoms. While I went through the automatic questions about her allergies and medical and family history, my mind scrambled.

OIL—Oxygen, Intravenous, Leads. OIL. The acronym I'd memorized long ago beat an insistent rhythm in my mind as I put her in bed and elevated her to a semi-seated position. I slipped on the O$_2$ mask, high flow, attached her to the vital-signs monitor and cardiac monitor from the crash cart. Too much to do, not enough hands, I thought as I pulled in a breath, slowing myself down. *OIL.* Intravenous. Where was Dr. Williams?

Nice veins.

Focus, Leslie, focus. I slipped the cannula in. *Nice and smooth,* taped it down and adjusted the flow. My mind ticked over my list again. *Oxygen. Check. Intravenous. Check. Leads. Check and check.*

I scribbled a few quick notes on a clipboard on the crash

cart as a lab tech came. I turned my attention back to Mrs. Harris.

"On a scale of one to ten, ten being the worst pain you ever had and one being a little discomfort, how would you rate your pain?" I asked, my gaze flicking over the information pulsing at me from the vital-signs monitor as the lab tech worked on the other side, drawing blood.

"It's about an eight," she gasped.

Her b.p. wasn't bad, but I gave her a shot of nitro, made a quick note, and glanced at my watch. I felt slightly outside of myself, watching myself going through the routine that so easily came back to me. In charge. In control.

A clatter of wheels announced another lab tech with the ECG machine. And right at that moment the daughter appeared by the bed. She didn't even ask, just went straight to her mother's side. It was getting crowded in here and Dr. Williams still hadn't shown up. I could use his help.

"I'm sorry, ma'am, you'll have to move," the lab tech snapped as he pulled out the leads for the ECG machine.

"I have to be here," she said firmly.

"You can move to the head of the bed," I said. "You won't be in the way there."

She gave me a thankful glance.

I checked the cardiac monitor. Classic wave form of an acute heart attack.

Arlene ran in. "I can't get ahold of Dr. Williams."

"Then try Dr. John," I snapped, torn between concern for this woman and pity for Dr. John being called back to the hospital after a full day on call. "He's probably still in the hospital."

"How is your pain?" I asked Mrs. Harris again as the tech pasted the leads to her chest.

"About a seven," she said, giving her daughter a weak smile. "It's going down, Linda."

Linda stroked her mother's hair. "That's good, Mom. You hang in there. We still need you around."

"Shouldn't have sold the farm."

"If you had kept it, you might be lying on the kitchen floor all alone right now."

"Maybe. But maybe I'd feel like I had a purpose."

"You have a purpose, Mom. That's to be with us yet." Their conversation registered in one part of my mind and I felt my heart tremble with yearning. I thought of my own mother and for a fleeting moment wondered where she was.

"Hello again." Dr. John was behind me, slipping on latex gloves. He gave me a tired smile that told me he would be okay. "What do we have here?" he asked as the ECG readout rolled off the machine. He pulled the paper, glanced at the patient then at me. "Morphine."

I drew it up and gave Mrs. Harris a small amount of morphine through the IV, my eyes constantly monitoring her blood pressure, oxygen saturation levels, and heart rate. I didn't have time to grab the chart and quickly scribbled what I could on the back of my hand.

"How is your pain, Mrs. Harris?" I asked again.

"Going down," she said, reaching up to catch her daughter's hand.

The lab tech came back with the results. Dr. John scanned them before looking up from the paper at the patient. "Looks like you're having a heart attack, or what we call a myocardial infarction. We're going to give you a drug to break up the clot in your heart that's causing this, but before we do, we need to ask you a few more questions."

Linda gasped. "Heart attack."

"Thankfully we caught things in time," Dr. John said.

As Dr. John went over the screening questions, I saw a faint track of moisture drift down Mrs. Harris's cheek. She pressed her lips together but made no move to wipe her tears away.

The words *heart attack* had such a deadly connotation for the average person. Such strong terminology striking at, well, the very heart of a person.

I sympathized, but as I injected the clot buster, I glanced at the clock and couldn't help but feel a flush of accomplishment. Twenty-two minutes from the time Mrs. Harris came into the hospital until we injected the clot buster. Not bad.

Dr. John must have caught my look, because he gave me a quick wink of understanding. I hoped the Harrises didn't catch it. This quick rush of adrenaline was what emergency-room nurses lived for. It was our drug of choice, and every time we handled an emergency smoothly or cheated death, the charge came. The more complicated the situation, the stronger the rush.

I tried to explain this to Dan once but I may as well have been speaking Urdu. Sometimes when a bad case had gone well, when once again I had helped snatch a patient from greedy death, I wished he could see so he could share my thrill, understand why I needed to be here as much as with him and my children at home.

For now I had John, and as he surreptitiously squeezed my hand, I felt a connection I never had with my own husband.

Mrs. Harris was stable for now and her daughter held her hand. Their eyes were closed, and Linda's lips were moving. "Thank you, Lord," she whispered over and over again, smiling as she did so.

Whatever gives her comfort, I thought, though at the same time I felt a flash of envy. She at least had someone to talk to when all was said and done. Well, she could keep talking to God—I still kept my eyes on the vital-signs monitor.

John laid his hand on my shoulder. "And again, nice work. Glad you're on my team."

I was still coming down from my adrenaline rush. "Thanks," I said, adding a smile. As he returned it, his eyes singing into mine, I heard a faint niggling voice.

He's coming on to you. Keep your distance.

I chanced a sidelong glance, surprised to see his eyes holding mine. A little too intensely. I knew I should listen. My rational self told me to be careful. But the lonely self, the one whose self-esteem had been battered by the woman who had held my husband's attention, and now by his family, who seemed to be drawing him away from me, not only continued to hold his gaze but lifted her hand up, covered John's hand with hers, and gave it an extra squeeze.

It's innocent. Means nothing.

He should be watching Mrs. Harris. So should I.

Confusion and professionalism fought with the basic need of any woman to know that she's attractive to a man.

So why do I have to remind myself of that? And why is this man so appealing?

Because he understands what you need. And these days Dan doesn't.

The ward nurses came to take Mrs. Harris away, and in the confusion, John and I ended up standing close.

"If things slow down here, we should go for coffee," he said. As he held my gaze I saw raw longing and yearning in his eyes. "I need to talk to you," he said hoarsely, his hand holding my shoulder. He lifted his hand to my face, his fingers trailing over my cheek. I couldn't stop a shiver—unsure of my reaction. Excitement? The knife-edge thrill of teetering on the brink of an abyss? I had always been afraid of heights. I got shaky standing on deep-pile carpeting. But each time I stood on a high building, I would inch to the edge and look down. And each time some perverted part of my psyche would wonder what it would be like to jump.

That was what I felt now. This steady, inexorable pull toward a place I knew I shouldn't be. A place I felt drawn to by a man who had made that fateful step past boundaries and borders and now invited me to do the same.

Unprofessional, my mind cried even as a very female part of me was drawn to this attractive single man desiring me, a married woman. A man who understood what I had to deal with.

I couldn't look at him anymore. I knew I was wobbling on dangerous ground.

And then, behind the warnings flashing in my mind, reared the indistinct features of Wilma. Gloria.

What would they think?

Their finger-wagging presence drifted a cool shiver down my neck and glided between John and me. And with them came Judy. Kathy. A host of other witnesses.

And on the periphery, Dan.

This is how it happens, I thought. This was how Dan got drawn into his relationship with Miss Bilingual. A smile, an argument with a spouse whose faults had accumulated over a period of six years, creating an unfair comparison with a sympathetic presence.

It would have been so easy to carry on, to slowly break down one barrier after another until there were none left to cross—no place left for retreat—no place left to hide.

Reality hit me like a fist.

I was no better than Dan. I could no longer accuse him from a point of self-righteousness. I had toppled as easily as he had.

I wanted to believe that my love for Dan was the force that finally pulled me from the brink of entanglement.

The truth was that fundamental and unwelcome notion of "What would other people think?" made me see this situation for the tawdry thing it was.

If love could be gauged by emotion alone, then what surrounded John and I almost fell into that category. But I knew I loved Dan. And sometimes love is simply a choice. A choice *for* a relationship.

And I wanted Dan and me to stay a couple. To stay married.

"I'm sorry, Dr. John," I murmured as I took a step away from him. I didn't look him in the eye, letting him draw what conclusion he would from my apology.

Chapter Fourteen

Can I come in?" I tapped on the open door of Tabitha's room, taking a few steps into the room. The only illumination was the light at the head of Tabitha's bed and the faint glow from the IV readout.

I had been done with my shift for over an hour, and during that time I hovered between going straight home to my husband and my children and wanting to talk to Gloria who, I knew, was with Tabitha in the ward.

Gloria sat beside her daughter, reading. She wore no makeup; her hair wasn't curled. In the reduced light, she looked drawn, tired, and vulnerable. Earlier, Gerrit had stopped by the ER, gave me a quick hug, quietly thanking me for what I did for his daughter. I didn't know what to say. Normally I wasn't involved with the aftermath of an emergency procedure. In Seattle the ER was often looked upon as a sorting house. Critical goes here, surgery goes there, others get a prescription and are sent on their way. Once we triaged and treated, we seldom saw our patients again, unless they were "regulars."

Now, here I looked at the clean and tidy face of a girl who had been much, much worse only a few hours ago.

"How is she doing?" I asked.

"She's fine. Still sleeping."

Tabitha's hair shone, and the faint sprinkle of freckles over her nose stood out against her pale skin, but thankfully, she looked as innocent as she had the day she and Allison had first burst into my kitchen.

"Did she wake up at all?"

Gloria nodded.

"That's good." I checked Tabitha's pulse, taking refuge from the awkward moment in my job as a nurse. Pulse. Normal. Temp. Normal.

"Will . . . will . . ." Gloria's voice faltered. She took a deep breath and tried again. "Will there be any long-term damage from this?"

"I believe we caught it in time. The fact that she woke up is good. Means she's not too deeply unconscious." I gave Gloria an encouraging smile. "She'll be fine."

Gloria nodded, then gave me a furtive glance. "I . . . I don't know what to say. Thank you for . . . for . . . what you did. It was a hard . . . situation."

I could see that Gloria was stumbling, and I wasn't sure what to say. Her hesitancy made me uncomfortable. But she was reaching out to me, and in spite of the jokes I had made at her expense, in spite of my frustration with her and, yes, my jealousy of her, I was thankful she wanted to make the connection.

"It's not that abnormal." I stroked a strand of hair away

from Tabitha's face. "I've seen it happen to all kinds of kids from all kinds of homes. And it doesn't mean she's a bad daughter."

Gloria sighed, her hand resting on the cover of her book. A Bible. Since Dan started reading the children's Bible in the evening, I had picked up the Bible from time to time in the evening, trying to make a connection with a man who was changing on me. I discovered I liked reading the Psalms and I liked some of the stories Jesus told, but a lot of the rest was hard going. All that finger-wagging from the prophets. I couldn't figure it out.

"You know, you do the best you can, and yet . . ." Gloria's voice faltered and she ducked her head.

I tried to imagine myself in Gloria's place. Tried to imagine what it would feel like to be sitting by the bed of a daughter who had messed up so publicly. Not only publicly but in front of the one person that you personally disapproved of.

"You didn't put the alcohol in her mouth, Gloria." I spoke quietly. After what had just happened to me, I was in no position to make any judgment.

Gloria flicked another curious glance at me, then sighed. "No. But I taught her better than this. We raised her to be a good Christian girl. I don't know what we did wrong."

I fingered Tabitha's hair again, soft and silky, all traces of what had happened washed out. Cleansed. "I don't know much about raising teenagers, and I don't know much about being a Christian. If Anneke did the same thing, I would be horrified and hurt. But I do know that kids are going to try things out, no matter what their parents teach them. They come to an age when their peers are more important than their parents. I've seen this kind of thing again and again." I paused, searching for something that I could use. "I also know that the kids we seldom see again are the ones who have parents who keep caring. Who keep loving their kids regardless of what they do."

I noticed the faint glint of tears on Gloria's cheek, and in that brief moment of vulnerability, I felt a faint throb of caring for this woman. She reached out and touched her daughter's cheek, and Tabitha became the bridge between Gloria and me.

I didn't want to leave. I wanted to maintain this fragile connection.

"Thanks for telling me that." She sniffed and swiped at her cheeks, glancing across the bed at me. "I do love her. But right now I am struggling between anger and plain, ordinary humiliation. She smelled so terrible. So common. She reeked of alcohol. And I'm supposed to be a Coffee Break leader." She laughed then and shook her head. "Pride. What a mistake."

Her admission and her soft laugh did more than any Bible lesson she could have taught me. I smiled at her, then took a huge chance and touched her arm.

"She's a good girl," I said. "Give her some time. Her behavior is not a reflection on you."

"I'll give her a good talking-to when she comes out of it," Gloria said, shaking her head. She squeezed my hand lightly, tweaked out a faint smile. "Thanks. This means a lot."

We shared a look, then she let go of my hand and fiddled with the sheet covering Tabitha. "Leslie, I know . . ." She stopped, bit her lip, then shook her head. "Leslie, please be careful with Dr. John. He's . . . he can be . . ." I caught a glimpse of confusion and regret. "Just be careful."

I clutched the bed as guilt and shame buffeted me.

Had she seen?

But she wasn't looking at me. Her words reminded me of how close I had come to doing something truly stupid.

Gloria stroked her daughter's cheek, graciously creating a space for me to regain what I had lost.

I nodded, understanding the suggestion subtly woven through her words. "Thanks, Gloria." And as she smiled at me I sensed a shift in our relationship. We now shared a vulnerability.

I had much to think about as I drove home through the night. On an impulse, I stopped on the hill overlooking our valley and pulled to the side of the road.

Lights winked at me through the darkness from various farmyards below. I could see ours, the VandeKams down the road. One of the many Brouwers whose names showed up above mail slots in the back of Harland church. I thought of the smiles I got when I accompanied Dan to church. Delores had given me a hug the second time I had gone, loudly proclaiming how glad she was I had come. As if I had given her a gift.

I turned off the car, killed the lights, and got out. The silence, now familiar, didn't hurt my ears like it did that first day. In fact, I even welcomed it.

I rested against the warm hood of the car, leaning back to look up. Stars winked like crushed diamonds tossed over a velvet sky that stretched from horizon to horizon. A wave of dizziness washed over me as my tiny mind tried to grasp the vastness of our galaxy and the universe beyond. If I looked any longer I would shrink down, disappear like a gnat.

Snatches of verse from an old song came to mind. "O Lord, my God, when I in awesome wonder . . . I see the stars, I hear the rolling thunder . . . how great Thou art."

I looked back over the valley, at the homes below, the people whose names and faces were becoming familiar. "Do You really care about all these people, God?" I whispered into the evening silence. "Do You really see them and love them like the minister said You do?" I shivered, then pressed myself closer to the car. "Did You see what happened with me and that doctor? Did You know how, for a small moment, I wanted to be with him? That I wanted to feel special to someone?"

I waited a moment in the cool silence of the evening for some kind of revelation to my whispered confession. Some judgment.

A small breeze teased my hair and tugged at my sweater, but other than that, nothing.

Well, it was worth a try, I thought, slipping back into the car.

As I drove down into the valley, I thought of Dan and my children and suddenly I pushed my foot harder on the accelerator. I wanted to be home.

From: tfroese@hotmail.com

To: lesismore@montana.net

U sound confused, sis. Stay the course, hand on the tiller. Don't get sucked into the cult. God is just a fantasy made up by people who can't explain things. Course, I can't explain things either but at least I admit it. Come to the light, sis. Come back to Seattle.

'Til Then Terra

Chapter Fifteen

'm glad you had fun," Kathy said with a self-satisfied smirk as she helped me load the large plastic dollhouse into my car.

It was late afternoon. Kathy had called me at work and asked if I wanted to go to a garage sale. I got off at four and Dan wouldn't be home until later on that evening. I had gotten used to having my husband around more often and didn't always like being home when he wasn't.

"Okay. You got me," I admitted, smiling as I set a large box of dollhouse accessories beside the dollhouse. "Pawing through someone else's used stuff was more fun than I thought it would be."

"It's the adventure," Kathy said. "You know exactly what you're going to get when you go to Wal-Mart or Costco. Garage sales are all about the thrill of the hunt."

As well as the dollhouse, I had also found a cute push-toy for Nicholas and a goofy farmer hat for Dan that the garage-sale lady had thrown in for free. But the best discovery was a couple of lily plants I found hiding in a corner. The lady who ran the sale told me they were perennials and if I wanted them to do really well next year, I would have to cut the blooms off. I had no intention of doing that. The lilies were beautiful and starting to open up. I had the perfect spot for them right outside the back door. Provided I could keep Sasha out of the bed, they would add a wonderful splash of color.

Kathy had bought a couple of lawn chairs, some clothes for her kids that Carlene was already trying on, and a large beach umbrella that Cordell dragged down the sidewalk.

"Good job, buddy," Kathy said as she took the umbrella from her son. She gave me a teasing smirk. "And are you sure you're done?"

I glanced back at the house, remembering the other things I had looked at but put back—the cute shirt I had found with the price tag still on it, and the funky lamp that would look so cool in our bedroom. "Yes. I am."

"And did Madame have a good time?"

I didn't change my expression. "You're liking this, aren't you?"

She nodded, her glance cutting to the amount of stuff I could barely fit in my car.

"I told you already, I had a lot of fun."

She yelped and made two fists. "Ladies and gentlemen, we have a convert." Her eyes sparkled at me. "Whaddya say? Hit town again next week? There's two happening in the new subdivision. Should be pretty good."

"Give me a chance to make the cultural shift," I said with

a laugh. "I'm still getting used to paying for things with a personal check." It still surprised me that the woman holding the garage sale took a check from a complete stranger with only my last name as security. "VandeKeeres are good for the money," she had said when I told her I had no cash.

The vehicles were loaded, the kids settled and bribed with some candy Kathy had brought along. As I closed the car door, I looked back at Kathy. "Thanks for bringing me."

"What shifts are you working next week?"

I told her and we chatted some more about inconsequential, drowsy subjects. A few flies buzzed lazily around our heads, and in the distance I heard the buzz of a lawnmower, the hissing tick-tick of a sprinkler. I wanted to hold fast to this glorious summer day. Me, spending ordinary time with a friend after a fun afternoon.

Life was good, and as I got into my car and waved goodbye to Kathy, I felt a sense of warm well-being. In Seattle, Josie and I had spent precious little time together outside of the hospital. Always our shifts interfered with the care and maintenance of a friendship.

Since coming here, I'd spent more time with Kathy than I had in the previous six months with Josie. She was the first good friend I'd had in a long, long time.

I glanced over at Nicholas, fast asleep in his car seat, his cheeks bright red with sun and fatigue. He'd been uncharacteristically quiet and patient with me as I poked and prodded and snooped through the sale items. He'd probably be up most of the night in payment for these few moments of peace, but I didn't begrudge him the rest.

The warm sun shone through the windshield as I drove, the purr of the car engine making Anneke drowsy, and I saw her head slump to one side as she drifted off, as well.

I hummed the song I remembered from church. I had gone again a couple of times when Nicholas was in a good mood or I wasn't working. I recognized a few people who had come through the emergency department and a few more from my shopping trips at the co-op. I didn't feel as much a stranger as I had the first time. Each time the minister spoke I discovered more about God, but I kept my guard up. No sense in jumping into this all the way without knowing where it would take me. Dan was happy, and it made his family happy, which, by extension, made my life a little easier.

I made the last corner out of town, then headed down the road toward home. Soon I came to my favorite part of the drive. Up and up through wooded hills, then cresting a ridge and then, suddenly below me lay our valley. A broad wide basin, mountains rising up on three sides, pale blue, snow-covered. Solid. Protecting.

I saw the patchwork of fields in the valley, some bright green from irrigation. The fields higher up looked as if a giant comb had raked through them creating green furrows alternating with brown cultivated fields. It didn't seem that long ago that Dan had planted the higher land and now it had been up for over a month, growing more every week.

Below us the silver ribbon of a creek unspooled through the pastures and fields heading toward the Gallatin River and then the Missouri.

I felt a beat of expectation as I headed down into the valley, thinking of Dan and looking forward to telling him about the garage sale when he got back from spraying tonight. He'd get a kick out of the hat.

As I drove into the yard, I slowed down by the garden. I had weeded it yesterday, taking peculiar pleasure in sorting out the bad from the good. Restoring order to the neat rows. The carrots were finally recognizable, and the peas were starting to crawl up the fence. I still found it semi-miraculous to see the changes every week brought. I looked forward to tasting fresh vegetables, harvested myself.

For now, I was excited to help Anneke set up the dollhouse. Like any mother of a little girl, I'd been wanting to buy a dollhouse for years, but we simply didn't have the space. It would fit perfectly in the corner of her room now, just under the eaves.

I parked in the yard and got out, a feeling of accomplishment flowing through me.

Dan came out of the house, and walked toward the car. Why was he home already?

"How was town?" he asked as I got out of the car. He glanced at our sleeping kids.

"Kathy and I went to a garage sale. I didn't think you would be back until after supper."

"That's why you didn't come straight home from work?"

"Yeah." I gave him a puzzled look. "Is something wrong?"

"Why isn't Kathy home yet if she went with you?"

"I don't know."

"And you really went to a garage sale?"

What was with the good cop–bad cop routine Dan was pulling off all by himself? "The evidence, Mr. CSI, is in the car," I said, an edgy tone entering my voice at the mistrustful one in his. "One dollhouse and three lily plants."

He looked from me to the car, his eyes narrowed, an unwelcome slant to his mouth, and a question breathed through me.

"Where did you think I went?" I asked carefully.

Dan blinked, then shook his head. "It doesn't matter."

"It does," I said, trying to hold his gaze. But he shoved his hands in the back pocket of his blue jeans, not looking at me. "You're angry, and I haven't done anything wrong."

"I don't know about that."

"Enough with being vague. Something is bothering you. What is it?"

Dan sighed, then turned to me. "What's going on between you and Dr. John?"

I endured an instant of guilt so intense and familiar, it felt like a friend. Right behind that came a mocking soundtrack, the velvet voice of Elvis singing "Suspicion" thrumming through my mind. I mumbled out a non-dramatic, "Nothing."

"Really? Then why did he have his hands all over you the other night?"

I pulled a face. "First off, that sounds gross. Second, that sounds *really* gross." He made Dr. John seem like a lecherous old man who couldn't keep his hands off me.

But other than the lecherous part, he did touch you a lot.

"That's no answer, Leslie. Is there something going on between you two?"

You two. Like we were a couple.

I knew I had been skirting along the edge of trouble when I encouraged Dr. John. Yes, he understood what I was dealing with. No, Dan didn't. Yes, Dr. John was caring and considerate.

But nothing really happened, I wanted to say, even as a small voice mocked my self-righteous protestations.

You liked his attention. You encouraged it.

Not much.

Enough to let him think he could carry on.

But I didn't want him to carry on. And how did Dan know?

I looked at Dan. Really looked at Dan. Saw the hurt in his eyes and felt my world twist and spin as the very things I had accused Dan of now faced me.

Did it really happen this easily? Was it so simple to slip into unsuitable relationships? A glance. A shared laugh. A spouse who was so busy with other things and other people that you felt a seismic shift of loyalty in your own relationship and desperately needed confirmation that you were desirable. Wanted. Needed?

"Leslie, you're not saying anything. He called here today. Have you and he—"

I swallowed my pride. I didn't really want Dr. John. Only support. I took a breath and started down the same road Dan had taken over half a year ago. "Yes, I thought he was attractive. Yes, we spent time chitchatting and visiting." I held his troubled gaze and saw the hurt I had felt with Miss Bilingual reflected in his eyes. "If I talked too much to Dr. John, it was because I could vent to him about Wilma and Gloria. Because he knew what I was dealing with. Because he sympathized with me and I could tell him things I could never tell you."

"Gloria said he could be like that," Dan said with a sorrowful note in his voice.

"Gloria? When did you talk to her?"

"She was the one who told me. Warned me, actually. She saw you and Dr. John."

My mouth opened and shut like a fish as I tried to find the right thing to say, the right thing to do. I had never truly understood the full meaning of the word *flabbergasted* until this moment.

The irony of it all. I had said nothing about Tabitha, wanting to spare Gloria. I assumed, from her hesitantly spoken words, she was going to allow me the same courtesy.

"I can't believe this," was all I could come up with. "I can't believe she would have the nerve . . . After what I had to clean up . . . what I had to do . . ." My voice halted as hurt fought with pride and shame.

Dan stood rock-solid, his arms across his chest. "She told me about Tabitha. Don't think she's not grateful for what you did." He glanced at the kids in the car. They were stirring. The statute of limitations was running out on this discussion, and I was trying to encapsulate my confusion, my anger, and, yes, my guilt, into something resembling a coherent sentence.

"Why didn't she talk to me?" was all I could come up with. I thought Gloria and I had come to an understanding. That gentle soundtrack moment in the hospital room had been wiped away by her self-righteous attitude. One step forward, two steps back. "Doesn't she care?"

"I know my family's not perfect," he said. "But you can't accuse them of not caring. They're involved in our lives. They care about our marriage. And I do, too. I had hoped that moving here would help us. I thought you wanted the same."

"I do . . ."

"Then why were you spending time with this doctor?"

"Why were you spending time with Miss Bilingual?" Guilt made me lash back.

"Her name was Julie. And I spent time with her because I was weak and because I was confused and because she was around and you weren't around," and once again we revisited ancient history.

"I was trying to keep our family financially afloat," I said.

"Like I am now. And you may not see it, but I appreciate the help we get from my family. I don't see your sister helping out. Or your mother."

My face stiffened as the blood drained to my chest and pain lanced through my very being. "Low blow, Dan. You know as well I do that I haven't heard from my mother in months . . ." My voice broke. Did he think I liked how dysfunctional my family seemed compared to his? Didn't I get to see enough disapproval from Wilma and, yes, Gloria? Had he moved so firmly over to their camp that he could no longer see my point of view?

"If she ever stayed in one place long enough, maybe you would hear from her."

"Don't you think I want that?" I cried, my voice breaking.

"Do you think Terra and I chose to have an absent mother? Do you think I enjoyed wondering if my mom was going to be home when I got home from school, wondering how we were going to make it through the week? Do you think it's easy for me to be surrounded by your family, who have always been here and probably always will be, a reminder of what Terra and I don't have?" I pressed my lips together. Dan knew about my past, but I seldom spoke about it. The past was, well, the past. I didn't want to spend too much time comparing memories. Dan's would always eclipse mine. "Your mother is far from perfect, either, Dan VandeKeere. And each time I see your family I see a family so different from mine, but yet not so different. From the first time your mother met me she made her mind up about what kind of person I was, and she doesn't seem to want to change it no matter what I do. Yes, my mother is a failure in the mother department, but I would be careful how you throw around accusations. They can come back and smack you in the face."

And I should know, I thought as Dr. John's face suddenly superimposed itself on Miss Bilingual's. Our combined failures.

"My mother has had her own difficulties . . ." Dan said, aligning himself on Wilma's side.

"Your mother had a husband who loved her and gave her a home. That was your father. That her second husband was a snake is hard. But she had and still has people around her. A community and people who care. My mother had no one. And maybe I'm not perfect, I've never claimed to be, but I hope that if Nicholas ever gets married, I don't treat his

future wife the way your mother treated and still treats me."
Dan blanched as my words spun like a cyclone, gathering
speed, words spat out in anger and self-defense. But I
couldn't stop now. "And if you're going to blame everything
that's wrong in your mother's life on the fact that some man
recently left her in the lurch, then you're only making it easier for her to be unkind, and uncaring, and controlling." *And
I should know*, I thought, but I wasn't going to give him any
more ammunition.

"She's not controlling, Leslie."

"If she's not, why does she insist on controlling the farm
accounts?"

"Because we were only going to be here awhile."

Were. He said were. "And now?"

"Things change." He drew in a deep breath. "In spite of
what you've just said about my mother, I don't want to
leave."

A wail from Anneke scattered the conversation. I
blinked, trying to ground myself back in the present. I
needed to retreat and regroup. Regain my own control.

"I can't talk about this now, Dan. I just can't." Too many
emotions churned around us, too many words had been
thrown on the ground. We needed some time and space before we took them up again.

The next few hours were painfully silent as we ate. Dan
read the story Bible again, but I couldn't listen. My feelings
were a patchwork quilt of guilt and pain stitched together
with anger. Not comforting at all.

Afterward Dan carted the dollhouse into Anneke's room

and helped her set it up, a job I had been looking forward to doing.

Instead I planted the lilies, watered them, and stood back to garner what precious enjoyment I could. The woman at the garage sale had told me that if I clipped them off they would grow better next year. I didn't care about next year, I wanted to enjoy them now.

Stay here?

I know my kids loved it here. They loved their grandma—correction, Oma—even if I didn't. They loved their aunties, the chickens, the dog, Dan's horses.

And you don't?

I couldn't fit my head around that yet. Didn't know where to put it.

What would I lose? What would I gain?

There are moments when you like it here. Admit it.

But so much would change . . .

I couldn't think about that yet. Not yet.

I put the kids in bed while Dan retreated to his shop. We maintained a quiet cease-fire, neither of us talking. Neither of us knew what to say, how to regain lost ground.

I tried to read a book, gave up and went to bed, lying between the freshly washed sheets, trying to find sleep. Dan joined me much later, but he turned away from me, presenting his back to me across the expanse of our bed, which now seemed as broad as the Atlantic and just as inviting. In minutes I heard him snoring.

Sleep, when I finally found it, was restless. Full of incoherent dreams.

I woke up in the early morning, unable to sleep anymore, and made my way back downstairs. Two o'clock in the hospital was usually a chance to catch up with some of the other nurses, catch up on paperwork. At home, it was an empty, lonely time with no one to connect with. I checked my e-mail. Nothing from Terra or Josie. Somehow it didn't matter as much as it used to.

I wandered around the house, restless, unsettled.

Then I saw the Bible sitting by Dan's chair. I snapped on the light and picked it up. I had read it a couple of times before, not sure of where to start. A piece of paper stuck out from the pages, so I opened it there. Psalm 23. I dropped into Dan's chair and started reading. The rhythm of the language and vaguely familiar words drew me in. ". . . He leads me beside quiet waters. He restores my soul." I took a long, slow breath as I read, letting the cadence of the words wash over me. Comfort me. ". . . You anoint my head with oil. My cup overflows. Surely goodness and love will follow me all the days of my life and I will dwell in the house of the Lord forever."

I dropped my head on the chair and stared at the ceiling. The house of the Lord. Did God really want me? Would He really restore a soul that had been tainted by wrong? Would the family really forgive me?

I felt as if my life were unraveling and I didn't know how to put it back together again.

Chapter Sixteen

nd when did you say you injured your back?" I asked my patient as I whisked the curtain closed around the bed. The day had been busy, thankfully. I didn't have time to spin through the endless circle of what I had said the day before yesterday—what I should have said, what I shouldn't have said. Dan hadn't brought it up yesterday or this morning.

I didn't know how to proceed from here and I couldn't mention it to Kathy or ask her advice. As for my magical book? Well, there was no chapter in *How a Marriage Can Succeed* that covered uneasy truces.

"Ten years ago. I was working as a roofer. Slipped on a shingle that some idiot had laying around and *wham*"—he smacked his hands together— "I was sliding down that roof and on the ground before I knew what hit me. Saw more stars than the Walk of Fame." He gave me a quick grin, then, as if realizing that he was supposed to be in pain, and winced. "I need to see the doctor."

Mr. Francisco wore scruffy blue jeans and a tattered jean jacket and his hair was pulled back into a greasy ponytail. Obviously not one of the more prosperous seekers of the American Dream.

"Before I get the doctor, can you do a few things for me so I can judge the extent of your pain?"

This netted me a sullen look and a shrug. "Sure. As long as you don't make me throw my back out. I'll sue, you know."

Of course he would.

"Can you lift your arms over your head?"

This was done with much groaning and moaning as I watched for any telltale signs. I knew that the motto of the justice system was "innocent until proven guilty," but I had a vibe about this guy.

I gave him a few more small exercises, which he performed mindlessly, his begrudging air slowly fading as I took notes.

"Can you touch your toes?" I asked the question casually, and when he easily bent over to do this, my vibe grew stronger. He should have been in agony.

"So, when is the doctor going to see me?" he asked, his voice growing quieter as he straightened. "I really need something for the pain, 'cause I lost my other prescription."

Of course he needed a new prescription. And as we went through the list of his allergies—big surprise—he named every common painkiller that could be acquired without a prescription.

With patients like Mr. Francisco, training and intuition collided. My training taught me to be sympathetic, to listen and to be nonjudgmental.

"Are you on any medication now?" I asked, injecting a pleasant tone into my voice. It was work, that injecting. I knew this guy's type all too well. We came across them day after day in Seattle, and it was always a struggle to deal with them professionally and courteously when you knew they were using and abusing the system.

He lifted his hands just a fraction. The pain, of course. "Well, I had some medication, like I told you. But I was with some dudes and we were hanging out at my place. One of the guys went into my bathroom. He's a big-time druggie. Loser," he said knowingly with a slow nod, pulling me onto his side. "I'm sure he's dealing on the side. Knows I'll squash him like a bug if I find out he's doing that stuff. I'm sure he took the stuff from my bathroom, 'cause as soon as he was done, he told this other guy they had to leave real quick. I was going to go to my regular doctor, in Missoula, but he's gone on some fancy trip to the Bahamas. You know doctors," he said, lowering his voice and angling his head with a quick jerk toward the cubicle where John was busy with another patient. "I had to come here anyway to see some guy about a truck that I was going to buy. I was gonna try to go without the pills, but the pain, it just got too bad."

"That's too bad," I said, forcing sympathy into my voice.

"Anyway, when can I see the doctor? I'm dying here."

I smiled politely as I carefully wrote out some notes on his chart. I'd seen dying, and Mr. Francisco was a long ways from hearing the angels sing.

"I'm in pain, nurse. You have to pay attention. You have to treat me."

Don't roll your eyes. Don't even make eye contact. Just keep writing.

"You hearing me, nurse? I got rights. I got medical insurance. I can pay." His voice rose with each declaration.

Relax. Don't take it personally. Don't let your emotions intrude on your patient-nurse relationship.

"I'll get the doctor," I said with a careful smile.

As I left, I massaged my temples, trying to push away the pain that had been steadily building since my confrontation with Dan. I couldn't push aside the angry words thrown down between us. What he'd said about my mother, what I'd said about his. What Gloria had said about Dr. John.

I worked the night shift after our fight, unintentionally underscoring his accusation that I put work before family. But I couldn't be at home with all that tension boiling beneath the quiet facade we kept up for the sake of the kids.

Once again our lives slipped past each other. I hated it.

In spite of my pique with her self-righteous gossiping, I set my own pride aside long enough to realize that Gloria was right. I had been edging around dangerous territory, encouraging Dr. John. And I had encouraged him for the wrong reasons. Pride. Selfish gossip. In spite of what Gloria and Wilma had done and said, I had no right to bring down their characters just to prop up my own weaknesses. What had been worse was realizing how easily I had slipped into the same territory where Dan had been. I had come here with a sense of pride and superiority. All lost. Swept away.

So I created a distance between me and Dr. John. I kept our conversation professional and didn't rise to the bait when he made a comment about Gloria. Thankfully he seemed to get the hint, but I felt as if I had lost my only ally.

I checked on the woman with the croupy cough beside Mr. Francisco. Thankfully she didn't ask when Dr. John was going to see her. I didn't have an answer.

As I stepped out of her cubicle, a noise at the front desk caught my attention. My heart sank when I saw the man carrying a child, a woman hurrying behind him. All the beds were full. Mr. Francisco had been triaged to the end of the line and was our last patient. If we had a real emergency, he'd be bumped back to the waiting room, which would make him even more cranky.

Then the frantic-looking man by the front desk glanced over his shoulder and ice slipped through my veins.

It was Dan . . . and he carried Nicholas.

Wilma was right on his heels.

Questions skittered through my mind. Why was Wilma here? Kathy was supposed to be taking care of the kids. But right behind those questions a larger one loomed, heavy and threatening.

What was wrong with Nicholas?

Go. Now. Hurry. Your baby. Your little boy is in trouble. You should have been at home. You knew he wasn't well. Dan was right. You do put your job first and now Wilma gets to see firsthand.

Nicholas had been fussing all last night and was a bit feverish that morning, but I had put it down to teething. Had I been so terribly wrong? Me? A nurse?

Guilty fear tumbled through my mind as I made my rubbery legs hurry to Dan's side.

"He's burning up, Leslie." Dan looked to me as if I had an answer. All I had at the moment was a flash of guilt that I hadn't been home to prevent this. Whatever this was.

"Bring him into the trauma room," I said, holding back from pulling Nicholas out of his arms myself. I hurried ahead of him, Dan and Wilma right behind me.

Relax. Assess. Triage. Treat.

I ran through the litany that always helped me during the harder cases that came into the emergency room in Seattle.

The words usually calmed me and pulled me back from the emotions of the situation. I had a job to do.

But I had forgotten about Mr. Francisco glaring at me through narrowed eyes as he sat on the bed we needed for Nicholas. "Where's the doc? I thought he was going to see me next."

"We have to move you back to the waiting room," I said firmly. "We have an emergency."

He didn't budge.

"Please get off the bed." I couldn't stop the edge in my voice. My son needed that space.

"I'll sue."

"I know a good lawyer. We have a very ill child." I didn't have time for this. "Now, get off that bed."

I didn't know where this fit in nurse-patient procedure, but as I stared at him, he finally moved. I was there in a nano-second, whipping off the sheets he had been sitting on, replacing them as he stormed out the door. He moved surprisingly fast for someone with severe back pain.

When Dan and Wilma came in the room, I saw Wilma

look from me to the retreating back of Mr. Francisco, then back at me, puzzled. No time to explain.

"Lay him on the bed," I said to Dan. "Take off his shirt and coat."

My heart stuttered in my chest as Dan undressed him, handing the clothes to my mother-in-law. I pulled the crash cart close, clipped a new cover on the thermometer, and checked his temperature. Sky-high. His breathing was fast, pulse erratic.

"Dr. John Brouwer!" I called out, knowing he was somewhere on the ward. "I need you *now*." Again, no time for niceties. This case now had priority.

Nicholas's chest was clear.

In spite of my training and my previous experience, I couldn't pull back far enough from this case. This body, burning with fever, lying so still on the bed, was my son. My baby boy. I called to Arlene to get a lab tech down here.

"What happened?" I asked as I started a chart.

My mind clicked through the possibilities as a faint whisper of a memory teased the back of my mind. The mother who had come in the other day talking about a suspected case of meningitis at the day care. We hadn't treated the child here, so I never thought of it again. Until now.

"Kathy said Nicholas was cranky when you left for work," Wilma said. "Then he started shivering a couple of hours later and he threw up. She called Dan, who called me, and we met at Kathy's place. When we picked Nicholas up, we noticed that he was all stiff."

Febrile convulsion?

Habit and training pushed away the emotions for the moment as I scribbled rough notes on the chart. I would translate later. I hooked him up to the vital-signs monitor, slipped the oxygen mask on, snapped a tourniquet on his arm, and swabbed the spot where I would start the IV. I was pushing things. O_2 and IV were not on the standing orders for a young child presenting with a fever. But I couldn't get rid of the doubt scratching repeatedly at the back of my mind.

Why was that cannula shaking so much? Why couldn't I hold it still? I swallowed and tried to relax.

Oh, God.

I took in another breath.

Oh, God.

The expression had always been simply that. An expression. A cry to a deity that I had conveniently sidelined, only to call Him out when things went wrong. God's name was an expression of fear, a cry for help.

It was only in the extreme situations of my job that I used His name. But now, as I gently pierced my own son's soft skin with a needle, I felt as if I mentally whispered to Him. Drawing on His power and strength.

"When he got drowsy on the way here, I knew something was really wrong," Wilma was saying.

Nicholas's eyes fluttered open. I didn't want to make eye contact. He was a patient. If I saw his eyes, if I saw tears or pain, he would cease to be a patient and suddenly become my son.

Check oxygen levels. Increase saturation. What would the doctor order from the lab? I started a requisition form.

Where was Dr. John?

I checked the vital-signs monitor, my mind still flipping through possibilities.

Chills. Fever.

Treat the fever.

I slipped him to his side and gave him a Tylenol suppository, then noticed how his legs were drawn up. That puzzled me as the whisper in my mind amplified.

Mother panic clawed at my nurse persona. I couldn't separate them. My little boy lay on the table, deathly ill.

Where was that lab tech?

I glanced at the clock again and made a snap decision. I couldn't wait another second. I wrapped a tourniquet around his other arm, tightened it, and once again slipped a needle into my son's soft skin so I could draw blood. A faint gasp from Wilma pierced my concentration but I couldn't lose focus. Every second counted to my fevered brain. Once the vials were full, I carefully set them onto the crash cart.

"What's wrong with him, Leslie?" Dan asked, weariness and concern edging his voice. "Why did you take his blood?"

I looked across the bed at him and eked out a reassuring smile as I pulled off the latex gloves. "The lab will need to run some tests."

I looked down at Nicholas and ran my finger down his soft cheek. He held his head funny. The whisper gained volume. I was about to extend his knee to check my suspicions as Dr. John swept into the cubicle. Dan's eyes narrowed when he saw John and I thought, *Please, no time for this, Dan. No time.*

"What do we have here?" Dr. John asked.

"High fever. Did up the blood work." I listed symptoms, turning my son's pain into something clinical. Detached. Simply another patient.

Just as I spoke, a tech came into the room.

I angled my chin toward the crash cart. "You drew blood already?" She frowned and Dr. John picked up on that.

"That's not part of standing orders," he said as he checked the chart.

"I couldn't wait," I replied, keeping my focus on my son. "I think this is serious."

"I know you may have done things differently in Seattle, but here we follow policy and procedure." Dr. John snapped on a pair of gloves and waited a moment, as if to let his words sink in. I realized what he was doing and I felt another flicker of panic, followed by anger. We had so often been warned about doctor-nurse relationships. I understood the full implications of it now.

"We don't have time for this," I said. "I'm suspecting meningitis."

Too late I realized what I had done. I had not only criticized Dr. John in front of other people, I had also stepped way out of the bounds of my job and delivered a premature diagnosis.

"I think you might be overreacting," he said quietly, his voice telling me more than either Dan or Wilma could pick up. He reached for the otoscope and checked Nicholas's ears himself.

I bit my lip and imagined myself grabbing the front of his

lab coat and giving him a shake. Why was he dawdling? Every moment counted.

Keep your mouth shut, Leslie. Don't say anything.

"His ears are red. He might have an ear infection," Dr. John said, ignoring me and giving Dan a patronizing smile.

I couldn't stay quiet. I threw away any shred of pride I had and looked him directly in the eye, pleading with him. "Please, John. This is my son. I know he has more than an ear infection."

Dr. John frowned again. "Is this going to be a problem, Leslie?"

"I think we should do a lumbar puncture."

Dr. John's eyes narrowed. "Last time I checked, that was my call to make, Leslie."

I had already gently rebuffed advances from him that I knew I had unwittingly encouraged. Now I had chosen to go toe-to-toe with him. If he wanted, he could fire me on the spot, could reduce my hours, could make my life here at the hospital miserable. But I was now nurse *and* mother.

"I know my son. He has never thrown up. He has an elevated heart rate. Nicholas is not teething, doesn't have an ear infection, and doesn't simply have a cold."

Down, girl. Keep your voice down. You're exhibiting classic signs of an hysterical parent who wants the entire health-care system to fix her child.

But it was my son who lay on the table, not my pride or my job. And I knew how quickly we had to act.

Then, with a sigh as if to show he was still in charge, he turned back to Nicholas and lifted his head.

It barely moved. *Nuchal rigidity,* I thought as my heart skittered like slippery shoes on ice.

Then Nicholas screamed, took a breath, and vomited all over the doctor.

"We'll need to do a lumbar puncture," Dr. John said. "If positive, we'll have to call an air ambulance."

"Lumbar. That's the back, isn't it?" Dan asked, panic in his voice. I didn't like to hear that. I wanted Dan the way he always was. Calm and in control.

"We need to drain some spinal fluid to confirm the diagnosis of meningitis." I could barely speak the words as I reached for the LP kit. This was my little boy they were going to do this procedure to. My chubby little Nicholas. Dan's wild gaze snagged mine, and I tried to give him a reassuring smile even though I knew, more than he did, what the potential complications for Nicholas were.

The next few moments were a flurry of busyness as I unwrapped the LP kit and laid it out, the lab tech returned to collect the fluid, and Dr. John prepped the site. A wave of fear pressed relentlessly against the thin wall of resolve I had erected. I couldn't let it get in. Couldn't let it wash over me.

Dr. John inserted the needle into his spine and as the fluid came out, the wave grew. Cloudy.

Dr. John called to Arlene to order in the air ambulance, ordered intravenous antibiotics. My hands weren't shaking as much as before, but even so I found myself concentrating fiercely on my job and then, while we waited, writing everything carefully down on the chart as if writing down the precise time and exact measurements would make all the difference for my son.

Son.

I looked down at Nicholas with his one arm strapped against the bar, his leg immobilized, the IV cannula sticking out like an obscenity.

As a father has compassion on his children . . . The Bible passage slowly filtered past the flickers of fear, eased them away. God loved Nicholas. I had to cling to that.

Finally, as if just now remembering that she was here, I looked at Wilma. She stood at the bedside, her eyes firmly on Nicholas, her fingers resting lightly on his leg. His grandmother.

"So, what now?" Dan asked, panic edging his voice.

"We wait for the air ambulance."

"That's it? That's all we can do?"

I nodded.

Waiting was an agony for parents, and even for nurses. As long as we had a task, as long as we were intervening, we felt as if we were pulling the person toward life. I needed a job to do. Something so I could feel like I was keeping my son alive. Keeping him healthy.

"If it's okay with you, I'd like to pray," Wilma said quietly.

I glanced at Dan looking down at our son, his hand clutching Nicholas's. Dan nodded slowly and closed his eyes.

I guessed praying was doing something, so I closed my eyes.

"Dear Lord, we know that You are a Father and that You loved Your Son," Wilma said, her voice surprisingly calm.

"We know how deep Your love is, that You know if even a hair falls from our head. Lord, we plead with You for this child. Be with the doctors who will take care of him. The nurses . . ." Her voice wavered, which almost made me lose it. She loved my son as well, I thought. And she loved God. She was a worthy intercessor.

Wilma cleared her throat and continued. "Keep him in Your care, Lord, we pray. Keep him healthy. Let us enjoy him again. Amen."

I took a long slow breath, my eyes on Nicholas. He still looked flushed, still lay deathly still.

Nothing had changed, no bright lights accompanied by stirring music, angels singing. No miracle. Yet I felt a whisper of peace sifting around the edge of my fear. Nicholas had family around him, interceding.

Then Nicholas stiffened and vomit spewed out of his tiny mouth. And the peace exploded violently out of the moment.

Chapter Seventeen

o answer at all?" My sweat-slicked hand clutched the headset of the phone in the parents' room of the hospital.

Where are you, Terra? I need you.

"I'm sorry, ma'am." The disembodied voice gave standard-issue condolences. I whispered an equally fake thanks and dropped the phone into the cradle.

I had dragged myself here after spending most of last night standing guard over my son, keeping death at bay. I fell asleep on the couch and had just woken up. My first thought was a desperate need to connect with my sister. But nothing. Had she moved already?

"Hey, there."

I jumped, then felt a hand on my shoulder. Dan crouched down beside me.

"Hey, yourself." I wiped my tired eyes.

Images of last night scurried through my mind. The flashing lights of the helicopter, and then it was gone into the air, taking our son away. Then the mad dash to Helena in the night and the long vigil by Nicholas's bed in the pediatric ICU.

Dan had left toward morning while I stayed behind. Finally, one of the ward nurses practically pushed me to the parents' room. The last thing I remembered was wondering if I could sleep while my son lay in critical condition in Pediatric Intensive Care.

"Have you seen Nicholas?"

"I just checked on him. He's sleeping." To my disappointment, Dan didn't come and sit beside me. Anneke had slipped in and found the toys. I called her name, and she got to her feet and slowly walked over.

I must look a wreck, I thought, pushing at my hair, which now nested around my face. I quickly finger-combed it, then held out my arms to my little girl. When she finally came, I pulled her into my arms, clinging tightly. Then I pulled away and looked her over, almost hungrily.

If it wasn't so pathetic, I would laugh.

She looked like a little refugee. She wore her favorite polka-dotted skirt—the one that was far too large for her—a plaid coat over a stained T-shirt, and rubber boots. Her hair was pulled into some semblance of a ponytail, and I saw a smear of jam on one corner of her mouth and dirt under her fingernails.

I cleaned the jam with a dab of Magic Mommy Spit but was helpless about the rest of her new look.

She had obviously dressed herself and Dan obviously didn't care.

Obviously, because his ensemble was hardly *GQ* material. Oblong oil stains decorated his pants, and his shirt had a darker spot on the chest where a pocket had once been and had since been ripped off.

If my family looked like this after two days away from me, I couldn't imagine what my house looked like. *Dan* and *neat* were not two words that dovetailed.

"How are you doing?" Dan sat beside me but kept his distance.

"I'm tired." I wanted him to hold me and let his strength wash over me, but I didn't know how to behave, what to say. Before this emergency we had been walking carefully around each other, my actions with Dr. John, the words I had spilled out filling a space between us that kept us apart.

Dan touched my shoulder lightly, then withdrew. He pressed his hands against his knees and got up. Paced the room. Turned to me, his truck keys in his hand. He wasn't going to go already, was he?

"Dan, what's—"

"Leslie, I need—"

I waved my hand at him the same time he told me to go ahead. An uncomfortable pause followed. He spun his truck keys around his hand.

"I'm trying to find the right way to say this." He stopped, his keys still jangling in his hands, a nervous habit of his I hadn't seen in a long time.

He sighed, then dropped the keys into his pocket. "You know, *sorry* isn't a big enough word for this," he said softly. "But I don't know what other one to use." He stopped, giving me a careful smile.

I needed him now. The past thirty-six hours had revealed my rant against his mother for the petty thing it was. With

Dr. John, I had stumbled into the very trap that had ensnared Dan back in Seattle. Down the hall our son clung to life. Everything else was swept away as inconsequential.

"I'm going to use it," I said quietly. "I'm sorry for what I did. I want you to know that that thing with Dr. Brouwer never went any farther than what Gloria saw, but I was wrong to even encourage that." I rubbed my forehead, wishing I could ease away the pain tentacled around my head. I needed him now.

Dan slipped his arm around me, then pulled me gently close. "Leslie, don't, please. I did the same thing. We've never talked about it. I didn't want to, and I know you didn't want details. But I finally understand exactly what I put you through." He sighed, and laid his head on mine. "I'm sorry for what I said about your mother. That wasn't right."

A knot of unbearable pain that had pressed on my heart slowly released its hold as Dan spoke, as he touched me. And with the release came the reality of what I had said.

"Well, we may as well keep going," I said, leaning into him. "I was wrong about your family. Wrong to resent their involvement." I thought of Wilma praying earnestly for Nicholas. She loved him, too.

Dan laid his finger against my lips. "I don't want us to fight. I don't want us to be strangers. Our boy is sick, and I want us to be together. Supporting each other. In spite of what I did, I love you. I always will." He stopped, his voice breaking. "I love Anneke and Nicholas. And you all need to be the most important people in my life. Not my mother or my sisters or the farm or the rest of my family."

My throat thickened, and I couldn't stop the quiver of my lip. But as I reached for him, he held up his hand. He had more to say. "I asked my family to stay away. To give us some space. And I want you to know that when this is over . . . when Nicholas is better, we're going to sit down and talk about what is going to happen in our lives, in our future. Whatever we decide, I'll stick with it. If we go back to Seattle, I'll try the garage thing again. The farm, well, it was really just a dream, wasn't it?"

I could read nothing in his eyes, but the muted yearning in his voice cut me like a knife. I knew how much he loved it here, how much of himself he put into the farm. For the first time since we got married, I saw my husband smile every morning. I saw him enjoying his work, playing with his kids. Home every night and sometimes during the day—a rarity even during his down times with the business.

"Moving to the farm wasn't so much a dream as a plan," I said carefully.

Dan gave a short laugh. "A plan that isn't turning out too great. Keith is entitled to some money. Not as much as he thought, thanks to the assessment we had done, but some nonetheless. I've used up the line of credit to put the crop in, and he doesn't want to wait. So, we'll have to look at selling something. Of course, if we move back to Seattle, that will have to happen anyway."

My mind flashed back to the auction we had attended. I imagined people digging through stuff from the farm. Bidding on Dan's equipment. His cows. Maybe his horse. I thought of Mrs. Harris in the hospital and how futile her life seemed now that she didn't have the farm. I never realized how connected you could become not only to a home but to the land itself and how it fit in with community and life beyond the farm. I had lived in a large city, but here, my world had expanded far beyond the confines of my own home. People here knew me, my kids, my husband, and cared about our family. For better or worse, they watched out for us.

"We don't need to talk about anything now, Dan." I gently shifted our conversation away from a decision I was unsure of at the moment. But I was thankful for the gift of freedom he had given me. "Right now our focus is Nicholas."

He gave me a careful smile, and then, thankfully, he came and sat beside me and pulled me close. I sank into his embrace, letting his warmth and strength hold me up.

And then, for the first time since Nicholas had been diagnosed, I started to cry.

"Is Mommy sad because of Nicholas?" Anneke's fluty voice slipped over my sorrow, making her presence known.

Dan kept one arm around me and held out his other for our daughter. "A little bit," Dan said as she insinuated herself between us. But Dan slipped her to one side so that he sat between Anneke and me, holding us both. He gently kissed my temple, his breath warm against my hair.

My sniffles subsided. I heard a nurse paging a doctor and I straightened, listening. Thank the Lord, it wasn't Nicholas's doctor.

"We should go," I said quietly.

Dan nodded, kissed me again, and together we got up and walked back to our son's room.

Chapter Eighteen

faint snuffle from the bed pulled me out of the dull sleepiness that dragged at my eyes. Nicholas lay on the bed beside me, the oxygen mask still covering his face. His IV dripped slowly into a tiny body that lay unnaturally still, the only movement the rise and fall of his chest. Two days without change.

On those days when his relentless busyness wore me out, did I think I would ever wish I could be back home vacuuming sugar out of the dog's hair? That I would yearn to be cleaning up food coloring, sponging pen marks off the linoleum, wiping out dirt from the inside of his mouth and hands?

Helplessness clawed at me.

I wasn't used to being a medical bystander. Emergency work was all about doing. Fixing. Immediacy. Results. The day-to-day maintenance and slow recuperation took place out of our sight, here, in the ward.

It was wearying beyond anything I had ever undergone before.

I stretched, trying to push the fatigue out of my body, trying to corral my stampeding thoughts. Silly pictures resonated through my head. Anneke's horrid clothes. The faint musky scent of old clothes from when Dan hugged me. I didn't know if I still had a job after my confrontation with Dr. John. Keith was pressuring Wilma for a settlement. I couldn't fix, plan, or work around the events of the past few weeks.

Beyond that welled a fear of what my house looked like even though I could do nothing about it. Once in a while, when I was alone, it would loom in my mind like a dark cloud, but I couldn't allow it to take over. I had the next hour with Nicholas to think about.

A movement beside me caught my eye and I spun around.

Dan stood at the foot of the bed.

"How is he?"

The deeply familiar voice pulled me toward him. He laid his hands, warm and strong, on my shoulders, his health and vitality pushing away sickness and fear.

He dropped a quick kiss on my cheek, then pulled me tight against him. I clung to him.

Sniffed.

The gown he wore masked but did not eradicate the fresh scent of clean clothes. In spite of his declaration that things were going to change, I knew it would take aliens and a body swap to get Dan to do laundry. And then I smiled, guessing that it was either Wilma or Gloria. Interfering in-laws. Thank goodness.

"Is there any progress?" Dan's voice rumbled under my cheek. I burrowed deeper, resisting the pull back to the lynchpin of our lives.

"Tomorrow they want to do an MRI to see if his brain—" I faltered, took a breath, and tried again. "To see if there's been any brain damage."

Dan held me tighter and I stopped talking. For now I wanted to enjoy the warmth of my husband's body, the strength of someone stronger than me holding me up. Supporting me. The nurses were wonderful. The counselor suitably concerned.

But they didn't care as intensely about the tiny body in the bed behind us as the man holding me did.

We had made this child together. Dan had clipped his umbilical cord. Dan had been the one to hold him beside me and announce his name. Nicholas.

He caught my face in his hands. "And how are you doing?"

I carefully probed my emotions, trying to pull out the ones I could describe. "I'm okay. Tired. Scared." That last word wasn't supposed to have slipped out. I was a nurse. Trained. I knew exactly what was happening with Nicholas's blood counts, his oxygen saturation, his intracranial pressure. Fear wasn't supposed to enter into the equation.

Dan looked surprised. "I didn't think you were scared of anything," he said quietly, touching my cheek. "You would talk about things that happened at work so easily . . ." He let his sentence fade away, and I filled in the blanks.

"I care; it's just that I can't care too much." I stopped, my throat thickening as my gaze cut to Nicholas, a small body with tubes and leads snaking out from him. Oxygen hissing, monitors bleeping, IV slowly metering out exact dosages, catheter draining. All so familiar, but so wrong. "Whenever emotions get engaged, I can't do my job."

"But watching you in the hospital, working on Nicholas— I've never had a chance to see what you do." He touched my cheek lightly. "I never realized how critical your job is. I tended to treat it like my job. Fix and walk away. It's not the same at all." His embarrassed smile showed me the revelation had been more than his guy self would admit.

He pulled me close in another hug. "Anneke is outside," he murmured into my hair.

I nodded, not wanting to say anything, not wanting to dispel this moment.

"Is she allowed to come in?" Dan asked.

Each time Dan and Anneke had come in the past couple of days, we had visited in the family lounge. I didn't want to take any risk of her contracting meningitis as well.

I looked sideways and caught a glimpse of my daughter standing in the hallway, clutching a brand-new teddy bear in one hand, leaning toward me, an expectant look on her face. She was being restrained by Wilma.

Over the past few months, a barrage of emotions and changes had bombarded our family from every direction, bringing us to new and different places.

Now our family's world had narrowed down to this small place. Dan, me, and our children moving carefully through the days, hardly knowing what we could expect. But we were still together. That had to count for something.

And, added to that, a family who was working in the background. Supporting. Helping where they could. I knew that Wilma or Gloria or Judy was feeding Dan. Taking care of Anneke. Probably cleaning the Day-Glo floor, as well. We didn't do this alone, and the thought gave me comfort I had never felt before.

"Mommy, where's Nicholas?"

Anneke's plaintive voice was my undoing. What could it hurt? She'd already been exposed to him. Already been dosed with antibiotics and sterilized and checked over until I was sure the only thing wrong with her was probably ear-wax buildup.

"She'll have to gown up," I said, pulling away from my momentary haven. "And when she leaves she'll have to wash her hands. She can't touch him, only look at him."

"That's all she wants," Dan whispered. He motioned to Wilma, who drew Anneke away to gown her up. It was then I noticed Anneke's corduroy jumper, the clean ruffled shirt, and the smooth braids in her hair. She looked like my little girl, not a waif, and one of the tight coils inside of me loosened. Wilma was taking care of her, keeping her looking the same as I had.

I walked to the doorway and motioned to Wilma. "You have to gown up, too," I said.

She looked from me to Anneke, then gave a brisk nod. I knew this wasn't going to be a Hallmark moment. Wilma was still Wilma.

But she had prayed for my son and was probably still praying for my son. He wasn't just mine and Dan's. Nicholas belonged to a larger group. Family. Community. It might not take a village to raise a child, but it sure helped.

As Wilma and my daughter entered the room, Anneke ran to me smiling, her arms held out. "Mommy, I miss you," she said as she clutched me around my neck.

She planted a wet kiss on my cheek, then grinned at me, then Nicholas, her world complete. *How bare-bones children's lives can be.* All she needed was her mom and dad and little brother and her contentment quotient was filled.

"Why does Nicholas have wires on him?" she asked in a matter-of-fact voice.

"You remember what Daddy told you," Dan said. "Nicholas is sick, and the doctors need to do all these things to him to make him better."

Her gaze ticked over each item and she nodded as if granting her approval. "Can I give Nicholas his teddy bear?"

"Sure you can, honey," I said. We kept our voices quiet. Anneke didn't know how tenuous our grip on normal was. We were all together, and that was enough for her. I glanced at Wilma in time to see her press her lips together tightly. Holding back even as she adjusted the mask on Nicholas's face and rearranged his sheets. I wanted to tell her it was okay to cry, but thought I would be overstepping a boundary that had shifted but still lay between us.

Anneke bent over and kissed Nicholas, her mask touching his cheek. Then she looked at him, as if waiting for a reaction from her little brother. When none came, she wriggled loose out of Dan's arms. "I want to go to the playroom."

Already? She had just gotten here. "Don't you want to sit

with me for a little while?" I asked Anneke. I wanted to hold my healthy child and smell her and feel her wiggling on my lap—life and vitality and everything that I wanted Nicholas to be again.

"I want to see the toys," she said, her lip starting to droop in a pout.

"I'll take her," Wilma said.

"I can go." I looked back at Nicholas, momentarily torn.

Noise and a sudden movement in the hallway caught my attention. Judy stood in the doorway, Allison, Tabitha, and a couple of Gloria's boys behind her.

"Hi there. I know we can't all come in, but the kids wanted to see Nicholas." Judy caught sight of her mom and her glance flicked from Wilma to me, her eyebrows lifted in a question. I nodded as I hurried to the door.

Judy hugged me and murmured her sympathy. I felt a gentle connection, an opportunity to release my tension to someone else. She stroked my face, then smiled at me, her hands still holding my shoulders.

"I'm glad you asked us to come," she said. "We all wanted to come and see him, but we didn't want you to feel over-whelmed. Goodness knows, we've done enough of that to you since you came here."

"Thanks," was all I could say through a throat thickening with grateful tears.

"You're okay with Mom being here?" she asked. "She's not rearranging Nicholas's bed or bossing the nurses around?"

"It's okay, Judy. She's his grandma . . . Oma, and . . . she does care."

"A lot."

My happy gaze touched on the kids gathered behind her looking solemn and concerned. So many of them here? It was a Friday night in a city a long ways from Harland, and they had foregone giddy teenage plans to see our son. *Their cousin,* I reminded myself.

"How is he?" Tabitha asked, giving me a shy, self-conscious smile.

"Thanks for asking, Tabitha." I returned her smile and touched her arm to reassure her that I still loved her. "He's had a couple of rough days. We're taking things one day at a time." I stopped there. I wanted so badly to assure them that everything was going to be fine, but the lack of progress had milked dry my own optimism. I knew the guarded looks the doctors exchanged with the nurses. I had read the charts. I knew the odds.

Douglas, one of Gloria's sons, flashed me a shy smile. "I'm sorry about Nicholas, Auntie Leslie. We've been praying for him."

"I got a card," Tabitha said, handing me an envelope. "I know it's kind of lame. Mom and Dad told me to tell you they want to come tomorrow, if that's okay."

"The kids really wanted to come tonight," Judy said. "The rest of the family would like to come, too, but we wanted to stagger it out. Kathy and Jimmy want to come. We had to tell other members of the congregation that, for now, it was family only."

The list of names, the group of faces looking at me with concern, slowly loosened another coil inside of me.

Dan and I weren't alone.

"Shotgun on going first," Allison said with authority, grabbing a gown from the cart beside the door. The kids argued over who would go next as Douglas stationed himself by the cart with the sterile gowns and started tossing them out. I saw one of the nurses at the desk lean over, her frown shooting disapproval down the hallway. But I didn't want to dampen the ebullient spirits. Their actions gently pulled me back to normal. To ordinary.

Judy tugged on my arm, then turned me around and untied the ribbons of my gown. "C'mon. You look like you could use a cup of tea."

"Anneke wants to go to the playroom," I said, torn between talking to an adult from the outside world and taking care of my other child's needs.

"I'll take her," Tabitha said, reaching out for her. "I can see Nicholas later."

I relinquished Anneke's damp, sticky hand with some reluctance as Judy took my arm and ushered me down the hallway toward the stairs.

A few moments later my hands cradled a paper cup filled with warm tea. We sat by a window. Still daylight. In Nicholas's room, time melted and turned into the shape of hands on a clock, the movement and routine of doctors' rounds and shift changes.

Through a space in the buildings I could see the solid peaks of the mountains. *He covers the sky with clouds, He supplies the earth with rain.*

My attention shifted gently from hospital and illness as

I turned back to Judy. "How are things going for you?" I asked.

"Fine. But I'm not here to talk about me." She reached across the table and laid her hand on my arm. "I want you to know that we're praying for Nicholas," she said. "I know that might not mean much to you . . ." She let the sentence hang, and I wanted to tell her that it meant more than she could know. But I was new at this God thing and at this family thing and wasn't sure of the proper protocol when people said they were praying for you. So I muttered a quick thanks and spun my plastic stir stick in my tea.

"So, what have the doctors been saying?"

"They're doing the vague doctor-speak. With meningitis, time can move things in either direction, good or bad." I sighed, gave Judy a tired smile, hoping she understood. "Can we talk about ordinary things right now? My life has been doctors and nurses and hospitals for so long, and I want to know there's a life beyond that right now."

Judy's eyes widened for a split second, then she recovered. Smiled. Nodded.

"Sure. You probably talk enough about Nicholas." But then she was quiet, putting the onus on me to come up with a topic.

I gave my tea another stir, trying to find the ordinary. "I'm guessing I can thank either Wilma or you for keeping things moving smoothly on the home front."

"Mostly you can thank Mom or Gloria. Gloria's also been watering the garden and flower beds for you."

My lilies were going to survive. My house wasn't going to rot away.

Judy leaned forward. "Look, I know Dan asked us to back off, but you know Mom and Gloria. They can't stay away. As for Gloria, she's not the easiest person to get to know, and I know that sometimes she wears her halo a little tight, but she has a good heart. It comes out a little differently with her than it does with most."

I thought of how, only a few moments ago, I felt I could relax when I saw Anneke's hair all shiny and neat. My out-of-control life was gaining control again, and Gloria and Wilma were giving that to me.

"I know she hasn't always been open to you," Judy continued, "but she wants to try. She just isn't sure how to start."

"There are a lot of qualifiers in that sentence," I said, picking up my cup of tea. I wasn't ready to relinquish the frustration I had nurtured the past few months—no, the past few *years*.

"I know. Gloria is one of those capable people who set your teeth on edge but at the same time you want in your corner in a rough spot. She's trying too hard to be like Mom. I keep telling her it's not going to work. Mom isn't one you can easily please."

Judy was talking this way about her mother? To me, the Imperfect Heathen?

"You look surprised." Judy laughed. "I know what my mom is like. And she's gotten worse since Dad died. He could always tease her out of her little control fits—get her to relax. Keith . . ." Judy sighed. "Not such a good match.

She's gotten more involved and nosy and controlling. She really needs to be put in her place from time to time."

"I've tried."

Judy gave me a quick stroke with her hand. "I know you have. And that's why there's been tension between you and her. She's not used to someone being so blatant about it."

"So, I should learn diplomacy, is what you're saying?" I countered with a quick smile to show her that in spite of what I was dealing with I hadn't completely lost my sense of irony.

Judy wrinkled her nose. "No. I think you should keep on doing what you're doing. It's good for her."

I almost choked on my tea.

"Seriously," Judy continued. "Mom's always had a hard time with boundaries. I'm sure that's why Keith bailed on her. She likes to be in charge and in control. Of everything. She had Dan's life all planned, down to the girl he was supposed to marry." Judy took a quick sip of her tea and waved her hand as if waving off my curiosity. "The girl doesn't live here anymore, so no worries. But Mom is coming around in her own stubbornly slow way. It helps that you come to church once in a while now. I know why you come, and that's good, but I also hope someday it will mean something to you."

I thought of the church services I had attended and the Coffee Break program Kathy had told me about. An entire world that I was learning to navigate without too many missteps.

I liked control, too.

"I think it's starting to happen," was all I could say. I

swirled the leftovers of my tea around the bottom of the cup. "There's a lot to learn, and I've never had any background in faith. Or God." And I wasn't used to living my life with a cloud of witnesses. I didn't want to examine my deeper feelings right now. I didn't want to think that I had maybe, perhaps, made any kind of commitment.

I could do qualifiers, too.

But even so, I knew that my initial hesitation to stay here was slowly wearing away, and I was willing to give our stay a bit more time. See where life took us in the next half year or more. And if I ran out of chocolates before we ran out of time? Big deal.

Judy lifted her shoulder in a careful shrug as if she didn't dare push too hard, either.

"It's a lot to put together." Judy brushed her cup aside. Folded her arms on the table in front of her. "But don't let people make it more complicated than it is. God loves you. He's perfect. We aren't. Jesus came to be the perfect bridge between us and God. Believe that, and you're on your way."

"He loves me, too; He loves me, too. . . ." the simple words of the children's song came back to me. Not so complicated after all.

"And that's your theology lesson for now," Judy said with a quick laugh. "I also need to tell you that Gloria was pretty impressed when she saw you with Tabitha, and working on Mrs. Harris. The woman who came in with a heart attack. Gloria knew she wasn't supposed to be watching, but she was amazed at how important your job is."

I felt a flush of pride. "I'm surprised she told you."

"About what?"

"Tabitha."

Judy laughed. "I was, too. But hey, I'm not going to say too much. Could easily be my Allison in a few years. Or less. Gloria really appreciated the fact that you didn't say anything to anyone about it. Dan didn't even know. Harland isn't a big town, and it only takes a spark to get the fire of gossip going." Judy gave me a quick pat on the hand. "Nice to know that if I come in roaring drunk it won't get put in the *Harland Chronicle*."

"Should I be worried?"

"Not yet. Depends on how the next year goes. We've got a major payment coming up, and the government keeps making noises about cutting back our water rights. So it's fight, fight, fight every step of the way."

"But you wouldn't change?" I asked, testing her commitment.

Judy laughed. "Not on your life. It's not just a job—farming is a way of life. I like it that Dayton and I are involved in each other's lives. That even though we fight when we do books, we always know where we're at."

Relief flowed through me. "I thought Dan and I were the only ones who squabbled over debits and credits."

"Are you kidding?" Judy looked incredulous. "Dayton and I usually have one major blowout at tax time and a few minor ones along the way. Nothing shock-and-aweish, but close."

"From the looks of things, Dan and I are going to have a few more of these squabbles on our hands. What with Keith demanding money."

Judy held up her hands. "Honey, you have enough on your plate—you don't even need to be sampling that witch's brew." She shrugged. "Besides, I don't blame you if you decide to bail." She held my eyes, her expression suddenly serious. "I mean that, Leslie. Don't feel like you need to hang on longer than you should. I don't blame you if you want to go back to Seattle and a regular paycheck and get away from us hicks. We can sell the farm and the animals, and Mom will be able to manage. But don't feel like you are responsible for us."

I was surprised at the mixture of feelings her comments created. Thankful that I had her blessing to leave. Hurt that she thought I would so easily walk away. Disappointed that she didn't think I could manage.

"I don't mind being on the farm," I said carefully. "And I don't think you're hicks."

Judy pulled a face. "Why not? I do."

I was about to say something more, when the sound of hurried footsteps, someone calling my name, sent my heart into overdrive. I pushed away from the table.

Dan appeared in the doorway of the cafeteria, saw me, and called out my name again. "It's Nicholas."

My heart plunged, again. *Get up. Get going.*

My hands wouldn't do what my brain told it. I tried to get up, and my knees gave way.

Then Judy's arms were around me, holding me up.

"I've got you," she said. "Let's go."

Chapter Nineteen

machine was breathing for my son. A sudden and unexpected seizure had plunged him further down. The doctor mumbled something about a stroke. I pretended not to hear.

The rash on his legs and arms was still there, cruel patches of ugliness on my son's pale white skin. The disease fought a winning battle in my son's small body, gaining ground inch by precious inch.

Dan stood beside me, watching the lifting and caving in of Nicholas's chest.

"I thought we'd see progress," I murmured. "I thought we were moving ahead."

Dan slipped his arm around me, and once again I turned to him, resting against him.

"We have to keep praying," he said quietly.

"I've been trying," I whispered. "I don't even know how to do it except to say please, please, please."

Dan laid his chin on my head. "If you look at most

prayers, that is essentially what they boil down to. That and thank You, thank You, thank You."

I touched Nicholas's face again, trying not to look at the endotracheal tube protruding out of our son's mouth like an obscenity.

"I'm hoping we can get to the thank You, thank You part," I whispered.

Dan's arm tightened. "Me, too." His voice broke. The sound cut the ground out from under me. Dan was never weak. He was the one I depended on. He was my strength.

He brushed a kiss over my forehead. "I have a little bit of a thank You. I got a letter from our lawyer in Seattle yesterday. Lonnie Dansworth settled with his creditors to avoid bankruptcy. We didn't get what he owed, but we got about twenty-five cents on the dollar. My lawyer suggested we take it."

I nodded, acknowledging his comment. Lonnie and the money was a part of another world that didn't concern me right now. At one time I would have been ecstatic, or depressed, depending on my expectations. But now? Nice to know, but unimportant.

We moved closer to the bed, and I caught my foot on a bag of books lying on the floor.

"I brought those. Just in case you might want to read." He gave me a weak smile, his arm still around my shoulder. I bent over and picked up the bag, then sat on the chair beside Nicholas's bed to look through it.

I pulled the first book, turned it over, and frowned when I saw the faded title.

"The Bible?" I asked, surprised that he would put that in.

"It gives me comfort," he said. "Gloria asked me to give it to you. It used to be hers."

I saw the sticky notes bristling out of one side of the book. Just like Dan's. Was this a VandeKeere thing?

Curious now, I turned to one. Psalm 139. I started reading aloud.

" 'O Lord, you have searched me and you know me. You know when I sit and when I rise; you perceive my thoughts from afar.' " I couldn't help but toss a nervous glance upward. I didn't think God bothered with perceiving thoughts. What kind of thoughts had He listened in on? I didn't want to contemplate that too much, so I read on. Then stopped and reread the words: " 'If I rise on the wings of the dawn, if I settle on the far side of the sea, even there your hand will guide me, your right hand will hold me fast.' " I lowered the Bible and drew in a long, shaky breath, glancing at Dan. The words touched emotions still tender and raw. For the past few days, fear had been breathing down my neck, hot, hard, and relentless. In the quiet of the early morning, I stood vigil over my son's bed, cocooned by a darkness broken only by the digital readout of the monitors. Utterly and indescribably alone. Clinging to trembling hope.

"So, the Bible is telling me that no matter where I go, God's hand is there?"

Dan tucked a strand of hair behind my ear in a curiously tender gesture. "That's what the Bible is saying. It's real, Leslie. It really is. I feel like I'm being upheld by the prayers of my family. Like God is nearer to me now than He ever has been." He stopped then and gave me a crooked smile. The self-conscious one he throws out when he feels like what he has said or done has trespassed some sacred guy-code.

I returned his smile but said nothing, giving him the space I knew he needed after such an intimate revelation. I read on.

" 'Even the darkness will not be dark to you; the night will shine like the day. . . . I praise you because I am fearfully and wonderfully made. . . . All the days ordained for me were written in your book before one of them came to be. . . .' " Again my eyes slipped to Nicholas. "So, how many days has God ordained for Nicholas?" I whispered as my gaze slipped over the array of equipment that kept my son with us. Such a complex organism, the human body, yet so fragile.

Fear gripped me then. "Would God take this little boy from me because of things I've thought? Because I haven't paid attention to Him? I've been a bad mother. I've yelled at him. Spanked him. Does God care enough to let us keep him?" Was this punishment for my foolish dalliance with Dr. John?

"Leslie, you don't have to fear God." He took the Bible from me, skimmed a moment, then read, " 'Search me, O God, and know my heart; test me and know my anxious thoughts. See if there is any offensive way in me, and lead me in the way everlasting.' " As Dan read those last words again, I slipped my hand over Nicholas's tiny one. It fluttered beneath my touch. A faint connection.

Dan's quiet voice washed over me as he flipped through the Bible and stopped, then read another psalm. This one was full of praise to a God who took care of nature. Who supplied the earth with rain and made grass grow. As Dan read, I looked off into the distance, thinking of the rain and the cows we had put out to pasture and the crop Dan put into the ground. God cared about that, too? I let the words settle, like the rain the psalm spoke of, into a parched portion of my life that I never knew needed moisture. Until now. This moment when I felt completely helpless and unsure of what to do. When I felt like I had reached the bottom of a place I could no longer find my way out of. I knew how this could end. I had stood at the bedside of enough children, some babies, fighting for lives that slowly slipped out of our hands. Who was I to think that I deserved to have my son's life given back to us?

Tears gathered in the back of my throat as I put my hand on Dan's. "I want to pray," I said. "Though I don't know how."

"I'm not an expert, either, but I think all we have to do is talk," he said. "And I think we're getting better at that."

I smiled back at him, grasped his hand, and let Dan go ahead. He simply asked for healing for Nicholas. For peace for us. For guidance.

Mine was simpler yet. *Please, Lord. Please.* And as I prayed, it was as if my hands, clinging so tightly to our little boy, trying to maintain control, were slowly releasing. Letting go.

He was God's child first. Mine second.

A moment of anxiety gripped me, and I clung tighter to Dan's hand, then released. "Please, Lord. Let Your will be done."

And slowly, slowly I released control. Gave our child over to God.

I knew I shouldn't expect miracles, but when I woke up the next morning, for the first time since this disaster dropped into my lap, I felt surging hope.

Nicholas still lay flat on his back, arms and legs splayed out, IV tubes still hooked up to him. The hiss and sigh of the respirator breathing for him.

When the doctor came on his rounds, I kept my eyes on his face, waiting for the surprise to come. But he only shook his head and patted me on the shoulder. Nicholas wasn't going down, was all he would tell me.

It was disheartening, to say the least. My major epiphany had resulted in a stall. Yet, in spite of the lack of miraculous results, as I stood by Nicholas's bed, the peace I had felt last night stayed with me. I didn't want to test it too hard, but when I helped the nurses give him a gentle sponge bath, I didn't cringe when I saw the sores on Nicholas's skin. I didn't cry when his head lolled like a doll's to one side when we moved him. I could feel God standing beside me, whispering in my ear that He knew what I was going through.

Of course. His Son had suffered as well.

I read the Bible some more. Skipped Lamentations. The title was a giveaway. I wanted direction and comfort.

I tried to find the piece Dan had read. Couldn't remember exactly where it came from, so I flipped to the back of the book, looked up *love* in the concordance of the Bible and had a *Whoa* moment. Column after column of Bible verses all referencing the word *love*. I didn't know there were so many. So, I started skimming the columns. "According to your unfailing love . . . Slow to anger, abounding in love . . . This is my Son, whom I love. . . ."

I glanced at Nicholas. I understood that part.

I continued. "Love your enemies. . . . This is my commandment: love each other. . . . Love one another. . . . Love one another."

I got the hint—love was obviously an important concept.

I finally found Dan's passage listed. I turned to it, wishing they'd given the page number instead of just the book of the Bible and the verse, but eventually I found it. I started reading, the words filling a yearning in me that had always lain there, restless and unnamed. Until now.

"Love is patient, love is kind. It does not envy, it does not boast, it is not proud. It is not rude, it is not self-seeking. . . ." I stopped there, keeping my finger on the words.

Self-seeking.

I sighed as I looked at Nicholas. I wanted him healthy for myself. For my happiness to be complete.

I wanted a lot of things for myself. My dream home. My family all to myself where I could control them.

Much control I have now, I thought as the respirator expelled Nicholas's air, then gave him another breath. And much control I would have once we left Harland.

But as that thought formulated, another one crept alongside on padded feet.

Stay.

I closed my eyes and gave in to the familiar, teasing thought. It had visited me before, I allowed it more time now. Let it play around in my mind for a while. I imagined us on the farm. Our kids growing up in Harland.

A bubble of claustrophobic panic burst in me, then dissipated, because with Harland came Kathy, who took such good care of my kids. Judy, who made me laugh. Gloria, who made me . . . well, take another look at myself. And Wilma. A mother who loved my husband and loved my kids. A mother who, unlike my own mother, was at least involved. Cared. Did something to help.

Family. Support.

Letting go.

I remembered what Kathy said about farming and control. Could I allow our family to be held hostage to the vagaries of weather and markets and tariffs and import agreements and countervailing duties? Things so far beyond our control you couldn't even face them down and demand accountability?

And yet . . . and yet . . .

I laid my head back against the chair, closed my eyes, and let a small prayer rise up in me. I knew I needed some direction. And as I prayed, I thought of Dan.

And I knew what I had to do.

Chapter Twenty

he next few days were a slow grind of doctor visits, nurses' maintenance, and family stopping by. Lots of family stopping by. Wilma came almost every day, and though there were times I wished she didn't, I had come to appreciate the long drive she made just to see Nicholas and me. Kathy came, as did a few of the women from church whom I barely knew. Judy and I had a chance to spend more time together.

Gloria came. There was an initial moment of awkwardness, but she kept things cool. I knew we wouldn't be swapping recipes anytime soon, but something important had shifted between us.

With each visit I felt as if Dan and I were being carried along, supported when we could do nothing more for our son ourselves. I looked forward to each visit, each opportunity to talk to a friendly face. To make another connection with people who cared.

And to rethink our decision to leave after a year. We

didn't need to be so hasty. We had nothing waiting for us in Seattle per se. We could take our time. Get to know the family a bit better.

I didn't mention my idea of putting our plans on temporary hold to Dan. I didn't dare put it into words yet.

Then, improbably, came the day when Nicholas turned a corner. When the rash started subsiding, leaving only angry red marks, an external reminder of the battle he had fought and won. When the last MRI showed no abnormalities, when he sat up in bed and pulled out his catheter and ripped off his oxygen mask, we knew we were on our way out of the dark pain we had been trudging through for the past ten days.

It was a miracle, plain and simple. Undeserved. Grace granted to graceless people.

As Dan drove the car up the driveway to the house many long, tiring days later, I glanced down at Nicholas on the seat behind us. He had been quiet all the way home from Helena, but as Dan parked the car, he gave me a loopy grin. Did our little boy know we were home?

I unbuckled my seat belt and felt the hard knot inside me loosen and open up. For some inexplicable reason I couldn't relax until I saw Sasha running toward us and heard the welcome whinny of the horses as we drove along the fence of the pasture. Normal had returned to our home and family.

Dan turned the key in the ignition and released a belly-deep sigh.

"We're home," he said, brushing a callused finger over my cheek.

I caught his face in my hands, his shaven cheeks smooth beneath my fingers. His face so familiar. So dear. Then I gave him a noisy kiss.

"I like home."

I pulled down the visor to check my face and flipped it quickly up again. Time may be a great healer but it was a lousy beautician. No sense in looking in a mirror until I got my hair cut again and had access to my own makeup.

I got out of the car, taking stock. The yard looked better than I did. Lawn neatly mowed. Flower beds weeded and tidy. Pots of geraniums, a new note of cheerfulness hung from the porch.

Home.

Stillness encircled my heart and settled there.

As I gently lifted Nicholas out of the car seat, I held him close to me, curling his warm head under mine. The fresh scent of his clothes couldn't mask the smell of hospital that still clung to him.

He shifted away from me, a hint of the old Nicholas, then drooped against me, as if that small rebellion was all he could manage for now.

We had our little boy back.

Before Nicholas's illness, that whole Valley-of-the-Shadow-of-Death concept sounded melodramatic. Today, with the sun pouring down bright promises, it became real. Spending time in the shadows gave me a vivid appreciation of light and grace.

I knew the situation could have turned out so differently.

Dan set Anneke down and looked over at me. "Here we are." I saw his gaze flit past me to the hills as the wind flowed over the growing grain. The smile on his face lifted my heart.

"They're here!" Judy's voice called out from the house.

She rushed down the same crooked walk Wilma had so sedately come down when we first came here. Gloria was right behind her.

"Welcome home." Judy gave me a quick hug, stroked Nicholas's head. Gloria hugged Dan and turned to me. A moment of awkwardness hung between us. I didn't know if we had reached the hugging stage in our détente, and if we had, whether I should make the first move.

She solved that for me by slipping one arm around my shoulder and pressing her cheek against mine. "So glad to see you all back," she said softly. She stroked Nicholas's head. He blinked at her and snuggled in a bit closer.

My boy.

I caught Gloria's arm. "Thanks so much for taking care of the house while I was gone. I was so thankful to know that things were under control here."

"I know how I would feel if I were in your position and my family looked the way they did." She gave me a quick smile. "Dan stopped by on his way home from the hospital, and I felt so bad that you had to see him and Anneke looking like refugees."

Surprise welled up in me. *I'm more like her than I thought.*

"I really appreciated it. Knowing that the house was well

taken care of made things easier for me." I looked around then. "Where's Wilma?"

"Mom's inside," Gloria said, giving me an awkward pat on my shoulder. "She's taking care of dinner."

Gerrit and Dayton joined us, followed by a crowd of kids and noise. The dogs barked, and a delightful chaos reigned as Dan, Anneke, Nicholas, and I were greeted, patted, slapped on the back, and in general drawn back into normalcy.

As I entered the house, the smell of roasting turkey teased my nose with the promise of the comfort of a home-cooked meal.

Wilma was bent over a roasting pan, basting a golden brown turkey. She looked up, her face flushed from the heat of the oven, but her makeup impeccable, her hair stylishly cut. Her eyes held mine a moment longer than usual. She gave me a quick smile, then her gaze moved to Nicholas in my arms and her features melted.

She put her oven mittens down and walked over, holding out her hands for my son.

"Here, let me take him."

I felt my arms involuntarily tighten around Nicholas. I hadn't had nearly enough cuddling time.

But my resolve to learn to let go returned, and I loosened my hold on him, moving him toward Wilma.

He frowned and puckered his mouth, pulling back toward me with a whimper.

Oh, how my heart beat high with joy.

This won't last, I reminded myself as I gave Wilma a regretful smile. "He's waking up," I said. "Not himself yet."

"Of course." She pressed her lips together, then eased out a dubious smile. "I'm glad he's better and I'm glad you're home again. Or, well, back at the house." Her small amendment caught me by surprise. It was as if she finally acknowledged the temporary nature of our stay.

"It's nice to be home."

Wilma gave me a curt nod, then turned to Dan and Anneke. They hugged each other and Wilma cooed over Anneke and lovingly stroked Dan's cheek.

As I watched mother and son together I thought of all she had lost. Thought of my own relationship to Nicholas and how fiercely I wanted him to be mine. All mine.

I didn't agree with her methods, but I felt a connection.

Dan pulled away and came to my side, slipped his arm around me, and gave me a gentle kiss. "I love you," he said quietly, laying his forehead against mine.

"I love you, too," I breathed, the words settling into my heart.

Judy urged me to sit down while the kids set the table and she and Wilma moved with purpose and calm through my kitchen finishing supper, delegating tasks—all done with the carelessness of experts.

Half an hour later we squeezed ourselves around the table, Dan at the head, me at his side. Nicholas still clung to me. I still savored his neediness.

As we all settled in, Dan looked from me to our kids to his family gathered around the table. "This is wonderful," he said. Then laughed lightly. "I'm not a speech maker, so, thanks for coming. For being a support." He paused and cleared his throat. "But I mostly want to thank our Lord for letting us keep Nicholas a while longer." He looked at me. "We don't know how long anything lasts, but I know Leslie and I have learned to appreciate each day we have together."

Of course, my throat choked up, and of course, all I could do at that touching moment was give him a silly smile and then look around at our family, blinking furiously.

But when Dan started praying, I let the tears flow. Happy tears. Thankful tears.

When he was done, people got caught up in the serious business of taking food out of bowls then passing them around. Conversation ebbed and flowed, punctuated by the clink of cutlery on china and I savored the belonging. I still didn't recognize all the names, and many of the stories were unfamiliar, but this time I didn't mind. In time I would "get" them.

"Judy, did you make trifle for dessert?" Dan asked, leaning back from the table after lingering over second helpings of his favorites.

Judy clapped her hand over her mouth, her eyes two horrified circles above her fingers. "I forgot. It's on the table at home and everything." She rolled her eyes. "Oh, well, you know what they say, brain cells come and go, fat cells stick around."

"Oh, no . . . Aunt Judy . . . I love your trifle . . . What about dessert . . ."

Dan sighed. "What's a good turkey dinner without the promise of chocolate afterward?"

"I could go home . . ."

"Don't bother, Judy," I said, "that's too far," though part of me hoped she would pooh-pooh the comment and get up anyway. But she shrugged and stayed where she was.

A thought slipped into my turkey-tired brain. I weighed it, measured it, then thought, well, why not.

"I'll be right back," I said to Dan. I ran upstairs and ducked into our cupboard, then came back downstairs carrying my once precious cargo.

"If anyone's interested, I have a box of Lindor chocolates. I believe there's about two hundred and fifty here. More than enough for seconds and thirds."

I could see Dan doing some quick calculations. He knew exactly how many I had bought and how many I should still have.

"What can I say?" I quipped, flashing him a smile. "Anything worth doing is worth overdoing."

But while I was trying to be smart, the teenagers whipped the box out of my hand and in seconds were inhaling the chocolates like they were air. Minutes later the box returned to me, half full, or half empty, depending on your point of view. It was like watching six months flash before my eyes.

Dan dug in the box and came up with a handful of chocolates as well. "Thursday, Friday, Saturday . . ." he intoned as he laid them out beside his plate.

"What are you talking about?" Judy's puzzled glance went from Dan to me.

"Tell you some other time," I said, digging out a handful myself. I could always buy more if I needed to.

If.

After checking Nicholas for the seventeenth time, I finally settled into bed.

"Are you done now?" Dan asked with a playful grin as I scootched into his arms and wriggled a moment, trying to get the pillow just right.

"For now." I pulled in a long breath and looked up at the ceiling, my eyes flickering over the water spots, barely discernible in the half light of the bedside lamp. I didn't think I would come to a place in my life where I would be happy to see their familiar shape. "Today was a good day."

"Today was a good day," he agreed.

"I like your family," I said.

"I do, too."

"In fact, I love your family. Judy is funny, Gerrit is kind, and Dayton is one of those solid people you can count on. The kids are nice. When Gloria has her guard down, she's a good person." My exuberance drifted off. What to say about Wilma? Would he notice that I left her off my little mutual-admiration-society list?

"It's going to be hard to leave," he said quietly.

I drew in a long, slow breath. "We don't need to talk about that yet." In the dimmed light coming in from the hallway, I saw a half-smile curve his lips.

"No. But we're going to have to face reality sooner or later."

"We've had our share of reality," I said, giving him a kiss. I slipped my arms around him and held him close, thankful for him, thankful for where we were now in our marriage. My love for him had been weighed and tested, and with the help of family and community it had held. "Let's live out some fantasies for tonight," I whispered.

"We could eat some more chocolate," he said suggestively.

"We'll save that for another fantasy," I giggled. Then kissed him again. And again.

Chapter Twenty-one

ou'll be drowning in zucchini come fall." Kathy yanked out another weed and threw it on the pile at the end of the row, then crouched back on her heels. "You'll be able to single-handedly supply the county with the stuff."

"I planted zucchini?" I asked, as I zeroed in on a plant. It rose above the rest, drawing attention to itself. Plus it stank. I guessed it was a weed and pulled it out. "One of the sisters must have put it in. I hate that stuff."

"Embrace the proliferation, honey. Whoever planted it put in a whack. And my goodness, could you have planted any more pumpkins?"

I looked up at my friend crouched in my garden a few rows down from me, her hair leaping up in glorious disarray. "I thought it would be fun to have some jack-o'-lanterns at Halloween."

"You have some scary idea of fun. Well, I'm done," Kathy said, getting to her feet and brushing the dirt off her pants. She walked over to Nicholas, who sat quietly in the bench on the side of the garden. "Hey, buddy, how are you doing?"

He lifted his hands to her, and she easily swung him up in her arms. He looked pale, but each day brought some new improvement. Some small triumph.

"He's going to be all right, isn't he?" The worried note in Kathy's voice resonated with the niggle of concern that lay tucked in a dark corner of my mind.

"The doctors gave him a clean bill of health." I dug out my last weed and looked over the garden, pushing my damp hair back from my forehead. All tidy until the next onslaught. I felt a rush of well-being that had everything to do with Nicholas watching us, Kathy helping me, and my garden's neat tidy rows growing and producing. Another miracle. "It's the only decent bill we have in our house these days."

"Tell me about it. We always have more month than money at our place. But we struggle on."

Kathy said this with a sigh of resignation, but at the same time I knew, as Judy had also said, that she wouldn't trade her life for anything. I looked over the yard again and smiled. Each time I left and came back, it was as if tiny tentacles caught and anchored me here. It wasn't paradise, but hey, what is? And even though it wasn't paradise, it still had its snake. Keith had phoned this morning demanding his money. When Dan had hung up the phone, he told me he had to go to town this afternoon to ask the lawyer what the reality was and what our final options were. I said I would come with him, for moral support. But all morning the meeting with the lawyer hung over me like a dark cloud. Questions and possibilities flew through my head like errant Ping-Pong balls. Finally I couldn't sit still, couldn't concentrate, so I took the kids outside and sought refuge in weeding the garden.

Kathy, who had come to babysit, found me crouched between the peas and the potatoes and pitched in. Nothing like pulling weeds to cement a friendship.

I glanced over my shoulder at the house, thinking of all that had happened since I reluctantly moved here. Thinking of what could happen if we stayed.

"If you were to paint this house, what colors would you use?" I asked Kathy, pushing my hair back from my face.

Kathy's eyebrows lifted only a fraction but she gamely played along. "It's a great style. You'll have to work with the shingles." She stopped, tapping her finger on her chin. While she contemplated my house, I heard Carlene's shriek and Anneke's laugh. Familiar sounds, softened by the open spaces around us.

Home.

"I'd go with a dark taupe-y beige, sage shutters, and dark grape trim," Kathy said, glancing over my shoulder as if to check my reaction. "Would up the resale value."

I ignored her last comment as I imagined the changes. "I'm liking that."

Anneke's shrieks grew louder, and in seconds we were surrounded by three children demanding something to drink. Something to eat. So, to the house we went.

"Wow, look at all the chocolates," Kathy said, zeroing in on the bowl on the dining-room table. "You win some kind of prize or something?" She unwrapped one and popped it into her mouth, sighing in bliss. "I love these. My favorite waste of time."

I poured iced tea for the kids, handed out useless stern warnings about spilling, and put the kettle on the stove. "Just call it an experiment that had its day." I glanced out the window just as Dan drove up the driveway. My heart kicked in my throat. "Hey, Kathy, I've got to go change. Dan is here."

"You go make yourself gorgeous. I'll just make a dent in these chocolates." She unwrapped one for Nicholas. "Here, buddy, this'll put some hair on your chest."

She nuzzled him, he laughed, and I felt pure joy pierce me at the sound. No matter what lay ahead of us, Dan and I had our precious son and daughter. We had family and friends.

I took a moment to kiss Nicholas and brush my hand over his head, then ran upstairs.

I showered in record time, brushed my hair, checked my lipstick, and pulled a face at my hair. Still needed a cut, still hadn't had time. I pulled out the scissors and trimmed my bangs so I wouldn't look like a badger had taken residence on my head, double-checked the makeup, and retreated ungracefully from the field of battle.

Dan had changed and was helping Kathy put a dent in my chocolate stash by the time I came back downstairs. He gave me a tired smile as I joined them. I gave him a hug. Me. Supportive wife.

"Are you ready?" He brushed some loose hair from my face and dropped a kiss on my forehead.

"I suppose." I touched him again, reconnecting, rebuilding one small step at a time.

"Then let's go," he said, pushing himself away from the table.

I kissed the kids, waved to Kathy, and as we walked down

the sidewalk, petted Sasha's head. The chickens were scratching in the yard, softly clucking to each other, and the horses, sensing our presence, started whinnying.

Our farm, I thought as I got into the car with Dan. *Our place.*

As we reversed out of the parking spot and headed down the driveway, I turned back toward the house again, imagining the colors Kathy had suggested. They would make the house look cheery. Welcoming.

Dan gave me a nervous smile and reached over and squeezed my hand. "How are you doing?" he asked. "Ready to face a new adventure?" Since we had come back from the hospital, Dan had made noises about making plans for our future, but I kept putting him off. I'd had enough adventure, I kept telling him. We could wait. But now, Keith's last and final phone call had brought us to a turning point. We had to make a decision, and my heart and mind had come to a place where they finally agreed.

"How much is Keith entitled to?" I asked. Dan and Wilma had avoided discussing Keith or the farm while Nicholas was in the hospital. It seemed unimportant at the time. I was thankful, but it meant that I knew very few actual facts and figures.

"Thanks to the assessment, not as much as he thinks, but enough that the farm doesn't have the cash on hand to satisfy him."

"That doesn't tell me anything, Dan," I said.

"We'll have a final figure once we talk to the lawyer, but for now we're looking at about thirty to forty thousand."

I drew in a careful breath. That was a lot of money. "And how is the farm supposed to come up with that?"

Dan shook his head. "The only way we can is to sell some land. And if we do that, our income goes down, which means the farm can't support two families." He blew out his breath as he stared out the window of the car. "So, we're pretty much looking at selling the whole deal. Nothing new there." In his quick sideways glance, I caught a glimpse of the pain that would cause him.

My heart folded at the thought. During our time here I had seen my husband change, soften. I had seen him grow connected to his family, connected to the land.

And, yes, connected to me.

I had changed. I had been exposed to how family and community works. I had been challenged and supported.

Once again I tried to imagine Dan and me going through what we had with Nicholas back in Seattle. I shuddered.

We came to the top of the hill, and I looked back over the valley. Could I leave this now? After all we had been through?

Dan and I had come here as married strangers, bound by our children and our promises. We had grown. Our marriage, once raveled and fraying, had been strengthened here and with the help of family and friends, slowly woven back together. Dan, Nicholas, and Anneke were my breath, my blood, my life. Not accessories in a dollhouse that I needed to make my life complete.

The thought that had taken up residence in my mind some time ago hadn't left. Instead, with each day, each experience it had grown, settled, and taken root.

I wondered if I dared voice the thought. Dared make it real. Once I did, there would be no turning back.

My mind flashed back to summer camp. Two guys had dragged me down the pier toward the lake. I wore a new leather coat and brand-new blue jeans, both of which I had saved my tip money for, all in an effort to impress the very guys who were now dragging me down the pier to the lake.

When we got to the end, they lifted me up and started swinging. I was still laughing. Then, to my stunned amazement, they let go.

I remember the surprisingly exhilarating feeling of being airborne, hanging in space over the water, stupefied that they had actually done it, yet realizing that the inevitability of gravity would soon make itself known.

That was what I felt like now. I was in the grip of fear, but at the same time, the exhilaration of wonder.

"I want to buy out Keith's share of the farm with our house money," I said quietly, taking the proverbial plunge. "With the bit we got from Lonnie Dansworth and what I have saved up, I think we have enough."

Dan laughed nervously. "What are you saying, Leslie?"

"I was speaking English, Dan," I said with a feeble laugh, surprised that I had finally spoken the words aloud. "But I'll say it again. I want to use our money to buy out Keith."

Dan slammed his foot on the brakes, pulled to the side of the road, and turned to me. He rested one elbow on the steering wheel, his other draped over the headrest, his expression full of confused wonder. "Are you saying what I think you're saying?"

I threw my hands up in happy exasperation. "I dunno. What do you think I'm saying?"

"The money. You want to use it to pay Keith."

"He can be taught," I announced to the roof of the car. "Yes. Money. Pay Keith. See Leslie. See Leslie use single-syllable words so husband understands." My growing nerves brought out my flippant side.

Dan bit his lip, ran his hands through his hair, and laughed lightly. "You're making a joke, but I think you're serious."

Okay, I have to confess this was very anticlimactic. I expected him to pull me in his arms, sweep me off my feet, and swing me around like they do in the best movies. Of course, I could have chosen a better venue than the cramped quarters of a sub-compact car.

"But what about the house?" he persisted. "All the plans you made?" He still looked surprised.

"I have a house," I said with a laugh. "I have a yard bigger than I could ever have in Seattle, or any city." I gave him a slow smile. "I have my small family, and in the past few months, I've discovered I have a bigger family."

"It's hardly a dream home," Dan said, reaching for my hand, excitement and wonder coiled around him even as his words added reality. "It needs work. We'll need new shingles in a couple years. The appliances are old. The water tank is rusting out . . ."

"I hope you're not trying to change my mind," I said in mock warning.

"No. Just making sure." He shook his head, amazed wonder in his voice. "I can't believe you want to do this. I can't believe you're serious."

"This time I am."

"Leslie, this is unbelievable! I can't believe it."

"You're repeating yourself," I said, taking refuge in teasing.

He grabbed my face and kissed me solidly on the mouth, his lips warm, hard, and real. Then he pulled back. "Are you sure?"

"I think I'm sure." Hardly words to go striding confidently into the future with, but they would do for now. "We'll have to draw up some kind of agreement."

"Of course," he said.

"And I want to make sure that the money I make from my job is kept separate from the farm."

"Ah, still wanting control." His grin belied the comment.

"Ah, still being smart." I made a fist and bopped him lightly on the chin. Then leaned over and cancelled my reprimand with another kiss. "I know I can learn a lot more about family. About Jesus and God." I gave him a self-conscious smile. I still felt awkward about the whole issue of faith and religion and a relationship with God. It still felt like talking to my mother about sex. It was intimate and real, and I didn't know the right words to share the emotions I had felt during those moments alone. When I felt as if I had felt the touch of a Father, the love of a Savior, and the breath of the Spirit.

Dan closed his eyes, then slowly drew me into his arms and squeezed and squeezed. "You are the most amazing woman," he said quietly. He cupped my face in his hands. "I wish there were better words to say than *I love you*. Because

I know millions of people have used those words, and I feel like I need something unique. Just for you."

"*You're* unique," I said with a smile and kissed him again. "Just like everyone else. Now, we'd better go before Keith thinks he needs interest, as well."

As we drove, Dan looked at me a couple of times as if making sure the woman spouting the strange ideas was really his wife.

We made it to the lawyers in record time. I'm sure Dan was worried I would change my mind.

But once we got there, it was the usual hurry-up-and-wait. We sat in the plush chairs and as we waited, Dan tapped his fingers on the arm of his chair, looking from the faux prints on the wall to me.

"I'm not going to change my mind," I said quietly, giving him a reassuring smile. And the more I said it, the more I knew it was true. There might come a time that I would regret this decision—that I would miss the busyness of the hospital in Seattle, but I also knew that I had done the right thing. Here in Harland was an entire new world to experience.

Finally a friendly woman came and escorted us into the lawyer's office.

We were greeted by a suavely dressed man, his suit perfectly aligned on his shoulders, silk tie knotted with mathematical precision. I couldn't help a quick glance at Dan's best corduroy shirt and jeans. He looked better. Manly. My dearest husband.

The lawyer smiled and held out his hand. "Hello, my name is Phil Brinks."

I looked at him, then grinned back. Finally. After all this time, here was my chance.

"Hello." I glanced at Dan and winked at him, tucking my arm into his, then turned back to Mr. Brinks. "My name is Leslie VandeKeere. And I'm a farmer's wife."

Reading Group Guide

1. How realistic was Leslie to you? Could you identify with her?

2. Do you think Leslie was right in her determination to create a distance between Dan and his mother? Why or why not?

3. Leslie did not grow up as a Christian. Discuss her feelings toward the church, God, and the community.

4. The bond between a mother and a child can, at times, be one of the strongest forces in nature. Compare Leslie's relationship with her son and Wilma's with Dan. How does one affect the other?

5. How do Leslie's relationship with her sister and feelings about her mother affect her interactions with Dan's family and community?

6. Leslie has a deep-seated need to be a nurse as well as a mother. Can you sympathize or identify with her needs? Why or why not? Discuss the difficulties working mothers have with their divided loyalties.

7. Leslie moved to the community with the idea that this was only a temporary move. Discuss her changing feelings toward Harland and how they affected her final decision.

8. Leslie had a dream—a house and a yard and a family—that had to shift and change during the course of her stay in Harland. Have you ever had to let go of dreams and plans? How did this affect your relationship with God?

9. During the course of the story, Leslie slowly gets involved in an unhealthy relationship with Dr. John. Could you sympathize with her changing feelings toward Dr. John? How do you think you would respond in her situation?

10. There are times that our life's circumstances push us into places we don't want to go. How do you think God uses these times in our lives to draw us closer to Him?

About the Author

Carolyne Aarsen was originally a city girl transplanted to the country when she married her dear husband, Richard. Thankfully, the move took. While raising four children and a number of foster children, assorted chickens, dogs, cats, and cows, Carolyne's résumé gained a few unique entries. Besides the usual challenges and joys of wife- and motherhood, she found out how to grow a garden, can the produce, sew, bake, pickle, and preserve. She learned to sort pigs; handle cows; drive a tractor, a quad, a snow machine; ride a horse; and train a colt. Through all of this, she came to appreciate the open spaces of the countryside, the pace of life away from the city, and the fellowship in the Christian community she and her family became a part of. She is most thankful, however, to be able to express her faith in God through the books and stories she writes.

From *All in One Place*

e angled me a light frown. "Leslie VandeKeere is your sister?"

"That's what I said." I could see the Feds wouldn't be begging to recruit this guy anytime soon.

This netted me a deeper frown. Okay, maybe Leslie, being a mother and all, wasn't the type to wear high-heeled boots, a halter top, and a diamond in her nose, but I knew my whole look was way tamed down from what my friends in Seattle were sporting.

"You don't look like her."

"I'm getting that." My turn. "How do you know her?"

"Harland's not that big."

Wasn't he the cagey one? "I wasn't asking for a geography lesson." *No, Terra. Bad Terra. Smart-aleck comments are not how you can win friends and influence policemen.*

His tight smile wasn't encouraging, which only underlined my cop petrinoia. "Leslie works in the emergency department of the hospital. My job gets me there from time to time," he said. "So she didn't quit her job?"

"Was she going to?"

I thought of the last e-mails we had exchanged. "She was getting pressure from the family to get all hearth-and-homey."

The cop frowned, and I shut my mouth. If I didn't keep myself in check, I would end up giving too much information and, by extension, too much ammunition.

"So, you sure you'll be okay?" he asked again.

"I'll be great." I gave him a casual wave, a quick smile, and threw in a 'hey, whatever' toss of my hair just to dot the i's and cross the t's.

Thankfully, he was convinced. He strode back to his car, his heavy belt shifting with each step, but then, just before he got into the car, he gave me one last look. As if memorizing who I was. "See you around," he said.

"Not if I can help it," I muttered as I forced a completely fake smile and waved. As he finally drove on, I felt my legs go shaky with relief.

Did I mention that I didn't like cops?

As he drove away, I heard the screech of another hawk, but this time I kept my eyes on the road. *No more distractions. Stay focused. Get to Leslie's in one piece.*

But the thought of Leslie made me stop again. I was on the last leg of this journey. Less than an hour away from her.

What if she didn't want to see me?

What would she say when . . .

"Keep going. Keep walking," I said aloud.

Luckily, I didn't have to focus long. Five minutes after my cop incident, I scored a ride. A rusty, beat-up pickup truck pulled up. A tired-looking young girl sat behind the wheel. Her short brown hair had that slick, unwashed look and the neckline of her faded blue T-shirt was unraveling.

"D'you need a ride?" she asked through the open passenger window as she leaned one skinny arm across the back of the seat. She sounded as tired as she looked. So, obviously not much of a threat.

"That'd be great." I threw my backpack into the back of the truck and pulled open the passenger door. As it protested with a rusty screech, I saw the baby in the car seat beside her.

I hesitated a moment.

"I'm not going to do anything," the girl said, laughing at me.

That did look kind of silly. So I got in. The baby was a little girl, I guessed, from the pink sleeper and the little pink bow attached to a wisp of hair on the top of her head. Adorable little girl.

I was glad she was sleeping.

"You headed to Harland?" the driver asked as she put the truck in gear.

"If that's where this road goes."

"This road goes nowhere," she said, steering the truck with her elbows as she lit up a cigarette. "Every morning, I look out the window . . ."

"And it's still there," I finished the old joke for her.

She gave me a weary smile and waved her cigarette at me. "You want one?"

"No thanks." I had enough bad habits. Smoking wasn't one of them.

"So, what brings you to this godforsaken neck of the woods?" Her question came out on the breath of a sigh. As if talking was too much work for her.

"I'm just passing through, seeing where the day takes me." Though I had told the cop who I was visiting, I got a different vibe from this girl. Better to keep things safely vague.

"Lucky you." She glanced down at her baby, as if to let me know that if it weren't for this tyke, she'd be doing the same thing. She stuck the cigarette into her mouth and reached her hand over her sleeping baby. "Name's Amelia." She didn't introduce the baby and I wasn't going to ask.

"Terra," I said, shaking her hand.

"I'm heading into town to meet up with some friends at the Pump and Grill. You want to join us?"

I guessed the Pump and Grill was a bar, and I guessed her friends were of the male variety.

"I don't think so," I said carefully.

"Suit yourself. I know I could use a drink."

I licked my dry lips and lifted my hair off the back of my neck as the wind swirled through the truck, dry and dusty and hot. The pavement shimmered in front of us, and through the heat waves, I caught a glimpse of the town of Harland. For now it was just a smudge on the horizon, but it was getting closer. And as it got closer, my heart fluttered.

Leslie didn't know I was coming. I had dropped out of her life the past year. When I last checked my e-mail at the Internet café, she had sent a ton of messages. I only had time to read the first few. Something about Nicholas being sick. That was all.

I had my own worries, though.

I glanced over at Amelia. She finished her cigarette and flicked it out the window, then looked at me again.

Maybe getting to know a few of Harland's residents wasn't such a bad idea. Give me a chance to scope out the place. Get the lay of the land, so to speak, before I faced my sister.